"You Can Do Anything You Want . . .

if you want to do it badly enough," Courtney whispered.

His grin was wickedly enticing. "Anything?"

"Within reason."

"Then tell me when we get past reason," he replied huskily. Then his mouth was on hers, searching for a secret she couldn't really understand. She moved against him until, with a small groan, his hands slid down her back to crush her even harder against him.

"Don't play games with me, Courtney, not now," he warned her.

"No," she murmured, her breath a sigh of surrender.

BEVERLY BIRD

is a New Jersey resident who makes her home near the Atlantic Ocean she loves. She has long been a writer of articles and short fiction but has only recently turned to novels as a way of depicting the fantasy of love.

Dear Reader:

Silhouette has always tried to give you exactly what you want. When you asked for increased realism, deeper characterization and greater length, we brought you Silhouette Special Editions. When you asked for increased sensuality, we brought you Silhouette Desire. Now you ask for books with the length and depth of Special Editions, the sensuality of Desire, but with something else besides, something that no one else offers. Now we bring you SILHOUETTE INTIMATE MOMENTS, true romance novels, longer than the usual, with all the depth that length requires. More sensuous than the usual, with characters whose maturity matches that sensuality. Books with the ingredient no one else has tapped: excitement.

There is an electricity between two people in love that makes everything they do magic, larger than life—and this is what we bring you in SILHOUETTE INTIMATE MOMENTS. Look for them wherever you buy books.

These books are for the woman who wants more than she has ever had before. These books are for you. As always, we look forward to your comments and suggestions. You can write to me at the address below:

Karen Solem
Editor-in-Chief
Silhouette Books
P.O. Box 769
New York, N.Y. 10019

Emeralds In The Dark

Beverly Bird

Silhouette Intimate Moments
Published by Silhouette Books New York

America's Publisher of Contemporary Romance

SILHOUETTE BOOKS, a Division of Simon & Schuster, Inc.
1230 Avenue of the Americas, New York, N.Y. 10020

ISBN: 0-671-47782-X

First Silhouette Books printing May, 1983

10 9 8 7 6 5 4 3 2

*This book is dedicated
to my grandfather, with love*

Chapter 1

SHE HAD HEARD THE CRUNCH OF GRAVEL ON THE driveway outside and should have been prepared. Without her sight, or with the little that was left of it, Courtney Winston had learned a valuable lesson early in her twenty-five years: Her ears and her hands were her most precious companions. They guided her tirelessly; she had learned to respect them and to follow their guidance unquestioningly.

Still, her thoughts were deeply concentrated on the piece of paper that lay on the desk in front of her when the gravel crunched outside and the sound of car doors slamming followed. She pushed the irritating noises away and concentrated on the words that Elizabeth had written on the paper in large, bright red letters. Dimly, she could make out some of the shadowy words: a name, Meryl Knight, and an age, thirteen. The girl would be older than most of the other students at the school, but Courtney was willing to admit any girl, rich or poor, young or old, so long as she was blind or visually impaired and in need of an education. When she had used her trust fund to found The Winston House for the Visually Impaired, that had been her whole philosophy. Courtney had grown up struggling to learn in a world where sight was everything, fighting against the narrowing of her vision, which seemed to grow worse daily. She had accepted the fact that her life was destined to be different, that she would never fit entirely into a sighted world, but she also knew that she had a right and a need to be educated. She had completed her teaching degree just as her sight had begun their final betrayal, making it impossible, even with glasses and magnifying lenses, for her to continue her studies. And then she had used her trust fund to buy this lovely old mansion deep in the Pennsylvania hills and to set up her home, her school. It hadn't been a dream for her so much as it had been a necessity. She had to make a living, to support herself. She refused to rely on her father to support her for the rest of her life, even if he could have done so on his limited pension. And the public schools didn't need a blind teacher. She had been forced to institute a school of her own.

Sudden screams sounded from the entryway and broke into Courtney's reverie. She pulled away from her ruminations guiltily; there was little time in her life to dwell on fate, and even less time to do so on a Saturday. She pushed the paper away from her, gripped the thick, beveled edge of her desk, and pulled herself to her feet as quickly as her limited vision and innate caution would allow. The screams could only mean that the new girl had arrived and that she wasn't pleased about it.

Carefully, Courtney moved down the corridor as quickly as she could, her hand gliding along the wall railing. Ahead of her, she could vaguely perceive three figures in the bright sunshine that was streaming into the entryway. Two adults, one child. As she drew closer, her brow knitted in consternation. Two women. Elizabeth . . . and who else? The screams of the child continued, making it difficult for Courtney to think. Her records had clearly stated that Meryl Knight was an only child, the daughter of an import/export magnate who lived in Valley Forge. Her mother had been killed in an auto accident when Meryl had still been very young. She had been raised alone by her father; there had been no mention in any of Courtney's records of a remarriage. So who was the second woman? It was customary—indeed, Courtney almost demanded it —that parents bring their children to her school and stay for supper on admission day to meet the other children, Elizabeth and herself. Usually, there were also several brief meetings early on between Courtney and the child's parents. This hadn't been so in Meryl's case, so Courtney had been sure— mistakenly, she now realized—that her father would accompany her today.

Elizabeth and the unidentified woman were struggling valiantly to calm the child. Kicking and screeching, Meryl clawed at both of them, trying desperately to break away, to flee through the open door. Courtney quickly moved around behind them and pushed the door closed.

"It's okay," she said to no one in particular. She reached out a hand to the girl, then gasped at the sudden pain of sharp incisors digging into her flesh, and she pulled it back, rubbing at it with her free hand. The child had bitten her! Stupid to reach so close to her mouth, with her jaws working furiously, her temper at a high pitch. Still, nothing was very clear with the three of them moving around so rapidly. Courtney's field of vision was a blur of moving body parts and swirling hair. Her poor aim couldn't have been helped.

"Enough!" Her soft voice came out strong and demanding, despite the fact that she very rarely shouted, knowing that it was the last thing in the world that her girls needed. Elizabeth, surprised, looked up at her but kept one arm protectively and confiningly around the girl's shoulders. The other woman, who appeared to be near Courtney's age and beautiful as well, with long silvery blond hair, held Meryl's arm in a viselike grip. Courtney reached out and tried to pull her away.

"There's no need for that."

The woman wouldn't let go. "That's what you think! If I let go of her, she'll be out of here before either one of us could blink."

"No, she won't. The door's locked. And unless there's been some mistake here, I seriously doubt if we can expect Meryl to see the lock. Am I right, Meryl?"

Strangely, her words seemed to quiet the child somewhat. Meryl stopped her twisting and screaming, but her words were sullen and angry. "I can't see it, but I could find it!"

Courtney shrugged. The girl, she remembered from her file, could perceive some movement, light and shadows. She hoped that she would pick up on her own signal of nonchalance. "I have no doubt that you could. But why would you want to?"

"Because I want to get out of here! I don't want to stay here!" She seemed close to tears again.

Courtney stooped down so that she was kneeling in front of the girl. "Why? It's not so bad here. Elizabeth is one terrific cook, and we have our fair share of fun. Maybe it's not as good as being home, but it's not a prison, either."

"I don't have to be here! I'm not blind!"

"You're not?" Courtney kept her voice mildly confused. "But I thought you just told me that you couldn't see the lock?"

"I said I could find it!"

"I thought you meant if you felt around for it."

Meryl's head dropped. Courtney reached a tentative hand out to the child again and this time succeeded in brushing off the other woman's restraining hand.

"I'm not blind. Not all the way. I can see. Some things."

"So can I. But I can't see everything, so I have to learn to work around my handicap. That's why you're here—so you can learn, too."

This brought on another fit of screaming. What did I say? wondered Courtney. Meryl broke away from Elizabeth and ran stumblingly to the door. She came up against it hard and staggered back a few steps, blood trickling from her nose where it had met with the unyielding mahogany. Her wails increased as she groped around for the lock.

"Now look what you've done!" the anonymous woman shouted.

Elizabeth broke in for the first time. "There's no need to get upset. We're used to little bruises around here." She moved forward toward Meryl and grabbed her hand, trying to restrain her as gently and kindly as possible. "Look, why don't you come with me so we can stop that bleeding? Then we can go back into Courtney's office and sit down and continue this conversation where we're more comfortable."

"I'm not staying!"

"Maybe, maybe not. But we're going to have to talk about it one way or another, and I can't for the life of me see doing that standing out here. There's tea and cocoa in the kitchen. You can have either one, but I'm not going to serve it out here."

For a moment it looked as though Meryl would acquiesce willingly, but that illusion was short-lived. She moved off down the corridor with Elizabeth, but Courtney could tell that she was going only grudgingly. Soon they faded into the shadows at the end of the hall.

Courtney turned to the woman whose silvery hair was gleaming yellow-white in the sun streaming in the window, blazing brightly into Courtney's eyes. Her temper flaring and close to erupting, Courtney snapped, "Where's her father? And who are you?"

The woman seemed taken aback. "I'm Andrea Vaughan. I'm the Knights' housekeeper."

"The housekeeper?" Courtney's voice was taut with disbelief. She wasn't sure what had astounded her more. It seemed shocking that domestic help would be enlisted to escort a child on an occasion such as this, but equally absurd was the idea of this svelte, attractive woman being someone's housekeeper. She looked more like a model, Courtney thought, and was sure that her impression was fairly accurate.

"You're the *housekeeper?*" she asked again.

"I don't know why that should shock you so," Andrea Vaughan replied, her voice like velvet.

"I'll tell you why it shocks me," Courtney rallied. "That little girl is about to be taken away from her home and placed in a new one. This is a big crisis in her life. It's for her own good, but it's a crisis all the same. And she's obviously not taking to it very well. How dare that man send his daughter here with his housekeeper?"

"How dare *you* say such things?" The woman was insolently amused.

"I want answers," Courtney replied hotly. "I don't make a habit of taking in children because no one cares enough to take care of them at home. I take them in because they need my help, and I work *with* the parents, not separate and apart from them. I resent getting off to a really bad start like this just because Mr. Knight couldn't take the time to come down here himself. I've never even spoken to the man on the telephone! All of these arrangements were made by *letter!* What kind of a setup is this?"

"Miss Winston," Andrea Vaughan said coldly, "I do believe you're jumping to some very presumptuous conclusions. We've brought Meryl here because she needs some help in adjusting. You have no right to assume, simply because Josh—Mr. Knight—couldn't be here, that it's because he couldn't take the time or because he didn't want to help Meryl at home. He is an extremely busy man, and it was simply impossible for him to get away today, although he had every intention of it until last night, when something came up. As for my presence with Meryl, I may be her housekeeper, but I'm the closest thing to a mother she's got. My bringing her here was not a symbol of neglect, I can assure you."

Courtney stepped back from the woman, momentarily nonplussed. Andrea Vaughan was right, of course. She had jumped to some nasty conclusions, albeit obvious ones. It had just been such a shock to see the child so angry and hateful at her new situation, and the absence of her father was glaringly inappropriate. Also, so many letters, all typed, had led Courtney to believe that Mr. Knight was an impersonal, cold man who had little time for his daughter.

"I apologize," she said softly, feeling embarrassed at her temper. "I suppose I did jump to conclusions. However, this is an entirely different arrangement from what we prefer. For obvious reasons, it's best to have the parents here when the girl is admitted. And I'll admit to being a little miffed at the way Mr. Knight has continually put me off."

"I doubt very seriously if he's been putting you off, as you say, Miss Winston. As I've mentioned, he is an extremely busy man. I was instructed to tell you, however, that he does plan to be here for supper tonight as you requested. He simply felt that it would be a good idea for Meryl to come along first and get settled."

"Which she isn't doing overly well," Courtney added ruefully.

"You must understand that the child has been fighting against her handicap for years. There have been countless operations, but then, surely Mr. Knight explained that to you in his letters. Unfortunately, the doctors held out a great deal of hope for Meryl, and now that they've failed and she's been consigned to a life of blindness, things seem unbearable for her. No, she's not adapting well. But that, of course, is where you come in."

"I'm not a miracle worker, Miss Vaughan. I'm a teacher, and I happen to share her handicap. I have some psychological training, but I won't delude you, as I haven't deluded Mr. Knight. It's extremely difficult to help these children unless they want to be helped."

"You came highly recommended."

Courtney nodded, not sure if she should feel flattered or not. The statement seemed to be more of an accusation than anything else.

"My school is a young one," she ventured, "and so far, I've had no real failures. All of my girls leave here fully prepared to cope with their handicaps. But I don't believe in teaching them that they're no different from anyone else, because they are. They can fit in, but it will take twice the usual work and effort."

"I'm sure you mentioned all of this in your letters."

Fleetingly, Courtney wished that she could see Andrea Vaughan's face more clearly. Such wishes were futile, and she usually avoided them like the plague, but the woman's words seemed strange, and she wished that she could, just for a moment, have the luxury of seeing the woman's eyes, of reading the sentiments there.

"Of course I did." Courtney's words were calm, betraying none of her confusion. "As I've mentioned, we've worked out all of the arrangements by mail, and, I might add, my letters were extremely thorough."

"And his weren't? Is that what you're implying?" There was a touch of defensiveness in Andrea Vaughan's voice.

"I'm not implying anything," Courtney snapped, suddenly tired of the whole strange conversation and itching to get back to Meryl. "But no, Mr. Knight's letters were not all that helpful. I gathered most of the information I needed from Meryl's school transcripts and her medical records."

"I see." There was a short silence. Courtney sensed that the woman was moving toward the door.

"Well, I don't imagine you'll be needing me any longer. I should be getting back."

Courtney whirled around abruptly toward the shadowy silver form that was Andrea Vaughan. "You can't leave yet! That child doesn't even know for sure if she's staying here! Elizabeth told her that we were going to talk about it. How will it look if I go back to my office alone?"

"Perhaps Elizabeth should have thought of that. Actually, I don't think it will look like anything to her, Miss Winston. If you'll remember, Meryl can't see much. Just lead her to believe that I'm standing behind her, why don't you?"

Courtney was stunned by the woman's casual cruelty. She opened her mouth to speak, then pursed her lips together again, afraid of the words that might come out if she let go of her temper again. Earlier, she had toyed with the idea of sending Meryl home again, of having her admission delayed until Joshua Knight could accompany her and calm her, or perhaps just talk to her some more about this drastic move. Clearly, the child wasn't prepared for it. But now she was beginning to think that the less time Meryl spent with Andrea Vaughan, the better off she would be.

"I really must be going now. You can expect Mr. Knight for supper at seven o'clock." The door clicked, and there was another sudden burst of light as the sunshine streamed in through the open door.

"I'll believe it when I see it," Courtney muttered, but the other woman was already out the door, too far away to hear her skepticism. The door swung shut again, and she was left in comparative darkness.

And then another thought occurred to her.

Andrea Vaughan had said that Mr. Knight would be arriving at seven for dinner. A slow anger burned inside Courtney. The man had never even set foot inside Winston House, and he was high-handedly rearranging their dinner hour! Those girls who hadn't gone home for the weekend would be expecting dinner at five. Joshua Knight obviously expected her to hold the meal for him just to accommodate his busy schedule. Well, she wouldn't do it!

She made her way down the corridor, gliding her hand along the railing, dreading the scene that she knew would be waiting for her back in her office. Surely Meryl would react explosively, if not violently, to the news that Andrea Vaughan had left her behind. Would it comfort her at all to know that her father would, theoretically, be arriving at seven o'clock? Would it be wise to tell her that at all? Or would it be better simply to leave the issue open, in the event that the man didn't show up after all?

Courtney stopped near the door to her office and ran a tired hand over her eyes. It was the first time she had been confronted with a situation like this, and she was at a loss as to how to handle it.

Then, suddenly, she realized that although she was standing right outside her office, she could hear no screams or sobs coming from the other side of the door. True, the door was heavy oak, and it sealed in a good deal of sound, but Meryl's screams had tended toward hysteria. They had been piercing and shattering, and no amount of oak could have restrained their echoes. Tentatively, almost afraid of what she might find, Courtney pushed the door open and ventured a look inside.

Elizabeth was sitting in the wing-backed chair closest to the desk. Courtney moved closer and saw that her white hair was disheveled and pulled loose

from the chignon at the nape of her neck. One lock
dipped low on her forehead, obscuring an eye. She
sat perfectly still and rigid, gripping the arms of her
chair with both hands as though she expected it to
launch into flight. Courtney felt a small smile pulling
at her lips. Elizabeth was somewhat the worse for
wear, but she obviously had risen to the occasion.
What would she ever do without her?

She turned away from Elizabeth to make out
Meryl's slight, slender form reclining on the davenport a few feet away from Elizabeth's chair and tried
to force her tired eyes to focus on the girl. Coming
close, kneeling down beside her, Courtney could see
that Meryl was a beautiful child, with thick, heavy
chestnut hair that fell to her shoulders and sooty
eyelashes protecting amazingly expressive amber
eyes. Flecks of gold seemed to radiate from them,
and they were still snapping and angry, although, at
the moment, Meryl seemed fairly calm as she held
one of Elizabeth's old handkerchiefs to her nose, her
head tilted back at a careful angle.

Courtney wondered at the brown-gold eyes, marveling at the way they seemed to stare deeply and
intently back into her own. It was impossible, of
course, for that to be happening. Despite Meryl's
protestations that she could see, Courtney knew that
her eyesight had to be a good deal worse than her
own. She had been in the same car that had careened
off the road, killing her mother. Shattering glass had
destroyed her eyes, leaving her only peripheral vision, fragments of sight and little or no remem-
brance of what the world had once looked like to
her. That Meryl was actually seeing Courtney's own
emerald eyes was very close to impossible. And yet
their gazes met, seeming to challenge and test each
other.

Courtney leaned back on her heels, pulling on the hem of her denim prairie skirt so that it fell down over her knees, almost to the tops of her boots. She studied Meryl for a moment before she spoke. "So how's the nose?"

Gold-flecked eyes stared back at her silently.

"It's not broken," Elizabeth contributed. "Not so far as I can tell, anyway. Then again, I'm no doctor."

"Well, it's a miracle if it's not, the way you came up against that door," Courtney said directly to Meryl. "You know, you can get a lot further in this world with planning and plotting than with out and out force, especially when you're in our condition. Which brings us back to the whole reason you're here in the first place."

She paused, wondering again just how to go about telling the girl that Andrea Vaughan had left, and if she should mention that her father might arrive after dinner. Courtney was still determined that she would not hold the meal for him. If he arrived in time, he could join them for coffee in the study.

Elizabeth inadvertently solved at least half the problem. "Where's Meryl's escort?"

Courtney rose to her feet. "You mean Andrea Vaughan. It seems she's the Knights' housekeeper."

"I should look so good," Elizabeth muttered almost inaudibly.

"She left." Meryl spoke up from the davenport. "I knew she would."

Courtney turned back to the girl in surprise. Stalling for a time to collect her thoughts, she felt for the ridge along the edge of her desk and followed it around to her chair. Letting out a heavy sigh, she sat down, resting her elbows on the mahogany and her chin in her hands.

"Well, then, you knew a whole lot more than I did," she said finally. "Her departure took me totally by surprise. Actually, I've been standing out in the hallway wondering how to tell you about it."

"I knew she would go," Meryl said again. Now her voice was somewhat choked as she struggled valiantly with the tears that seemed to be right below the surface. "I'm not going to stay here, you know. I don't care if she did leave. I'll get back home somehow."

"Well, Elizabeth could take you, I suppose, but is that really what you want?" Courtney asked. "There are certain advantages involved in going to school here, you know."

"I don't belong here!" Meryl's voice was strident now, and tinged with anger once more. "I can see. I keep telling you that. I don't want to stay here with a bunch of people walking around into walls! I'm not like them!"

"Whoa!" Courtney spoke quickly, her own pulse accelerating. "First of all, nobody walks into walls around here. Only a few of the girls are totally blind, and we've taken measures to make sure that they can get around as comfortably as possible. As for the rest, they're pretty much like you and me. For one reason or another, they can see some things and not others. But none of them can see everything, so instead of going to some school where everyone else can see—and where they probably wouldn't learn all that much anyway—they come here. What I told you out there in the hallway was true. This isn't a prison, Meryl. I couldn't keep you here against your will even if I wanted to, and I certainly don't want to."

There was no response from the prone figure on the davenport. Meryl kept the handkerchief pressed firmly against her nose, and the only sound in the room was that of her heavy, agitated breathing. Courtney got up again and walked over so that she was close enough to the girl to see her.

"Why don't you just give it a shot, Meryl? What have you got to lose? I think the least you can do is give us a chance." Her voice was calm, rational, but she was seething inside. Damn it! This conversation should have been taking place between Meryl and her father! It simply wasn't fair that no one had bothered to find out what Meryl thought of coming here. Just what kind of a father was this Joshua Knight? Courtney suddenly found herself hoping that he *would* show up at seven o'clock. She had quite a few things that she wanted to say to him.

She stepped away from the davenport and spoke to Elizabeth in hushed tones. "I imagine that Lewis has already taken Meryl's luggage up to Corinne's room. I had thought it might be best to put the two of them together, since Corinne's closest to Meryl's age. But on second thought, maybe that's not such a great idea."

Elizabeth nodded knowingly. Corinne was one of the few girls at Winston House who lived in a world of total darkness. And, at eleven, she was a frisky, lanky child with a seemingly endless supply of energy. She often reminded Courtney of a caged bird, wild and untamed, but trapped. She was sweet mannered and fun loving, but she was constantly pushing herself, trying to do things that her lack of sight simply would not permit. Her fall from the old oak tree was one such incident. Insistent upon climbing it, despite Courtney's firm refusal to allow such a thing, the girl had managed to slip away one day and climb halfway up before she reached out for a branch that wasn't there. The fall had resulted in a broken wrist and a concussion. Minor enough injuries, but they had taught Courtney a lesson or two in responsibility. Corinne had been entrusted to her care, and Courtney felt that the fall had been the result of negligence on her part. She was convinced that she should have understood Corinne's nature and known that a simple admonition wouldn't thwart the child's efforts.

Now, when she thought of subjecting Meryl's precarious acceptance of Winston House to the high-spirited Corinne Klein, she decided against it. The eleven-year-old would undoubtedly walk into a few pieces of furniture, if not walls. She murmured another mild epithet, again thinking of how blindly she was groping with Meryl. If only Joshua Knight had seen fit to talk to her, to explain his daughter's foibles to her and to arrange an earlier meeting for the three of them!

"How about if we give her a room to herself? Near one of ours, of course." Elizabeth whispered her suggestion.

Courtney sighed. "That's so much extra work for you. I know it took a good portion of last night to get Corinne resettled. And the whole situation may only be temporary." She looked at Meryl and sensed more than saw that the girl's startling eyes were directed at her again.

"Well, if it is, both of us will have gone to a lot of trouble for nothing," Elizabeth said. "Under the circumstances, I'm not going to be the only one wasting my time. Meryl? Come along, I need your help."

"No! I told you, I'm not staying!" Her ears were obviously much sharper than her eyes. She seemed to have followed their entire conversation.

"Well, you're going to have to stay through to-night, at least, because I'm not driving you back to

Valley Forge today. You might as well come help me get a room together for you."

Meryl remained on the davenport, unmoving and silent.

"Oh, for heaven's sake!" Elizabeth sputtered. She reached down and took Meryl's hand. "If nothing else, it will help you kill some time while we decide what we're going to do about you. You can't just stay here in Courtney's office. She's got work to do."

Courtney watched their retreating backs until the incongruous pair faded into the shadows near the door. Meryl didn't go willingly, but she went. Courtney sat down hard on the edge of her desk and ran trembling fingers through her long, mahogany hair. Absently, she wound a thick strand around her index finger, staring straight ahead yet seeing nothing.

Her first really difficult student, and everything was getting off to such a terrible start, she thought. Was she really qualified to deal with this? Would her specialized training and her instincts be enough to help her deal with Meryl Knight and her anonymous father? There was more than Meryl's near-blindness at issue here. Joshua Knight was emerging as an extremely indifferent father; Meryl seemed to have a whole cache of problems to prove it. And Courtney was sure that the car accident couldn't have helped matters much. Not only had it resulted in Meryl's handicap, but it had also subjected a very young child to the firsthand ordeal of her mother's death. And then there were the countless operations that Andrea Vaughan had mentioned. Perhaps, Courtney thought, she really *was* unqualified to deal with Meryl Knight. Perhaps what Meryl needed more than Winston House was good psychological help.

She was startled out of her despondency by the loud ringing of the telephone behind her. Her nerves had been so strained by the time spent with Meryl that Courtney found herself literally jumping at the sound. She shook her head as though to physically dispel some of the doubts that were attempting to roost there, then went around to the back of the desk. Slipping into her chair, she slid her hand across the desk until it came in contact with the telephone.

"How are things at Tara?" came the melodic male voice that answered her greeting. It was Peter Tomlinson, of course. Even if Courtney hadn't long since memorized his soothing, tepid voice, no one else ever referred to Winston House as Tara. It was an old, teasing jibe at Courtney's Southern roots. Although Winston House was situated well above the Mason-Dixon line, Peter had pounced on the nickname.

"Everything's fine," Courtney answered him. "Well, maybe not fine, but it will be, I'm sure, after I get my hands on a certain Mr. Joshua Knight."

"Knight?" came Pete's voice. "Isn't that the name of your new student?"

"It is, and it's also part of a very long story. Suffice it to say that I've got a few things to square away with the girl's father, if and when he finally arrives. Meryl is here already, incidentally, but her father has yet to make an appearance. I'm told that he'll be here somewhere in the neighborhood of seven o'clock, which may or may not turn out to be true."

"Seven?"

"So his housekeeper tells me."

"Does this mean our plans for tonight are off?"

"Oh, no!" Courtney grimaced at the telephone. She had completely forgotten! She was to have met both her father and Pete at the Englewood Inn at seven o'clock.

"I'm sorry, Pete, but I've really got to speak to

this man. I'm afraid I just won't be able to make it. If he were coming for dinner at five, as planned, then I'd be able to slip out by seven or so. But as it is, he won't even be getting here until then." And that's if he gets here at all, she added to herself. "Why don't you and Daddy go on ahead without me?"

"Because it's you I want to see, not your father. Honestly, Courtney, if you would just marry me, we might be able to see each other more than once a week or so, despite your busy schedule."

"No!" she said more sharply than she had intended to. Then, to soften the harshness of her denial, she added lightly, "Somehow, Peter, I just can't picture you living here with thirteen girls. You don't even like children that much."

"Living there isn't exactly what I have in mind."

"Well, I certainly can't discuss it now. Look, if I can get away later on, I'll give you a call." She knew that she probably wouldn't, even if Joshua Knight didn't show up. Peter was getting so possessive these days, pressing her more and more for a marriage that she really didn't want. On top of Meryl's arrival, politely sparring with Peter Tomlinson over brandy tonight was something that she just didn't need.

As though reading her mind, Peter's voice drifted over the telephone line, sounding annoyed and edgy. "Well, I don't intend to hold my breath."

"Pete . . ."

"Look, let's just forget about tonight. Scratch it. We'll reschedule the whole thing for tomorrow night."

Courtney hesitated, feeling herself being backed into a corner. "I don't know if my father's free. I can always call and check with him, then get back to you."

"Courtney, I told you, I don't want to see Matthew. I see him five days a week at the college. I want to see you. Alone. Without any little girls and without your father." Suddenly his voice softened. "Please. I just want to talk to you without a peanut gallery in attendance."

Courtney felt her breath leaving her in a small, helpless sigh. "Yes, fine, of course," she murmured, feeling defeated and guilty at the same time. "Seven o'clock tomorrow, then."

She said her good-byes and replaced the receiver gently. She wasn't exactly sure what she wanted or expected of Peter, but she knew that it wasn't marriage. It wasn't even a romance. What was more, she hadn't really had time lately to decide what she wanted to do about their relationship. Maybe she wasn't leading him on, but she wasn't doing much to break off with him, either.

She got up from behind her desk and moved toward the shadows that marked the door, then headed down to the very end of the hall and out onto the loggia. She moved to the edge of the vast balcony and rested her elbows on the marble balustrade.

She really couldn't see them, but she knew that they were out there: the rolling green hills of Collegeville, lush and verdant with the advent of spring. Emerald lawns would be stretching out as far as a healthy eye could see. Courtney was content to know that they were there and to remember what they looked like. She had to be.

She swallowed a deep breath of clean air and willed herself to relax. Gradually some of the tension eased from her shoulders as the cool breeze ruffled her hair and teased the hem of her skirt. She really would have to do something about Pete. Their relationship couldn't go on indefinitely; it was a dead-end street for both of them.

She wondered, not for the first time, why he would want to resign himself to a life with a woman who would never know if she would be able to see anything at all next week, next month, even the next day. The life expectancy of her remaining sight was something that Courtney refused to dwell upon, but the specter of total blindness always lurked like an evil shadow in the back of her thoughts, begging to be acknowledged. Her eyes were getting worse. Someday her sight would be gone, even the meager bit she had left. Courtney shuddered at the image that flashed before her mind's eye: an older version of herself, with eyes that were completely blind, and totally dependent upon Pete for everything if she married him.

No, that would never happen to her. Never! She couldn't prevent herself from going blind, but she could control her life, and she didn't intend to marry anyone. Even when her eyes fully betrayed her, she would still have Winston House and a way to take care of herself. She would be a burden to no one. She wouldn't have anyone tied down by her, feeling sorry for her, living only half their life because of her.

A serious romance, thought Courtney, was a luxury that she could not afford.

But how to convince Pete of that? How could she make him see that Winston House was to be her whole life? How could she convince him kindly to move on to other, greener pastures?

The sunlight coloring her field of vision was golden now, less intrinsically bright. The afternoon was ending; dusk was on its way. Time for dinner, and later, perhaps, to face Joshua Knight. She decided suddenly that she would change for dinner tonight. The prairie skirt and cowboy boots were nice and comfortable, but she wanted to appear businesslike and professional when she confronted Mr. Knight. She had a feeling that professionalism would be the only language that he would understand.

Chapter 2

COURTNEY SPENT AN HOUR CAREFULLY DRESSING for dinner, although she had to wonder if she were wasting her time. Would the anonymous Joshua Knight arrive at seven? A part of her doubted it, but she wasn't taking any chances. She chose a sedate mauve pleated skirt and matching sweater that was formfitting yet somehow prim. Plain black leather heels and her mother's pearls created an ensemble that would have befitted the most austere school-teacher, yet Courtney was uncomfortably aware as she peered into the mirror at close range that she looked more like a well-dressed student. Her green eyes were bright and young, her lips full and almost pouty. Her hair was a tumbling dark mahogany

mane that fell about her shoulders. In a last-ditch
effort to achieve the look she thought would best suit
an encounter with the busy Joshua Knight, she
pulled it back to the nape of her neck and fastened it
into a severe chignon.

The dining room was filled with a babble of shrill
and excited voices when she finally went downstairs,
although only a few of the girls were in residence.
The majority of them were, as usual, spending the
weekend with their families. Courtney felt herself
succumbing to their infectious relaxation almost
immediately. She could almost feel the teacher
persona physically slipping away from her. She
stumbled slightly when someone crawled unexpectedly into her shins, but even that didn't seem to
bother her much, although there were times when it
would have. She detested it when her other senses,
including her balance, failed to compensate for her
eyes.

Now she knelt down to touch a soft cap of short
curls and recognized who it was immediately. "Lilith? What in the world are you doing down here?"

"My spoon fell down. Corinne knocked it off
when she was making it walk, and now I can't find
it."

Courtney helped the little girl to her feet. "Well,
there are more where that one came from. Where's
Elizabeth? We'll ask her to get you another. In the
meantime, troops, watch where you walk. We've got
a runaway spoon on the loose."

"I hardly think they can be expected to watch
where they're going, under the circumstances. Miss
Winston, isn't it? Courtney Winston?"

The smooth voice startled her, coming from behind her as it did. It was quiet and hushed, as though

meant for her ears alone, but it was equally unrecognizable and most indisputably male. It had a feeling of leashed power to it that caused Courtney to catch her breath slightly. She whirled around in the direction of the voice before she thought better of it.

Almost immediately, as she should have known it would, her head seemed to spin, gallivanting off into an orbit all of its own. She detested the spectacle she knew she was making of herself, but she couldn't help it; her untrustworthy balance made her reach out instinctively for something stable and unmoving to hold on to.

Even as she cursed softly beneath her breath, her hands found a hard, muscled arm covered in what felt like soft brushed flannel. Beneath her grasp, the sheer hardness of the muscles that she found there corded and rippled as the man tensed himself to catch her.

It was then that she found the spoon. She took a few, uncertain steps backward, only to come down on it hard with the relatively high heel of her shoe. Her ankle twisted painfully, and she knew, helplessly and with a sick feeling in the pit of her stomach, that she was going to fall into the vortex of light, fuzzy shapes and movement that was surrounding her.

Another powerful arm joined with the first one to catch her as she went down. The sudden force of that coiled strength breaking her fall made her gasp and grab once more for the muscles beneath the soft flannel.

As her head stopped spinning, she looked into the most vivid, golden brown eyes that she had ever seen—eyes so captivating that they mocked even the beauty of Meryl's. They were so very much like the eyes that had stared back at Courtney from the davenport earlier, and yet they were different. Meryl's gaze, though blind, had been hungry and devouring. The golden eyes that glinted back at Courtney now were hard and bright.

Greedily, in the mere split second of time that she allowed herself, Courtney drank in the man's appearance while she was still close enough to see him. His physical similarity to Meryl didn't end with his eyes. He had the same thick chestnut hair that Meryl had, although his was almost unruly in its waves, curling down over the collar of his shirt and falling rakishly over his forehead. The same sooty eyelashes blinked back at her; they would have looked oddly feminine and out of place had it not been for the rugged frown lines etched around his eyes and the cold, unnerving brightness that shone from their golden depths. The only outstanding difference between the face of this man and the girl who was obviously his daughter was the deep dimple in the chin that was now directly before Courtney's eyes. That, she thought, and a rugged, almost weary masculinity that seemed to be permanently engraved on his face, as though he had seen everything the world had to offer and wasn't impressed by any of it.

She drank all of this in quickly, storing it away in her memory, before bits and pieces of reality came storming in on her. Suddenly her other senses became acutely sensitive, and she was uncomfortably aware of odd, fleeting impressions: the crush of his hard chest against her breasts and a certain alien tingling there that felt both delicious and frightening; his hands, strong and gripping, as they held her upright and bit into the flesh of her arms. Inanely, she wondered at the bruises she might find there tomorrow before the silence that had descended upon the room finally reached her. She gasped again and began to struggle against the strong arms that held her.

"I can stand now," she protested, her voice sounding thin and tremulous even to her own ears. The tingling that had begun in her breasts had found its way to her legs, and she felt weakly excited, as though all her energy had ebbed away before crashing over her again with all its force. Butterflies of confusion and vague fear began beating their wings in the pit of her stomach, and she could feel the searching eyes of the girls boring into her back almost as strongly as she could feel the hardness of his chest crushing her own. His voice came to her distantly, as though it had to travel miles to break through her confusion.

"I suppose you can, but if you don't mind, I'd like to enjoy this moment just a bit longer. I can't remember the last time I had this effect on a woman." His voice held more than a tinge of mockery, cool and quiet and, to Courtney's sensitive ears, outrageously clear. Her confusion shattered at the sound of it, and she put her hands up against his chest to push him away. Her reaction, she was sure, was not so different from that of a hundred other women confronted by him in such a manner, although she had the misplaced spoon to blame rather than his unnervingly rugged good looks.

"The girls!" she hissed at him. Oh, God, surely they were all drinking this in, their eyes wide with amazement. What a spectacle she was making of herself! Her pride was feeling more bedraggled by the second; she was rattled and unsure of herself in a way that was completely new to her. She was also

incredibly grateful as she remembered in a rush that
Meryl had refused to come down for dinner. At least
she wasn't witness to this absurd scene.

"I doubt they can see you," the man was saying,
and his voice broke through her confusion once
more. "Don't worry about it."

Suddenly, with a strength that surprised even her,
Courtney pushed him away roughly. The air felt cool
and soothing against her skin where his touch had
been.

"You're deluding yourself, then, Mr. Knight, because only one of the girls present is actually blind,"
she whispered coldly. "You are Mr. Knight, aren't
you?" Who else could he be, with those eyes?

"None other." He sounded complacent and smug.
"You were expecting someone else?"

"I wasn't expecting *you*," she retorted. "And
most certainly not at this hour."

Elizabeth's voice sounded from the doorway.
"Oh, Courtney, I'm so sorry. He slipped right past
me. I told him to wait in the study—"

"It's all right, Elizabeth. It's not your fault. We
already know that Mr. Knight doesn't follow direc-
tions very well."

"Now what in the hell is that supposed to mean?"
His words were sharp and indignant, but his tone
was genuinely curious.

"Please!" Courtney hissed at him again. Instinctively, she reached out for his arm to lead him into
the corridor. Once again awe filled her at the
strength and power she felt there. Confusion steeped
through her, and she felt something quivering low
and deep within her. She had to forcibly fight off an
urge to run her hand up his arm and over his
shoulder, to touch and soothe his tense, coiled
muscles. She was appalled at herself! What was the

matter with her? Men weren't an alien species to her, not even good-looking ones. And yet, here she was, feeling weak and shaken and titillated by this particular man, almost aching to touch him and admire the hard contours of his body. Certainly Pete had never induced this sense of wonder in her. But this definitely wasn't Pete. This was the father of one of her students, for heaven's sake! She didn't know him from Adam, and she was behaving like a man-starved adolescent!

Determined to triumph over the tumultuous reactions that were racing through her, she yanked her hand free of his arm, crossed her own arms in front of her and tucked her hands safely against her sides. Her voice was still thin and not at all authoritative as she spoke.

"If you don't mind, I think it's best if we continue this discussion in my office." She was acutely aware of too many things here in the dining room: his proximity and the strange things it was doing to her; those amber eyes gazing mockingly down on her; Elizabeth's hushed amazement at this man, who blithely broke her rules of etiquette and whose presence seemed to fill every nook and cranny of the dining room. But most of all, she was regretfully conscious of the excited whispers that were beginning to buzz at the dining room table behind her.

"Whatever you say, teacher." He hooked his arm through hers, and the gentle solicitude in his touch was such a contrast to his haughty indifference that it took her by surprise. But, of course, there was Meryl. He was undoubtedly well versed in the details of leading the blind.

She snatched her arm away from him again, feeling angry and flustered. "I'm fine. If you had read my letters, you would know that *I'm* not blind,

either. I can certainly see well enough to get to my
office without your help."

"Now you sound like Meryl," he observed mildly.
She heard a touch of amusement in his words.

Courtney's anger turned immediately into embarrassment. How right he was! She sounded more like
an impatient schoolgirl than the adult she was. How
many times had she heard one of the girls squeal
indignantly, "I can see!" How many times had
Meryl repeated those very words that afternoon?

She grabbed the hall railing and knew that her
knuckles must be white with tension. She felt mildly
satisfied that her original assessment of Joshua
Knight had been correct after all. He had caused
problems that afternoon by not being there, and was
causing even more problems now with his presence,
although she had to admit that his was no mere
presence. She couldn't see him as he walked beside
her, but she was undeniably aware of him.

She came to her office and pushed open the heavy
door, her anger seeping back into her with each step.
He hadn't even asked about Meryl! Mentioned her,
yes, but he hadn't asked about her obvious absence.
And his condescending attitude! His ignorant suppo-
sition that since the girls couldn't see him clearly,
they had no idea of what was going on! No wonder
Meryl was as disturbed as she was, if her father
constantly treated her as a nonentity!

She rounded her desk quickly, her hand gliding
gently over the edge, then sat stiffly in her chair.
Now what? Oh, damn, there had been so many
things that she had wanted to say to him, carefully
prepared words that she had practically memorized.
All the words were gone now, lost in the confusion
that this man had created within her. And what was
he doing there, anyway? It could be no later than

five-fifteen; Andrea Vaughan had stated clearly that he would be arriving at seven.

Courtney floundered in her confusion, searching her mind for sensible, businesslike words, but came up with only snappish indignation. "In case you're wondering," she said finally, stiffly, "your daughter is still upstairs in her room. She preferred not to come down for dinner. In fact, she generally prefers not to be here at all. I don't suppose you were aware of that before you sent her here with your house-keeper?" She spat out the last word with such venom that it surprised even her. True, Andrea Vaughan was hardly her favorite person, but that hardly explained why the thought of her rankled so badly. Housekeeper, indeed.

"I was aware of it," he said smoothly, settling himself in the chair usually used by Elizabeth, the one closest to Courtney's desk. Courtney closed her eyes, for once preferring blindness to her limited sight. This would be so much easier if she didn't have to *look* at him, at the way his thick, muscular frame barely fit into Elizabeth's diminutive chair, at the way his thighs pressed against the worn fabric of the arms.

Courtney rubbed a shaky hand over her eyes, then quickly laid it flat against her desk, hoping that he hadn't noticed her trembling. My God, she had been an emotional wreck all day thanks to the Knights! First Meryl, and now her father, just as troublesome and thought-provoking. And as much as she was incensed by him, she was also shocked at her reaction to him. Even as she sat there, the words she had at last recollected wanting to say to him vanished from her mind again. She found herself noticing instead that he was dressed casually in the flannel shirt that she had been so acutely aware of earlier, jeans that strained over his thighs—or was that only her imagination taking over for her eyes?—and boots that looked like they were made of expensive leather. Well, Andrea Vaughan had mentioned only that he had been busy. She hadn't said exactly what he had been busy at. Clearly it hadn't been his import/export business!

"If you were aware of how she felt about coming here, why did you send her?" Courtney asked at length, struggling to keep her voice even and to concentrate on the business at hand.

"It was the best thing for her. Why else?"

"Mr. Knight, you don't seem to understand that this is not the best place for your daughter if she doesn't want to be here," she said coldly, her voice stronger as her anger returned to galvanize her. "What do you possibly expect me to do for her when she's this resentful of being here? That's quite a barrier to break down before I can help her."

"You'll think of a way to do it, I'm sure. I don't need to tell you, Miss Winston, that you came highly recommended to me. It was Dr. Farber who suggested that I look into your school, as a matter of fact. I believe he's your doctor?"

Courtney only nodded. What else did he know about her? Not enough, obviously, to realize that she had some limited eyesight. Her indignation at this stung her, and puzzled her as well, because it was an indignation that she had banished long ago. Why was it creeping back up on her now? The issue at hand was Meryl's eyesight, not her own.

"Miss Winston, I have all the faith in the world that you can work more wonders with Meryl than I ever could." His voice was cold and hard now, not at all smooth or mocking. Courtney had no doubt that if she could see his eyes clearly, she would meet with an icy, golden brown glare. She was surprised when a latent restlessness erupted in him and he sprang out of the chair suddenly to pace the room.

"Believe me, she'll be much better off with you." He spat the words out as though it were Courtney's fault that this was so. "Anything you can do will be an improvement! Now, I really have to get going. I haven't time for this nonsense. I only came because Andie insisted that you had to see me, and now that I've arrived, I find that you've got nothing but vague insinuations to throw at me. Good night, Miss Winston."

For the second time that night Courtney moved too quickly, but this time she was prepared for the sure-to-follow dizziness. She grasped the edge of her desk tightly and jumped to her feet, all her incredible anger burning in her green eyes.

"Just wait a minute!" Her voice rose to a shout. It seemed to echo off the wood paneling and reverberate in the room. "I think, Mr. Knight, that if you could salvage just a bit of your precious time for her, Meryl wouldn't be such a problem for you! That child needs love and understanding! Instead, you've dished out numerous operations and flimsy hope, so that when it became evident that she's not going to be able to see, she was devastated and resentful. And then what do you do? You push her away from you, send her to me, and don't even take the time to accompany her! It seems to me that you never had the slightest intention of trying to help her yourself. You just seem to want to get her off your hands! You're a despicable excuse for a father, Mr. Knight, and if I weren't so concerned for Meryl's welfare, I'd send her right back home with you. As it is, you haven't even asked to see her. I thought it was the height of negligence when you sent her here with your housekeeper, but your audacity just keeps getting worse!"

He had crossed back to her desk and was standing directly in front of her, his eyes shining with the most incredible anger Courtney had ever seen. Instinctively she flinched away from him, but the reflex came just a second too late. One rough hand caught her chin, holding her still and trembling. As he touched her, shock waves rippled through her flesh, and she felt her knees giving out beneath her, her heart hammering wildly within her. She tightened her grasp on the edge of the desk until the raised edge bit into her hands; the pain was real and pure and it distracted her. Feeling it, she felt her breath escape her, and she tried to concentrate on it, on anything but this man, so strong and virile as he leaned across the desk toward her, as he touched her, his anger burning brightly in his eyes.

"Are you quite through, teacher?" His cold fury chilled her to the bone.

Courtney opened her mouth to speak, but no words came, only more breath, heavy and catching in her throat.

"Awfully high-and-mighty, aren't you?" His voice was flat and cold. "Maybe you ought to let go of that facade. Maybe you ought to let that hellfire come out a bit more often. It might bring you in touch with reality. It's a cold world out there, teacher. People aren't always eager to live up to your little schoolmarm ideals. The world won't end because I didn't bring Meryl here myself."

Suddenly his hand was gone, and he moved slightly away from her. Courtney gasped, feeling her lungs burn with the force of her breath.

"I don't give a damn what you expect of me. I

don't give a damn what you think of me," he continued. "Just help Meryl. That's why she's here, whether she wants to be or not. And that, teacher, is all I expect of you."

"My instincts—" she began, then stopped, horrified to realize that her voice was choked and ragged. She gripped the edge of her desk still more tightly and looked away from him, determined to finish what she had started. In a voice that was softer, but still strained, she continued. "My instincts tell me that Meryl needs more than special schooling, and now that I've met you, I can certainly understand why. If it becomes apparent that I can't break through her resentment on my own, I'd like your permission to call in a psychologist. There's no way I can help her without her cooperation."

Joshua Knight reeled away from the desk in one fluid, animalistic movement. Again Courtney was frozen by the subdued strength which seemed to course through his muscles. She was grateful, for the sake of her thundering heart, that he moved closer to the door, where she couldn't see him clearly.

"Send the necessary paper work to my office. You have the address," he said shortly, as though her response to his cutting fury was no more or less than he had expected. "I don't care what you do or how you do it. Just help her. I should think you'd have plenty of success if you'd just concentrate on teaching her Braille or whatever the hell it is instead of worrying about my relationship with her— something, incidentally, that should be no concern of yours. Go ahead and hire your psychologist, Miss Winston, if that will help. Just send the bill to my office."

"You can rest assured that I will, Mr. Knight."

Her voice, though soft and hushed now, matched the iciness of his own.

"Fine," he answered, his words clipped and controlled. "Now, if you'll excuse me, I've got work to get back to."

He was halfway out into the corridor when Courtney heard herself calling out to him again. "You really have no intention of seeing Meryl before you go?"

"All things considered, Miss Winston, I think not. From what you tell me of her attitude toward this place, she probably wouldn't let me leave without her. And now that I've met *you,* I'm beginning to understand her attitude! If you didn't come so highly recommended by a man I happen to trust, I *would* take her back with me right now."

"You could probably save us both a good deal of aggravation by doing just that. However, Meryl would certainly be the one to suffer for it."

"Well, it seems we finally agree on something, then. I don't recommend that you tell Meryl that I was here, by the way. What she doesn't know won't hurt her."

In the next second the shadows in the corridor seemed to swallow him. Courtney was left alone in an echoing silence.

Her knees gave out, finally and suddenly, and she dropped back down into her chair. Hot tears burned her eyes, and she fought them with everything she had. There was no room in her life for self-pitying tears, none at all. Not even horrendous men like Meryl Knight's father were worthy of them. She swiped angrily at her eyes with shaky fingers and found herself breathing in short, staccato gasps in an effort to hold back the tears. They were just beginning to win the battle when Elizabeth's soft voice came from the door.

"Lordy, but that was some scuffle. What in heaven's name was going on in here?"

Courtney not only lost the battle, but the war as well. Her sobs erupted with a startling urgency, wracking her thin frame as she tried to gulp them back. Elizabeth quickly shut the door and hurried to her desk.

"There, there, what is it? What did he say to you?"

Courtney only shook her head as she tried to find her voice. "Oh, Elizabeth, he was horrible . . . I was horrible. . . . I was totally out of line. What's wrong with me? I virtually accused him of hating his daughter! Although"—and some of her anger surged back into her with the thought—"sometimes it would seem that way. Do you know that he didn't even want to see Meryl? He said he thought it was better if he didn't."

She sighed, the anger draining out of her again. "Unfortunately, now that I've blown up that way, he'll probably never come back. Not that I can blame him. But Meryl won't understand that. All she'll know is that her father won't be coming to see her and that she's stuck here." For some reason the thought that Joshua Knight would probably never come within a mile of Winston House again almost brought fresh tears to her eyes.

"Perhaps you ought to call him and apologize? It's just an idea," Elizabeth suggested tactfully.

"Not a bad one, either, I suppose," Courtney admitted. "Except for two things. First of all, I don't seem to have a whole lot of luck getting Mr. Joshua Knight on the telephone, and second of all, while I might have been out of line to say it, everything I said to him was right on target. I can't apologize for being honest."

Elizabeth laughed softly. "Oh, Courtney, what am I going to do with you?"

Courtney smiled at her wearily, then stood up unsteadily. The long day was beginning to take its toll on her. "Well, I guess there's nothing more I can do about it tonight. Elizabeth, I hate to ask, but would you mind sending the girls to bed and locking up? I have a terrible headache."

"Of course, I can see to it. But there's still the matter of Meryl. I was thinking of taking a tray up to her."

The realization that Meryl hadn't yet eaten hit Courtney almost forcibly. She sat down again, hitting the chair with a thump. "Oh, no. I'm as bad as her father. I can't believe I didn't remember that she hasn't eaten."

"It's understandable. It sounded like World War III in here a little while ago. You obviously had other things on your mind."

"That's just it! I had Meryl on my mind."

"No, I think you had Meryl's father on your mind. There's something of a difference between the two." Elizabeth winked and started off toward the door.

"Wait!" Courtney called out, getting to her feet again. "I'll take something up to her. I was going to check in on her anyway."

Elizabeth looked vaguely disapproving when Courtney joined her in the doorway.

"She's got to eat, Elizabeth. We can't add malnutrition to the list of her problems."

"I know that. It just annoys me that she's putting all of us out with her little tantrums. And I can't help wondering how long it's going to continue."

Courtney sighed audibly. "It's not just her, Elizabeth. It's her father. If he had just talked to her about coming here, or if he had forewarned me . . ." Her voice trailed off. What else could she say? She had picked the problem apart all day, and it wasn't getting her anywhere at all. All she had gained was a walloping headache.

She slipped through the door at the end of the hallway and started downstairs to the kitchen, holding the railing on the steps to offset the steep pitch of the shadowy stairs. She began counting silently on the top step, but when she reached five, she faltered and hesitated. Inexplicably, for the first time in years, her concentration had failed her. She found herself wondering instead if Joshua Knight was sleeping with Andrea Vaughan. Were they lovers? Was Andrea, with her silvery blond hair, sensuous shape and perfectly good eyes, sharing Joshua's bed?

She tried to remember how many steps she had taken, tried to push the unnecessary, irrelevant issue from her mind, but bitter, unwelcome envy of Andrea's sight was burning through her, making it impossible. Worse, hot tears were burning at her eyes again, melting the nondescript shadows that were all she had to guide her now that she had lost count of the steps.

"No!" she protested aloud. What the devil was wrong with her? Of course Andrea Vaughan could see. Most people could! Courtney just didn't happen to be one of them, and that was all there was to it. And if Andrea was Joshua's lover, well, then, so what? What difference did it make to *her* life?

She banished her self-pity bitterly, hating it and angry at herself for giving in to it. She had the steps to deal with, and she was damned well going to do it, eyes or no eyes.

She wiped a hand across her forehead and tried to concentrate. She had been on five or six, maybe seven. That meant there were four to six steps left to go. She resumed her counting, and when she reached four, she held a hand out in front of her. No door. One more step. The tips of her fingers brushed wood. She took one more step and pushed through into the lighted kitchen.

The blurry light revealed that Elizabeth had already put together a tray for Meryl. It sat on the butcher block table in the center of the room. Thick slabs of roast beef vied for space on the plate with a heaping mound of coleslaw and two biscuits. There were a small bowl of tapioca pudding and a glass of milk near the plate.

Courtney's stomach rumbled at the aroma of the cold yet tempting food. She realized with a start that she hadn't eaten, either. That could be half of the reason for her headache and her unexpected tears as well. She cut some of the beef for herself and voraciously swallowed a few pieces before she slipped the rest between two slices of wheat bread. She scrounged around in the refrigerator until she came up with some mayonnaise and Swiss cheese. It wouldn't be the most nutritious meal in the world, but it would fill her up. Damn Joshua Knight anyway! On top of everything else, he had stolen her dinner right out from under her nose!

As soon as she reached the second floor she could tell that Meryl's door was closed and the room dark. Inky blackness filled that end of the hallway. It occurred to her belatedly that Meryl might be sleeping. She had raised one hand to knock tentatively on the door when she heard a low, muffled sob from inside. Something deep within her wrenched. More pity, but not the selfish variety this time. Still, she pushed it away. Meryl needed many things, but pity wasn't one of them.

Balancing the tray on one hand, she pushed the door open gently. "Meryl?" she called out softly. "It's Courtney. I brought some dinner for you."

The sobs stopped; only thick, miserable silence filled the room.

Courtney ran her left hand over the wall, feeling vainly for the light switch. The room was darker even than the stairs had been, and without any light to guide her, Courtney could see less than nothing. And still she couldn't find the light switch. She tried in vain to remember if this room was laid out like her own; after all, the rooms were joined by a bathroom, so it was a possibility. If that was the case, the switch would be to her right. She moved the tray to her other hand and felt along the other wall.

Just as her fingers located the switch, she felt the tray pushed roughly from her hand. Courtney jumped as it landed against something hard and unyielding. She recognized the clatter of plastic against wood and the tinkle of glass breaking, and she gasped involuntarily. Soft light filled the room, and as a result she could see Meryl standing in the middle of the room.

Courtney crossed to her slowly, at a loss for words. The girl's face looked swollen and red from crying; her arms were crossed belligerently over her chest.

"Did I say I wanted dinner?" Meryl's voice was hard and hateful. "I don't want your lousy old food! Just go away and leave me alone!"

Courtney took a deep breath and tried to hold on to her temper. "Well, I'll admit that I thought of doing just that. It really didn't seem fair to either Elizabeth or myself that you were getting special treatment. But I thought you'd probably be starving by now. Anyway, if you're not, you're not. You want to help me clean this mess up? I don't dare ask Elizabeth. She might not take this as well as I'm trying to."

"Clean it up yourself." Meryl threw herself face first onto the bed and lay there with her face pressed into the pillow. It was only instinct that told Courtney that her back was rising and falling with the heavy weight of her sobs.

Courtney made her way slowly into the bathroom. Her headache was blooming now, reaching tenacious fingers throughout her skull. She squeezed her eyes shut against the pain and bit her lip. Now what? Should she humor the girl and clean up the mess? Leave it there until she cleaned it up herself? It didn't seem right to cater to her temper by cleaning it up.

Finally she settled on a compromise. She went back to Meryl's room and picked up the few shattered pieces of the milk glass and the tapioca bowl that she could find, those that could be dangerous if Meryl decided to roam the room again. She left the rest of the mess where it was, the tray overturned on the floor, the roast beef taking up residence in the oddest of places. Only her sandwich was salvageable, she discovered. The two pieces of bread sat at slightly different angles, and a slice of cheese had escaped, but all in all, the result was still edible.

Carrying the wastebasket full of glass in one hand and the sandwich in the other, she moved back to the bed where Meryl was still lying. Sensing her presence, the girl rolled over.

The angry amber eyes met Courtney's own, startling her again with their intensity. I know you, Courtney thought. I know what's going on behind those eyes. I was like you once, Meryl. I fought it, too. But it doesn't do any good in the long run. It only wastes precious time.

Though she wanted to, she didn't say any of these things to Meryl. She simply couldn't bring herself to. They were her own private revelations, special and sacred to her. Instead, she reached out and brushed a lock of heavy brown hair off the girl's forehead. Meryl flinched at her touch, and Courtney felt the familiar wrenching in her stomach again.

"It gets better," she said finally, softly. "That's about all I can tell you, honey. You get used to it."

She didn't give Meryl a chance to answer, to lash out at her with more angry words. Quickly she got to her feet and placed the roast beef sandwich on the nightstand.

When she was back in the doorway to the bathroom, ready to close the door and slip into her own room, she called out to Meryl again. "I left a sandwich for you on the nightstand. It survived somehow. Anyway, it's just to the left of you. You might get hungry later."

She pulled the door closed quickly and stepped back into the bathroom. For a second that stretched into a minute, she stood there in the darkness, listening to the silence on the other side of the door.

At least, she thought finally, she's not crying.

Thoroughly drained now, Courtney flicked on the bathroom light and leaned close to the mirror to peer into her own eyes. Did they ever look like Meryl's anymore? Were they ever angry and bitter? If someone had handed her a mirror half an hour ago, when she had been trapped on the stairs, would she have seen resentment burning bright and uncontrolled there?

Peter had once told her that her eyes had always

been like that when she was younger, that they had snapped with a hellion spark of pride and perseverance, as though trying to make up for their uselessness with pure energy and spunk. He had told her that he had first fallen in love with those little-girl eyes. They were more complacent now, more accepting. The green fire smoldered rather than burned, and still he said he loved her. The pride was still there, but now it had become his enemy, keeping him at a distance. Poor Peter, she thought. I just don't love you in the right way to give in. And even if I wanted to, I couldn't. I wouldn't let myself.

She straightened, and with muscles and limbs that almost ached with fatigue, she began to wash her face free of the makeup that had been totally lost on Joshua Knight. She had managed to look fairly professional, and all it had won her was his scorn. The simmering fury within her fed on the memory of his words and burned more brightly.

Back in her bedroom, she peeled off the sweater set and dropped it on the pink velvet Victorian chair near the fireplace. She reached into a drawer for a nightgown, then went back to the vanity to brush out her hair. It was very nearly as tangled as her thoughts about the Knights, which simmered just below the surface of her calm. She pushed them away from her, telling herself that the problems would still be there tomorrow, and that there was nothing she could accomplish before dawn, even if she had some idea of where to start.

She slipped between the sheets and turned off the bedside lamp, letting precious relaxation seep into her. Sleep, that was what she needed. Many undisturbed hours of it. In the morning she would figure out how to approach Meryl.

One last conscious thought fought free of the

tangle of impressions in her brain before sleep claimed her. It was more of a memory than anything else—a startling memory that made her roll over and stave off sleep for just a moment more, for it wasn't something that she had consciously noticed before. What she remembered was the shocked, miserable look on Joshua Knight's face as he had leaned across the desk at her, before he had touched her, before her few logical thoughts had whirled away from her like helpless leaves on a strange, new wind. Unbidden, a sharp stab of sympathy shot through her. She tried to push it away, tried to summon back the slow, burning anger that lay in wait for her whenever she thought of the man and the agony of the new emotions that he stirred up within her, but she couldn't do it. All she could see was the naked pain in those fiery yellow-brown eyes.

Chapter 3

Golden sunlight streamed through the crack in the bedroom curtains and burned into Courtney's eyes as she struggled against pending wakefulness. The amber light insinuated itself into her vision, enveloping her in its glare, reminding her of Joshua Knight's leonine eyes.

The thought, sliding in on her so casually and unexpectedly, jarred her awake. She sat bolt upright in bed, turning quickly away from the window with its brightness and its reminders. When she ran her fingers over the face of her bedside clock she was surprised to find that it was only six-thirty. Too early to be thinking about the Knights. But then, she hadn't been thinking about the Knights. Not really. She had been thinking about *a* Knight, and, as Elizabeth had said, there was something of a difference between the two.

Determined not to dwell on her preoccupation with the man—for at some point during the night she had decided that her chaotic emotions concerning him were merely a matter of preoccupation with his virility—she untangled her legs from the sheets and stood up. Stretching cramped, sleep-congested muscles, she shielded her eyes and turned back to the window. Sunday morning. What delicious potential the day had! Perhaps she would go into town and have breakfast with her father, or maybe she would organize a picnic of sorts for the girls who had remained at school over the weekend. They could go down to the creek and—

Her thoughts broke off suddenly as the glimmering, early morning light outside forced another realization upon her. Before she did anything else, she would have to call Joshua Knight and make her apologies. The thought rankled and stirred a queasy nervousness in the pit of her stomach, but she knew that it had to be done. For Meryl's sake, there had to be peace between Courtney and her father, although Courtney wasn't entirely hopeful that a phone call would do the trick.

She turned away from the window, pulled on a pair of jeans and a sweater, and moved into the bathroom. As she washed up, she listened hard for any trace of sound from the room next door that would tell her that Meryl was awake, but there was only silence. A good sign, perhaps, but then, it was still very early.

She used what had once been the servants' stairs to go down past the first floor into the kitchen. She held on to her concentration this time and counted down the twenty-four steps without mishap. Although images of Meryl's father hovered near the brink of her thoughts, they seemed less pressing than those of the night before. Andrea Vaughan wasn't so much a part of them this time, and Courtney had managed to convince herself that her envy of the housekeeper was only normal, although not necessarily acceptable. Joshua Knight was an incredibly self-possessed, intriguing and attractive man, and Courtney admitted that she was only human. Naturally, he would have an effect on her, and naturally, she would be somewhat envious of the lucky woman he loved.

She did not for a minute accept the fact that she also envied the 20/20 vision that made Andrea Vaughan both worth loving and able to accept that love. The idea was so preposterous that Courtney literally scoffed aloud as she entered the kitchen. Her self-pitying tears of the night before had been simply a childish railing at fate and had nothing to do with Andrea, her eyes, or her relationship with Joshua Knight. What was more, Courtney did not intend to give in to such sniffling again.

The kitchen was steeped in early morning quiet, so Courtney swiveled around in alarm when Elizabeth's voice shattered the silence.

"That was an unladylike sound if I ever heard one," Elizabeth said, looking up from the newspaper she was reading at the butcher block table. As Courtney watched, her heart slowing to its normal rhythm, Elizabeth's shadowy shape lifted a cup of coffee and sipped.

"What sound?" Courtney turned away in the direction of the counter and felt along its worn smoothness for the coffeepot, genuinely confused.

"That little snort you made when you walked in,

before you noticed me sitting here. Was it Meryl you were thinking of, or Joshua?"

"Neither," Courtney denied, not quite truthfully, as she brought her coffee to the table and slid into the chair across from Elizabeth. "Actually, I was thinking about myself and my reactions to both of them," she admitted.

"You're talking about the argument you had with Joshua last night?"

"That's part of it. I've decided to take your advice. I'm going to call him."

"That could be a good move."

"I'm doing it purely for Meryl's sake," she said musingly as she sipped her coffee.

"Of course," Elizabeth answered. The three feet that separated them prevented Courtney from seeing the unveiled amusement in her eyes.

"It certainly can't help her much if her father and I are feuding," she continued absently.

"How is she this morning, by the way?"

"Who?"

Courtney started slightly at Elizabeth's laughter and felt the blood rush to her cheeks. She shook her head. "I was lost in other thoughts," she explained lamely.

"I don't doubt it."

Courtney ignored Elizabeth's good-natured jibe, chiefly because she didn't know quite how to answer it. She retreated to the comparatively safe subject of Meryl. "Well, we took a major step backward, I guess. She threw the tray across the room when I took it up to her last night."

"That's outrageous!"

"Well, actually," Courtney amended quickly, "she just pushed the tray out of my hand. She's miserable, Elizabeth. She doesn't know where or who to strike out at. She's all alone in her dark little world, and even her father won't—or can't—get through to help her."

"Can't? That's an added dimension since we talked last night."

Courtney didn't answer. She was staring into her coffee cup, swirling the liquid around in circles so that it almost slopped up over the rim. Elizabeth was right; it was a new dimension, and it was a concession that Courtney hadn't really been aware of making. She just couldn't seem to forget that haunted look in Joshua's eyes. Courtney suspected that, in some way, Joshua had met his match in his daughter. There were many possible theories behind her suspicions, but none of them made much sense to her. She only knew that in one of them there was an element of truth, and that quite possibly she had stumbled upon it in her diatribe the night before.

Suddenly she looked up, aware only that Elizabeth had said something that had fallen on deaf ears. Courtney shook her head. "Sorry, I wasn't listening."

"I was just suggesting that you might mention the birthday party to Joshua while you have him on the telephone. I'll have an invitation sent out to him, of course, but it may be late in the week by the time he receives it, and the party is a week from next Saturday."

Courtney nodded, her thoughts in chaos. She should mention the birthday party. Ordinarily she would have thought of it herself. It was going to be a big day for the school; the second anniversary of its opening, and naturally the parents were invited. Courtney was simply afraid that Joshua would take it as a personal invitation. She remembered his bantering comment about her reaction to him when he had saved her from falling. Had he been serious? Had he somehow sensed the turmoil that he had started within her? It was a remote possibility, but one that had to be considered. Still, Courtney had no choice in the matter—not really. She would have to invite him personally. If they waited for him to receive the invitation in the mail, he might not get it in time to keep the evening free. He certainly seemed to have enough of a social life, and a business life, to keep him pretty occupied. Oddly, the thought that he might not attend bothered her, and she had to admit that it was a very real possibility. After all, how far could an apology go toward smoothing over their nightmare confrontation?

Courtney got to her feet and carried her cup to the sink, dashing its contents down the drain. "I'll be in my office if you need me," she said vaguely, unaware that Elizabeth's shrewd eyes were scrutinizing her, unaware of everything save the tangled thoughts and impressions that were beginning to pound at her brain once more.

"Before breakfast? On a Sunday?"

Courtney stopped by the stairs. "I've already told you that I plan to call Joshua in a little while," she said, more sharply than she had intended to. "And I'll do that from my office. Besides," she added more softly, already regretting her snappishness, "I've got a lot of work to catch up on, things that I didn't get done yesterday, what with all the confusion."

"Speaking of which, do you suppose our little friend will grace our breakfast table with her presence this morning?" Now it was Elizabeth who sounded snappish.

Courtney sighed. "I don't know. If she doesn't come down, let me know. I'll take care of it. God only knows how, but I'll think of something."

"How about letting her stew in her own juices up there for a while?"

Courtney couldn't suppress a small smile. Elizabeth's indignation was almost funny. No one had ever dared to upset her carefully built routine before, and within twenty-four hours the Knights had turned it upside down.

It seemed as if she had no sooner reached her desk than Elizabeth's gray head popped around the door frame. Courtney looked up blankly, her thoughts already deep in her lesson plans; even if she couldn't see the woman's chagrined expression, she could read her sentiments loud and clear in her stance. She was annoyed.

"Twelve heads at the breakfast table," she announced. "Guess who's missing? Besides yourself, that is."

"Well, you can forget about me. I'm not hungry. And as for the other . . ." The words trailed off as she got to her feet.

"What are you going to do?"

Courtney shrugged and summoned up a smile. "Wing it."

The smile faded as soon as she reached the stairs. Something's got to be done, she thought desperately, and I don't have any idea of where to start. She certainly couldn't let Meryl hide in her room forever. But how to put an end to her hermitlike behavior? It was, Courtney knew, only a symptom of the girl's many other problems. Still, something told her that it was where she would have to start. She knocked loudly when she reached Meryl's door.

"Go away!" Each syllable was loud and indignant.

It was more the response of a petulant child than one who thought her world was caving in. The realization fueled Courtney's determination; no longer worried about kid gloves, she threw open the door.

"Sorry, Meryl, but I own this place. I pretty much come and go as I please."

Meryl was still in bed. Boldly, knowing that she might be inviting trouble, Courtney went to sit next to her. "So what gives? How come you're still up here? Everyone else is downstairs having breakfast."

"I'm not going to do anything with them! I don't care if you make me stay here forever. You can't make me hang around with those idiots!"

The insult was more than Courtney could stomach. She leaned close to Meryl, her voice dangerously quiet. "Fine. You just stay up here, then. But if you think I'm going to keep bringing you trays to throw across the room and being real nice about it and giving you my sandwich, you've got another think coming. What I told you yesterday still stands, Meryl. I'm not going to *make* you do anything. But I'm not going to pander to you, either. So I'll tell you what. If you want to eat, the dining room is downstairs, the third door to the left. We eat lunch at twelve-thirty and dinner at five. If you ever decide you want to come down, you're more than welcome. Then again, if you want to stay here in your room, feel free to do that, too." She paused, out of breath, her anger diminished somewhat.

Meryl was gaping at her, wide-eyed. "I'll just do that!" she said finally. "I'll do whatever I want to!"

"That's the idea, Meryl. I keep telling you this isn't a prison. But nobody is going to go out of their way for you. It's something of a tit-for-tat system around here. You don't give, you don't get. Okay?"

Courtney got to her feet but paused near the door. "By the way, you might want to consider cleaning up this mess that you made last night if you're planning on staying in here for any length of time. It's going to start smelling pretty awful soon."

She pulled the door closed as she finished speaking, leaving Meryl no time to reply, then stood in the hallway, listening. There wasn't a peep from the other side of the door. She had half expected to hear something crash as it was thrown across the room, but there was only silence.

Courtney made her way back downstairs, her white knuckles on the railing clearly revealing the tension that she hadn't allowed herself to show to Meryl. Although she felt no sense of accomplishment, she was glad that she had at least developed some plan of action where the girl was concerned. It remained to be seen if she would come down for lunch. Personally, Courtney doubted that she would, and she wasn't even hazarding a guess on dinner. But breakfast tomorrow? It was a long shot, but even long shots sometimes won races. She promised herself that if no progress had been made by then, she would seriously consider calling in a psychologist.

Satisfied with her decision, Courtney turned her thoughts to the flip side of the problem: Joshua. She felt the hands of her watch, found that it was only eight-thirty, and let out a small sigh. She could procrastinate with the phone call, then. It was inhuman to call anyone at this hour on a Sunday morning.

She went to her office and sat back down behind her desk. Then, unbidden, a new image flashed into her mind's eye, one that totally blocked out her blurry view of the lesson plans which were scattered in front of her: Joshua, Andrea, breakfast in bed. Andrea's silvery hair would be spread over the pillow, glistening in the sun spilling into the room from a window. And Joshua, those hard, corded muscles of his chest and shoulders relaxed, would be reclining next to her, his skin warm and silken as it touched hers. And, of course, she would look up at him with those huge bright eyes. She would be able to see him; she would see herself in his eyes, and she would have no reason to run from him.

"Stop! Just stop!" She startled herself by saying the words aloud. Quickly she looked up at the door to see if she could discern any human shape among the shadows there. There was no movement; no one had witnessed her outburst. She got to her feet and went to close the door.

None of it made any difference, of course; not the question of what they were doing at this hour of the morning, or the fact that, whatever they were up to, Andrea had a lot to offer him, much more than Courtney herself ever could. Her jealousy, this crazy obsession with Andrea, would simply have to go away. It was useless, a waste of emotion and energy. She was going blind; she was better than halfway there. She was in absolutely no position to vie with Andrea Vaughan for the attentions of a man who had every reason to despise her anyway. And on what was she basing such a preposterous desire in the first place? His good looks? Certainly not the cool mockery that kept him distant and apart from everything that mattered! She didn't even like him much, and yet she was simmering with jealousy of the woman who *might* be his mistress!

Angry with herself, Courtney returned to her desk, but even as she gathered together the papers in front of her, even as she bent to the task of trying to decipher Elizabeth's large printing, she found her fingers tapping at the hard wood, beating out an irregular rhythm not entirely different from that which her own heart was setting. She took a deep breath, but it wrenched free of her throat in a helpless sigh, heavy with confusion. Impulsively, she reached for the telephone with one hand, flipping open her address book with the other.

Call him, she thought. You've got to call him. You've got to apologize, to invite him to the party. This is business. Think of Meryl. Remember that he's the father of one of your students. Remember that you're going blind. Remember that his golden eyes and that hard, unyielding flesh probably belong to Andrea Vaughan. Remember that they have nothing to do with you.

Her headache was threatening to come back again. She pressed her free hand to her temple and pushed the little buttons on the telephone as quickly as her sight would allow, without giving herself a chance to think about what she was doing.

The voice that answered the telephone on the third ring was unmistakably his. Low, fluid, warm, it rippled across the line, sounding somehow harried even at this early hour. Courtney cleared her throat and found her voice.

"Mr. Knight?"

"Speaking." The single word was short and clipped, almost impatient.

The butterflies in her stomach had spawned off-spring; they took flight through her limbs, tickling her throat. She coughed and started again. "This is Courtney Winston. I need to speak to you . . . about last night."

There was a short, derisive laugh from the other

end of the line. "Yes, well, it was a night to remember. I'll grant you that."

"I think some apologies might be in order here."

"Unfortunately, I'm not prepared to give you one."

"Give me one?" Momentarily nonplussed, she stared blankly at the milky form of the telephone. The butterflies hesitated in confusion, then were drowned out in a fiery deluge of rage. Of course. The insults had flown both ways last night. What was it he had called her? A schoolmarm? Instinctively her free hand went to her chin; even the memory of his hard grasp set something to burning in her flesh, and she closed her eyes, struggling with her anger. So he wasn't prepared to offer an apology. The fury that had bubbled within her the night before at his cutting words returned full force, smothering her. She had been so consumed with her own guilt that she had forgotten it, pushed it aside; but now it raged through her, making her grip on the receiver viselike and her voice thin.

"Somehow, I really didn't expect one from you. That would require a certain *savoir faire* that I'm sure you don't possess."

The chuckle that came from the other end of the line was throatier now, less derisive. "Well, I suppose I could give you the chance to reverse my opinion. Why don't you let the wolf out of the sheep's clothing, teacher? Hmmm? Drop your schoolmarm facade and have dinner with me tonight. We can start all over, pretend last night didn't happen."

"I'm sure that won't be necessary." Fury filled her words, making them precise and tight. How dare he? What an insufferable, egotistical man he was! She bit her lip hard to keep herself from gasping aloud, and the metallic taste of blood teased her tongue.

"No?" he asked idly. "Well, suit yourself. You're the one who called to talk about apologies, if I remember correctly."

"I've changed my mind. They're most definitely not in order anymore. Have a good day, Mr. Knight. I'm sorry to have disturbed you."

Without thinking, without knowing that she was going to, she slammed the receiver down with a crash. She trembled with anger that ran hot and furious through her veins. Only a small, distant part of her recognized the stupidity of slamming the receiver on him.

Her heart still pounding erratically beneath her ribs, she bent over her papers again, then, in another burst of temper, shoved them away from her. It was useless. She couldn't concentrate, couldn't think, couldn't see anything but his mocking, leonine eyes as they had looked down at her the night before, couldn't remember anything but his derisive laugh and his cutting words. Abruptly, she got to her feet and paced toward the door.

Well, there was always Peter, safe, sweet Peter, to retreat to. She was going to see him that evening, and it was just as well. She could escape into his bland and polite friendship, back into a world where she belonged, far from the alien butterflies and unquenchable rage that Joshua Knight managed to evoke in her. She had to stop thinking about him, had to stop dwelling on him. As she climbed the stairs to her room she began the almost familiar litany to herself once more. He was the father of one of her students. He was of no concern to her. She couldn't have him, even if she wanted him. Which she didn't. Of course she didn't. He was outside the realm of possibility.

But he was playing havoc with her well-ordered world, making a maelstrom of her carefully guarded emotions.

"Enough already," she murmured to herself as she pushed through the door into her bedroom and went deliberately to her closet. For lack of anything better to do, she began to pick over her wardrobe, contemplating what to wear that night, but vague stirrings of guilt began to thread their way through her confusion. She was using Peter, just as she had been using him for months, running to the sanctuary he provided when things got rough and out of hand, leaning on him for his support while she was willing to give him nothing in return. She had been dreading this date the day before, and yet, in the face of another bout with Joshua Knight, she found herself suddenly looking forward to it. She would spend yet another night leading Peter on by simply not breaking off with him, feeding on his safe, always predictable friendship. And he would savor that, encourage that, because he loved her.

She had to set him free. She knew it even as she pulled dresses from her closet, squinting to see which was which. She had to be one hundred percent honest with him; she had to tell him that she wouldn't marry him and give him back his freedom. The problem of their relationship had been nagging at her, whispering guiltily at her, for months. It was time to do something about it, both for her own peace of mind and for Pete's benefit.

The dress that she finally settled on was of mint green jersey. The neckline was high and sedate, but the dress clung sensuously to the curves of her body, belying the modesty of the bodice. At six-thirty, when Courtney looked into the mirror, she liked what she was able to see. The color complemented her eyes, eyes that did not tell the secret of her handicap. They smiled, they met other eyes, and they wandered. They simply didn't see very well.

She was halfway down the stairs when the knocker on the door sounded. Peter. It had to be, she thought, as she crossed the foyer. Who else would knock so tentatively, as though convinced that he was probably interrupting something?

Still, when she pulled open the door, Courtney found that for once Peter looked quite determined. He stood outside holding a small bouquet of baby's breath and rosebuds that were beautifully delicate. Courtney smiled her thanks and sniffed them, but she couldn't meet his eyes.

"I've decided to pull out all the stops," Peter announced with forced humor, stepping into the entryway. "I'm a very determined man, Courtney." He bent to kiss her lightly, then straightened to fuss with his tie. "Before the month is out, you'll be my wife. I'll put money on it."

Courtney should have caught a warning in his words, but she was preoccupied. She studied his tall, rangy frame, a small frown creasing her forehead. Did he have to start in on the subject so soon? She squinted up at him, took in his perfectly coiffed blondish-gray hair, the eyes that she knew from past experience were crystalline blue, his casually preppie attire. He smelled vaguely of something woodsy and clean. She could do a lot worse than Peter, Courtney knew, but the fact of the matter remained: As far as marriage was concerned, she didn't intend to "do" at all. She couldn't afford to.

She sidestepped his opening remark with a cool smile that she hoped would show something of her displeasure, if only gently. "Well, I'm glad we could get together tonight. I do want to talk to you about that." It was best, she thought, to keep everything up front. A line from a song had been buzzing around in her head all evening. Sometimes you had to be cruel to be kind.

"Well, that's good. I've been waiting forever to have this conversation." He whisked her coat out of the hall closet with a gallant gesture and held it up for her. Even as she slid into it, Courtney felt stirrings of misgiving in the pit of her stomach. This was not, under any circumstances, going to be easy.

She was silent in the car, wrapped up in her thoughts of Joshua and Meryl and the problem with Pete that lay before her. When they pulled up in front of her favorite restaurant, an overly expensive place nestled into the lobby of a local hotel, Courtney grimaced. Being cruel to be kind was one thing, but spending an atrocious amount of Peter's money while she was at it was quite another. For a quick moment Courtney considered putting off her mission for yet another night, but she caught herself firmly before the thought could bloom. No, the time had come. She did not intend to continue to use Peter as a convenient puppet, and that was what it had come down to.

As she slid into her seat, she smiled up at him. "And I was expecting the Englewood Inn."

"Not tonight," he answered, and again there was a vague warning in his words.

In the dark, candlelit room, she didn't see the leonine eyes that were watching her from behind Peter's head. She didn't recognize the hard set of

Joshua Knight's jaw or the rugged imprint of the dimple in his chin as he sat at the table directly behind them.

Courtney gave Peter some rough, sketchy details about Meryl over her *escargots,* but she couldn't see the shrewd eyes that drank in the information from the table behind them. If she had, it would have shattered the tenuous hold she had on her composure. As it was, worries about what she still had to discuss with Peter were filling her mind, along with worries of Meryl and a sense of disquiet over the girl's father.

While the last two problems were far from being solved, the first came to a head over their after-dinner brandy.

"I'd tell you to close your eyes now, but I imagine it would make very little difference," Pete said. It was the kind of light joking that Courtney could accept from only a few people. She offered Peter a funny little half smile that wavered in confusion and cocked her head.

Then, suddenly, she felt it: a small velvet box nestling in the palm of her hand. She recognized it immediately for what it was and her heart froze. Her time for casual procrastination had run out.

"Oh, Peter," was all she could manage to say. Gentle tears, barely discernible, made her emerald eyes glitter. At the table behind them, Joshua Knight's face was clouded with a strange speculation.

"Wrong words," Peter said quietly. "You're supposed to say, 'Oh, yes.'"

Courtney shook her head slowly, the words she wanted to say clogged up in her throat. Finally she spoke, and her voice was choked with regret. "Oh, Peter, I'm so sorry. Really, I am. But I can't. I was going to tell you tonight. Oh, God, I wish I had done it sooner, before I let you go to all this trouble."

"You can't?" he repeated dully. "I suppose all the old excuses still stand?"

Courtney nodded miserably.

"They're not good reasons, Courtney. I love you. I don't care if you go blind and deaf, too. It wouldn't matter to me. I *want* to be the one to take care of you."

"Peter," she said quietly, reaching out to take his hand. The little box sat dejectedly alone in the center of the table. She hadn't opened it. She couldn't.

"It's not a matter of *anyone* taking care of me," she told him carefully. "I can't do that to you. I care about you very much. You're one of my dearest friends, and marrying you might be nice, but I can't be selfish about it." She swallowed hard, knowing that her words were hurting him, but knowing also that there was no help for it.

"That's not really the point," she continued. "I am *not*, under any circumstances, going to marry anyone at all. I can't. I've tried to tell you this, but it was so hard. I'm not going to tie anyone down to someone who might end up walking into walls two years from now," she said, borrowing Meryl's phrase and realizing it with pained humor.

"You don't know that! You don't know that that's going to happen. Your eyes could stay just the way they are now. And besides, it wouldn't make any difference to me."

"It would make a difference to *me*, Pete. A big difference. I'd have to depend on you. You'd have to take care of me, cater to me. I couldn't live with that." Why wouldn't he listen? Why couldn't he understand instead of fighting her? Her composure was slipping badly. An ache over what she was doing to him squeezed mercilessly at her heart. She found herself putting her face in her hands, feeling heartless and cruel.

Finally, finding some small amount of inner strength and courage, she pulled out another indisputable fact to close the subject once and for all. "Besides, Peter, I don't dare have children. I wouldn't risk passing this on to them."

"You have no reason to believe it's hereditary in the first place," he answered her gruffly, his own voice clogged with emotion. "And in the second place, I'm forty-four years old, and I have absolutely no desire to start a family at this late date. Of course, if it meant a great deal to you, I'd go along with it. But it's something I can live without."

"I hope I can, too. At any rate, I'll have to. Besides, I have a houseful of thirteen children to love and take out my maternal instincts on. I can't give that up, Peter. I love those girls, and I love what I'm doing. And we already know how you feel about Winston House. Almost every time you've mentioned getting married, you've mentioned closing the school in the same breath."

"Not closing it, Courtney. Just not living there. You can't make those kids your whole life."

"I can, and I intend to. Oh, Peter!"

"Courtney, just think about it some more. Don't say no yet. That's all I ask."

"I've done nothing *but* think about it for months now! Don't you see that? Peter, I just can't marry you!"

Suddenly she knew that she had to get away from the table, knew with a deadly certainty that if she didn't she was going to cause a scene. Her eyes were sparkling brilliantly with unshed tears. For someone who didn't cry often, she had been choking up entirely too often lately.

Without saying another word, she got to her feet, clutching her handbag against her as if to ward off any further argument.

"Where are you going?" Peter asked, alarmed.

"The rest room. I'll be back."

"Do you want me to go with you?"

"Oh, Peter, please. Give me some credit. I'll get there." She was instantly sorry for her waspish tone and for the crushed, defeated look she knew he would certainly be wearing, but her nerves were stretched to the breaking point. She muttered a vague apology and turned in the direction of the rest rooms.

The dining room was unbearably dark. Snapping all of her senses into high gear and listening hard to the voices around her and gauging their distance, she somehow managed to make her way down the aisle without bumping into any tables. Joshua Knight could have told her that her walk was sure and regal, but she wouldn't have believed him. She felt as though she were stumbling aimlessly in a world darker than it had ever been before.

Out of sight of the other patrons, in the narrow corridor outside the restaurant door, she allowed herself the luxury of guiding herself with one hand against the wall. When she came to the elevators she began her old trick of counting steps. Seconds later she slipped into the rest room.

She dropped down onto one of the hard wrought-iron chairs near the vanity mirror and took a deep breath. If only Peter hadn't taken her by surprise, she might have handled the situation better. She had tried to find the right words, but her effort had been flimsy and ineffectual in the face of her panic.

Finally, her pulse steadying and her remorse ebbing just a bit, Courtney got to her feet again. Hastily she ran a comb through her hair and leaned close to the mirror to touch up her lipstick. Somehow or other she had to ride out the rest of the evening. Thank goodness she had almost finished her brandy. Unless Peter insisted on staying for another, the ride home was virtually all that remained.

She slipped out of the bathroom, feeling buoyed by a vague hope that she could still salvage their friendship out of all this, and walked straight into the hard chest of Joshua Knight.

In the low lighting of the corridor she didn't immediately recognize him and was only appalled that she had walked into a stranger. She staggered back, holding on to her balance precariously. When his strong arms steadied her for the second time in twenty-four hours, realization and familiarity struck her an overwhelming blow. She looked up into his flashing amber eyes and groaned, her embarrassment stronger, for the moment, than her shock.

"Are you all right?" His voice was low and solicitous. His hands didn't leave her arms, but held her there against him, his fingers biting into her flesh much as they had the night before; but the trembling that started in her knees was stronger this time, rocking through her and gathering force.

Her voice was tight and angry, but she knew, somewhere deep inside herself, that it was only a reflex, something hard and unyielding to cover the treacherous chaos that was swamping her once more at his touch. "Of course I'm all right. You tend to get used to bumping into things after a while, although I seem to be doing it more than ever with you. You have the damndest way of turning up in the wrong places."

"That's not what I meant. You seemed upset when you left the table."

She stared up at him, her forehead creased in a baffled frown.

"I should explain. I'm at the table right behind you. I'm sorry, but I couldn't help overhearing your conversation." His tone was idle, almost disinterested, but his eyes were roving down the clinging folds of her dress with unnerving familiarity, as though everything beneath the soft jersey belonged to him, as though he knew every inch of her soft flesh. Courtney felt almost naked under his steady perusal; it seemed to caress the swell of her breasts and the soft curve of her hips. Impulsively, instinctively, she pulled away from him, crossing her arms in front of her.

"I had no idea that eavesdropping was one of your countless vices," she snapped unfairly, feeling flustered. Her heart was thumping irregularly again, pounding against her chest in an effort to get free, and she was uncomfortably aware of the warmth on her arms where his hands had been, and where his eyes had been devouring her.

Something in his eyes sizzled, and he turned away from her with a shrug so calculated that it spoke volumes about his anger. "You're no less disagreeable out in public, I see." Suddenly he turned back to her again, his eyes raking over her once more as a small, tight smile settled on his lips. He reached out to flick a cloud of hair away from her shoulder with one finger, but before she could react his hand was back in his pocket and he was speaking again. "Although I must admit that you're beautiful without your schoolmarm clothes." His voice dropped lower, an intimate caress meant only for her ears. "I had a strong hunch that would be the case."

Defensive, angry words were hot on her tongue; she could feel them there, ready to explode and protect something that was quivering dangerously within her, something that was burning hotter than her temper. Then, suddenly, an image of Meryl flashed into her mind. Courtney took a deep breath and swallowed back the words. Despite her own personal feelings for the girl's father, she had a responsibility to Meryl for as long as she was her student. That precluded temper and . . . yes, desire. It precluded everything.

She forced a contrite smile to her lips, although it resisted all the way, fighting her good intentions. "I'm sorry," she said, somehow pushing the words out with a regret that sounded genuine. "I know that those tables are practically right on top of each other. I shouldn't have accused you of eavesdropping."

He stepped closer to her again. "I followed you back here to tell you that I think you'll be needing a lift. Your friend stormed out of here right after you left the table."

"Peter did that? Oh, no!" Her final, harsh words had been the icing on the cake, then. She bit her lip, wishing that she could somehow go chasing after the words and reclaim them. Peter was a kind, patient man, but there was only so much a man could take. His pride and his ego were badly bruised. In a way, Courtney was relieved that he had left. She supposed that it might afford him some small sense of satisfaction, and he deserved that, even if leaving her stranded was pretty low. Still, she felt only the most remote, mild anger at him and was vaguely glad that she wouldn't have to face riding home with him after all.

"I'd be glad to take you back to Collegeville," Joshua offered carefully. Courtney was close enough to him to see that his face clouded over and grew distant with his words. For heaven's sake, why?

"Don't be silly," she answered. "It's out of your way. I'll call a taxi."

"Now *that's* silly. It so happens that I have to go in that direction anyway."

Suddenly, inexplicably, his hand was under her chin, pulling her face up so that her eyes had no choice but to meet his. She was so close to him that she was sure that the amber sparks would flash out and burn her. Something electric charged through her at his touch, similar to that of the night before but infinitely more gentle and provocative, and at his unwavering stare, which was open and revealing now. Again she had a sense of many things crowding his eyes, among them something that looked like the mockery she had already learned to expect from him.

"Let it go, Courtney."

"I . . . I don't understand." She felt herself reeling inside. His hand was still under her chin, warm and rough, and it started a chain of other reactions in the far reaches of her body. She jerked away, trying to step past him, but her legs were slow and heavy, and she couldn't move fast enough. He reached out for her again, pulling her toward him until she was crushed against his chest, much as she had been the night before, her breasts warm and tingling against the strength of him, her knees all but useless. She clung to him; she had no choice in the matter. The lights in the corridor were spinning around her in a way that had nothing to do with her lack of sight.

"You're so amazingly adept at analyzing the feelings and emotions of others," he murmured, "but you don't seem to be very in touch with your own. That's not pride you're flaunting, Courtney. It's fear. I'd recognize it anywhere. You're just afraid of letting yourself go, afraid of what might be waiting for you if you do."

He was so close to her, holding her so tightly, that she could feel his breath warm and silky against her face with each of his words. Weakly, ineffectually, she tried to pull away from him again, but it was useless. He refused to let her go. He held her more tightly as she struggled; then, with a small groan of exasperation, he brought his mouth down on hers.

Courtney froze, stunned, before something feverish erupted inside her. For the briefest of moments she felt herself spinning away from any semblance of control, felt only his lips against hers, his tongue running smoothly against her teeth, then finding her tongue, teasing, chasing into corners of her mouth that she hadn't known existed. A small moan escaped from her throat. She heard it distantly, as though it had come from someone else, but she heard it. It was enough to make her rear back, breaking away from him, but even as she did, even as she found relief in the distance between them, something hollow washed over her.

"What . . . what are you doing?"

His chuckle was low and mocking, enough to stir the anger within her again. "Come on, teacher. If you don't know the answer to that, perhaps you ought to go back to school."

She wrenched free of his grasp with a strength she hadn't known she possessed, the old fire in her eyes. "You have absolutely no right to say . . . to do

. . . such things. I'd say you're being pretty damned presumptuous on many counts, considering that you only met me last night!"

"You should know about being presumptuous, teacher. How long had you known *me* last night?" His voice was tinged with the mockery she had expected. It didn't help at all to know that he was right. The apology that she had planned for that morning seemed especially impossible now. She would have choked over it.

"Come on, Courtney. Take a chance. Let me give you a ride home. I can't promise you that I won't bite, but I can guarantee that it won't hurt a bit, if that's what you're afraid of."

"I'm not afraid of anything!" she snapped back at him. With her right hand flat against the wall for guidance, she rushed back up the corridor, putting as much distance as possible between them before she paused. "I'd just rather not trouble you for that ride, Mr. Knight. I'll be fine. I'm perfectly capable of taking care of myself."

"So I overheard. Too bad you're not as good at accepting favors." His voice was low with smoldering sarcasm.

She paused a moment longer—just long enough to glance over her shoulder at him one last time. His shadowy form seemed to fill the whole corridor. "It's a matter of necessity, really. If I accepted that ride, we'd probably end up arguing all night, and I've got some little girls I'd like to tuck into bed. Incidentally, in case you've forgotten, one of them is your daughter. You might be interested to know that she still hasn't left her room."

She was much too far away to catch the wounded look that flashed across his face with lightning speed before his cool control took over again. She turned into the lobby before he could answer, her blood coursing through her wildly, throbbing through her very soul. Just as she passed the door to the restaurant she nearly collided with a tall, statuesque brunette who was scanning the lobby with bright, observant eyes.

"Oh, Joshua, I was just beginning to wonder what had happened to you," the other woman purred as she looked past Courtney.

Courtney stopped in mid-stride. She turned quickly back to him, her heart lurching into her throat for the thousandth time, but he wasn't looking at her. He had hooked one arm through the brunette's and was leading her back into the restaurant.

So he had to go back to Collegeville anyway. Lovely. The three of them would have been downright cozy stuffed in his car together for the ride.

The doorman looked at her, and she turned on him, her temper blazing. "Would you please stop gaping at me and just call me a taxi?"

"Of course, ma'am. Just calm down." He was watching her warily.

Well, that could be the best advice she had received all night, she realized with a good dose of embarrassment. She was making an utter fool of herself, and all because of some egotistical, rude man who had somehow managed to get under her skin.

Within minutes she was in the back of a taxi, hurtling toward Collegeville. As she settled back against the worn leather seat she forced away her anger at being in the cab in the first place. She couldn't blame Peter. Actually, she should just consider herself lucky that she wasn't trapped in a car with Joshua Knight and his friend!

As they passed the town limits she told herself that it was just as well that Joshua Knight was the elusive, conceited playboy that he was. If Andrea Vaughan, with her bright, seeing eyes, couldn't hold on to him, then nobody could. Once again Courtney reminded herself that she wouldn't even want to try.

Chapter 4

COURTNEY LEANED DANGEROUSLY OVER THE BALUS-
trade of the loggia, trying in vain to see something of
the game of blindman's bluff that was going on out
on the lawn. The late afternoon sunlight glowed
through her eyes in various hues of gold and orange.
It was a delightful kaleidoscope of color, but it did
nothing toward enabling her to make out any of the
frenetic activity on the lawn.

The gentle sunshine, just on the verge of being
warm, drifted into the loggia, mingling with the
high-pitched sounds of girlish laughter. Courtney
wished desperately that she could capture it all and
hold it close to her heart to try to warm away some
of the cold, nagging uncertainties that had been
hibernating there for days.

As she went down the marble steps and left the cool, dappled shadows of the loggia, Courtney flicked days off on her fingers for the thousandth time in two weeks. It was Thursday; eleven days had passed since the evening at the restaurant. Peter hadn't called, and she had been hesitant to call him. There had been no word from Joshua, either, but then, such a hope was pure fantasy. He had no reason to call her. Meryl was doing as well as could be expected, and short of that, they had no common ground. All in all, there had been nothing but silence from either of them, and Courtney was more than a little troubled by it. Against all logic, she found herself feeling bereft and abandoned.

Although she had worked diligently through the weeks, hiding behind classes, preparations for the party and her problems with Meryl, not once had she been able to put either Peter or Joshua from her mind. They were always there, perched on the perimeters of her thoughts, watching her, waiting for her to acknowledge them. In her daydreams Peter inevitably looked heartsick and shattered. Joshua merely smiled his mockery.

At four o'clock Courtney had finally succumbed to both of them. She had sent the children out to play after the last class of the day, knowing that they would be well supervised by Mark Kendall and Barbara Rolphy, the two college students who worked weekday afternoons at Winston House. Elizabeth, who had been obviously but silently troubled by Courtney's reticence of late, had retreated to the kitchen without a word, hoping that Courtney would reserve the idle hour before dinner for herself and perhaps do something to cheer herself up. Courtney was more than glad to take the hour, but she was under no illusions. Cheerfulness was way down the pike. All she wanted right now, all she dared to hope for, was a little perspective that might chase Joshua Knight from her thoughts.

She cut a wide berth around the area of the lawn where the voices were coming from, intent upon staying to herself and not getting involved in the game. She had walked for a good ten minutes when she realized that the excursion had been a mistake. The kaleidoscope was enveloping her, with considerable help from the late-day angle of the sun. The shadows of the trees in the thicket that she had somehow managed to reach were long and slender rods that were no help at all when it came to locating the numerous real trees. Courtney felt frustration boiling up inside her as she was forced to spread her arms out, her hands searching for the feel of the bark that would tell her a collision was imminent. Was it just her imagination, or were things harder to see these days? She had just been to see Dr. Farber on Monday. Surely if anything had changed she would have been the first to know. No, it had to be her paranoia, and nothing physical, that was clouding her vision even more this afternoon. That, and the brightly burning sun that was sending out long shadows to tease her with their quick, misleading flashes of darkness.

"Damn!" The word slid out of her, ragged with aggravation. Courtney folded her legs under her in defeat and sat down hard on the ground. Lying back against the smooth, mossy turf, she pulled her wide-brimmed hat off her head and shielded her face with it. She had to think.

She wasn't lost. After two years the grounds, or at least most of them, were as familiar to her as the house was. Of course, there were areas where she had never ventured, but that was simply because she had no need to. They lay on the borders of the property like mystical black wastelands she couldn't even imagine. Courtney knew that she hadn't walked that far, if only because she hadn't been walking long enough.

Still, this myriad of trees so close together was something new, and she wasn't entirely sure where she was, even if she knew where she wasn't. Her first error had been in cutting such a wide berth around the playing children, rather than taking her regular, straight path to the creek. She tried to relax and consider her alternatives but was able to come up with only one. She would have to wait until dusk settled, when she would be able to see better without the full, blinding strength of the sunlight. She'd get back eventually, she knew, but Elizabeth would worry, and there would be vague whispers between Mark and Barbara, undoubtedly speculating on the obvious depression that she had been laboring under lately. Worst of all was the embarrassment of getting herself into this predicament in the first place. It was so understandable, and yet so unforgivable. She could hear the voices of the three of them, wise and compassionate in the security of their eyesight: Of course, Courtney could have gotten lost. She's blind, the poor thing.

"Damn!" she muttered again, more vehemently this time, and rolled over on her stomach. Her hat fell off to the side, and her skirt hiked up a bit, exposing long, trim legs to the sun. If only she knew where the devil she was, she would be able to enjoy the moment of respite.

Again she contemplated battling the elongated shadows to get back to the house, and again she realized that they could well end up leading her into the never-never land that she had never visited before. Giving up, she laid her head down on her forearms and closed her eyes.

As she had known they would, her thoughts rushed to take their own path. Images of Peter faded away completely, taking his long, sorrowful look with them. Joshua's mocking smile came front and center. Courtney's sun-drenched face creased into a scowl that had nothing at all to do with the light that was playing havoc with her vision.

She was helpless against the memories that were knocking demandingly on the door to her consciousness. With a strange feeling of wary exhilaration, Courtney remembered Joshua's strange words about pride and fear.

Go ahead, Courtney, said a demonic voice from somewhere deep inside of her. Think about it. Find out if he was right.

She fought against the voice with everything she had, but idle time rendered her efforts impotent. Maybe she hadn't always been overjoyed with the pride that had held her back from so many things life had to offer, but she knew that it was a necessity. Even if it sometimes hurt, she had always gratefully accepted the armor that protected her from embarrassment. Was that fear? No, of course not. It was dignity. It was a matter of being her own best friend, her own protector. What was more, it had absolutely nothing to do with Joshua Knight, his kiss, or his offer of a ride home. While the impact of all three had stunned her, she wasn't afraid of him, and she hadn't been protecting herself from him, despite what his ego might try to tell him. No, of course she hadn't been doing that.

But what about Joshua? He had said that he would recognize her attitude anywhere, but that could only be possible if he, too, were at its mercy, Courtney thought. It takes one to know one. Wasn't that how the expression went?

For weeks, ever since Meryl's arrival, Courtney had found herself recognizing the similarities between the girl and the child she herself had once been. Of course, their mutual pride had to be just as much a product of their inborn personalities as their blindness. After all, it hadn't been obvious in any of the other students Courtney had worked with. Everyone handled their perpetually dark worlds a little differently. Corinne simply refused to acknowledge hers. Lilith was complacent and accepting. Meryl was angry. Where did those attitudes stem from? The answer came to Courtney with simple clarity: their upbringing, their parents. Meryl's anger, the struggling embryo of a full-fledged and self-protective dignity, was quite possibly something that she had learned from her father, just as Courtney had learned hers from her own father.

But what does *he* have to be so self-protective about? Courtney wondered as little fingers of indignation spread around her heart at the mere thought of Joshua. There was nothing wrong with his eyes, and there was nothing difficult about his life. He was a carefree, hard-boiled and devoted bachelor—that was apparent enough!

Then, just as quickly as her indignation had surfaced, it skulked sheepishly away again. The answer was so obvious! It had been right under her nose for weeks, right there in Meryl's consistently snapping eyes. It was so easy to forget that Joshua had lost his wife in the same accident that had stolen his daughter's eyesight. A double blow, Courtney realized. Aching memories on one hand, and blind reality on the other.

Miraculously, in the space of the minute that it

took for a single leaf to flutter down and come to rest
against her outstretched hand, Courtney lost her
fiery anger at Joshua Knight. She grappled with it,
but it twisted free. She begged it to come back, for
she was more than a little afraid of where she would
be without it, but it fled from her, running free into
the orange and gold light. An undefined sense of
protectiveness and tenderness for the man replaced
it.

Courtney confronted this new feeling warily, un-
willing to accept it. She scorned it, she ridiculed it,
and then she ignored it, but just as Joshua's cool
smile had refused to leave her thoughts, her sympathy for him would not go away now.

She flipped over onto her back again, then
reached for her hat and planted it squarely over her
face, hoping to block out more than just the sun. She
let out a deep breath, and her breasts heaved with
the effort of it; she crushed the moist, green leaf she
still held in her hand. The stickiness clung to her
fingers, and a warmth clung to her heart.

She was so lost in her thoughts that it took her
more than a full minute to realize that the shadow
preventing the sun from sneaking in under the edges
of her hat was not that of a tree. Trees didn't move.
They didn't suddenly stand beside her and block out
the sun, which had been there just a few moments
before.

She pushed herself upright with her elbows, her
skirt falling upward in frothy pink clouds over her
thighs. She pushed it down over her knees, then
groped around on the surrounding grass for the hat
she had lost. Something close to fear shimmered
through her. Who was it? Why didn't he speak? The
bright light from the sun seared her vision, serving

only to make the situation seem more frighteningly unreal.

"Who is it?" God, how she hated to ask that question! All the carefully guarded-against insecurities brought on by her dark world flooded into her with the words. She felt so helpless, so vulnerable, and it was a feeling she loathed. It made her snarl out her demand with more than mere fury. "Answer me, damn it!"

"I'm sorry. I really didn't think I would frighten you." The words were genuinely repentant, but Courtney didn't notice. A surge of something unnameable—excitement? . . . disbelief?—filled her as she recognized the voice. It was Joshua Knight.

"You? What are you doing here?" Her confusion destroyed any chances she might have had of remaining cool and calm. She realized in some far part of her soul that she must look terribly ungainly trying to get to her feet while holding her skirt down at the same time, but there wasn't sufficient space in her thoughts to worry about it. Tiny shock waves brought on by his unexpected presence, so sudden on top of her thoughts about him, jolted through her, leaving her feeling exposed and vulnerable.

His strong hand was under her elbow, pulling her to her feet; each tiny nerve ending recognized and remembered that touch, rough yet soft, demanding yet gentle, hard yet warm. Even as she got up, she quickly stepped back from him, her heart lurching up into her throat and stopping her breath. The loss of her anger made his touch an uncertain proposition, something infinitely strange and dangerous and provoking. The very thought of it frightened her. If she could no longer despise him, would that stirring feeling of electricity she had felt before grow even stronger? If it had consumed her then, what would it do to her now? She was genuinely afraid to find out.

She replaced her hat, and blessed shadows cooled her vision. Feeling awkward and unnerved by the hammering of her heart, she pushed her hands into the pockets of her sweater and bent her head. More shadows, even more welcome.

"Elizabeth told me that she thought you had taken a walk. The people out on the lawn pointed me in this direction. Even so, it took me a while to find you."

She remained silent, her head still bent. A strange new breed of panic, tingling and exciting, prevented her from answering him. She simply couldn't find her voice. She groped for some semblance of her old control, only to find that it had vanished without a trace.

In a gesture that was reminiscent of the one he had used the first time they had met, he put his hand under her chin and tilted her face up.

"Why won't you look at me?" His voice was curious.

Courtney jerked her head away and pulled the hat further down on her brow. "Because I can't see you!" she snapped. "Because this stupid light is making everything else invisible!"

She knew instinctively that he was shaking his head, wrestling with his own brand of confusion. "I thought you could see. You said—"

"I know what I said! And it holds true whenever I'm inside. Outside, in the sunlight, that's a different matter." She bit her lip against the humiliation that filled her. To have to admit it to him! To have to admit it to any stranger, she amended quickly.

"Well, I double my apology for sneaking up on

you, then. I had no idea that you wouldn't be able to see at least some of me."

He sounded so contrite, so sorry for her! Courtney couldn't refrain from muttering an oath under her breath. She hugged her arms to her protectively, turning away from him and taking a few steps further into the trees. Immediately she realized that she had no idea where she was going, and she stopped to turn back in the direction she had come from.

"This is something of a surprise," she said finally, her words coming carefully and with her old, scrupulous control. "I mean, after our last two meetings, and what with the way you've been avoiding Meryl, I never expected you to show up here of your own free will." She spoke out of honesty and a need to say something businesslike, rather than with the anger she had so unwillingly relinquished in the copse of trees.

"I was going to call," he said at length. Her ears and sixth sense told her that he was moving around restlessly. With unnerving clarity, she remembered the taut muscles beneath his jeans and flannel shirt on their first meeting and the harnessed power she had sensed there. She remembered his mouth on hers and his hands holding her so tightly, so roughly, in a demanding embrace. Her breath escaped her abruptly, as though someone had knocked the wind out of her, and she retreated from him again, savoring the coolness of the few shadows she could find, seeking comfort in their distance.

"Then I decided that the things I have to say would be better spoken in person," he went on.

"What things?" She moved back in his direction cautiously, praying that she wouldn't stumble yet again.

Suddenly he grabbed her hand, and it happened,

as she had known it would. Her reaction was deeper, stronger, more overpowering. The weakness in her knees was no longer content to stay there; it ran rampant up her legs, through her thighs, into the most intimate corners of her being. Something full and floating settled there; still she did not allow herself to pull away from him.

And yet, when he spoke, some of the mockery she remembered so well was back in his voice.

"Let's walk. And don't bother telling me that you don't need me to guide you. If you couldn't tell who I was earlier, you're certainly not going to be able to find your way through these trees now."

"I know that." Her own voice was an odd blend of annoyance and contrition.

"You're admitting it?" He seemed surprised as he tucked her hand under his arm.

The weakness spread again, further and more tenaciously, with his touch. It flooded upward, its waves crashing through her, drowning her. All her concentration, each and every functioning sense, seemed to be aimed and coursing toward the corded muscles beneath her hand. So this was it, she realized. This was what she had been afraid of when she had let her anger go. And with due reason. She felt helpless and pliable in a strange way that she was only just beginning to know. With great effort, she collected her thoughts and found her voice.

"Only because I have no choice," she answered him, her preoccupation and panic making her voice almost cold. "It would be pretty ridiculous to insist that I can see when I've already told you that I'm just swimming around in sunlight out here."

"You were lost, weren't you?" he asked suddenly. "That's why you were just lying there."

Her heart thumped wildly against her breastbone.

Her every instinct was screaming out a denial. And yet she couldn't seem to force herself to speak the lie. Her silence was an admission that she begrudged with every ounce of pride she had ever known.

"You're so secure about this, so trusting," he mused finally, more to himself than to her, and she was just as glad to drop the earlier subject, even if she wasn't sure what he was talking about now.

"Whenever I try to walk with Meryl," he continued, "she pulls against me, hesitates, you know? Like she doesn't trust me to lead her, to keep her from harm. You don't do that."

"Meryl's young," Courtney answered carefully, knowing she was treading on ground that she didn't quite understand. His feelings for his daughter seemed so cold and remote, and yet she knew that they couldn't possibly be. Without any explanations from him, she couldn't be sure of his feelings, and she was hesitant.

"It's like that at first," she explained. "When it first comes, when things first go fuzzy and dark and you're not used to it yet, it's just human nature to pull back into yourself. It's frightening. All your instincts tell you that there's something dangerous out there. We're all raised with the idea that darkness is something bad and threatening, and when you're faced with it on a constant basis, for a while you just feel threatened all the time."

"Then, after a while, you get used to it?" he suggested, a question mark in his voice.

"No, not really. I wouldn't say that you ever get *used* to it, but after a while the fear isn't quite so intense and you learn to cope with it. You end up forcing yourself. A little voice inside of you battles with you at each step, saying, 'There's nothing out there! Go on! Move!' And on those very rare occasions when you allow someone to lead you around—" She paused, not able to keep the almost embarrassed smile out of her voice or off her face. "You start to remember that that's a pretty safe way to go. You start to allow yourself to depend on the other person's eyes. But it's never easy. That's the hardest part of all for some of us, learning to give ourselves over to someone else's vision."

"But you've done it." There was a trace of admiration in his tone, but it was carefully shielded.

"For the most part, but not always. Sometimes my baser instincts take over, and fear makes me drag my feet every step of the way."

Courtney was listening to herself with amazement. Something inside her rebelled at the easy way she was admitting all this to him. These were things that she had never said to another living soul, things that her pride had never before allowed her to reveal. She had never before admitted to a fear of her dark world to anyone, not even to Meryl on that night when she had thrown the tray. And yet an urgency of sorts was forcing the words from her now; although speaking them was painful, she felt compelled to say them. He had to know. For Meryl's sake, he had to know what it was like.

She didn't even acknowledge the sense of personal peace she felt by telling him. Nor did she allow herself to scrutinize why it had happened so easily and suddenly, after years of silence.

"Meryl's young," she said again, "but eventually I think she'll get a grip on things. I hope she does!" she added fervently. "She's got to! Her only chance is to stop fighting against it and try to work with it."

A strange groan came from him, and instinctively Courtney hesitated in her steps, pulling back against him. Close by, she could hear the soft gurgling of the creek, and to cover the break in her stride she stopped and asked, "Is there a big boulder anywhere around here?"

"Hmmm?" His response was distracted.

"There's a place down here by the creek where I always go. Out of necessity, really, because the path to the creek that I just happen to have mastered leads me right to it. But it's a great spot, peaceful and quiet. There's an enormous boulder there which crops out over the edge of the water. I just wondered if that's where we are."

She knew he was looking around, knew it only because she was so aware of him, so conscious of and alert to his every movement. It was another phenomenon that she hadn't analyzed yet; for the moment, at least, she could only accept it.

"It's down the way a bit," he answered finally. "Do you want to walk over there?"

Courtney nodded. Despite what she had told him, her nerves were beginning to frazzle a bit from the forced necessity of following his sight. She almost ached with a physical yearning to be able to sit down and be still so that she could go back to relying on herself.

They walked to the boulder in silence. Out of habit, Courtney pulled herself up on the rock and tilted her head back to catch the sun on her face. She was savoring the sensations of the tepid sunlight glancing low off the horizon and the feel of her long hair tumbling down her back when something told her that he was watching her. She tried to ignore the certainty that his golden eyes were studying her and to somehow hold on to the self-confidence that had been skipping in and out of her reach ever since he had arrived, but when he slid up on the rock beside her his thigh brushed against hers and her control shattered. A small thrill tripped through her again; intuitively, like a small animal sensing danger, she found herself pulling away from him before she could stop herself.

But the small space she had put between them did nothing to assuage her tight nerves. Every part of her was blazingly aware of his proximity. She couldn't help remembering how she had thought her attraction to him was so natural, so simple. It wasn't. It had the strength of Hercules. It was out of the realm of her experience, and it was frightening her badly.

She sat up straighter, pulling her knees up tightly under her chin, realizing too late that the gesture would send her cotton skirt sliding up her thighs until it was only a small pink puddle concealing virtually nothing. She yanked it over her knees again even as Joshua sprang up off the rock with abrupt intensity to stand behind her.

She started at his movement, surprised by it. Had he felt it, too? But if he had, surely he wouldn't have jumped away. Not Joshua Knight. Not the man who had so suavely and smoothly offered her a ride home when he was already with another woman. No, if he had felt it, he would have known what to do about it. He wouldn't have jumped away from her.

Just as she felt sure that she would drown in her own confusion, Joshua began to speak again.

"I came here because I felt I owed you a few explanations," he murmured. "I had no intention whatsoever of ending up here, like this."

She had twisted around on the rock and was watching in the long-awaited dusk when he waved a shadowy, blurred hand at their surroundings. She tried to gauge his voice. Angry? No, more confused, she thought. It didn't mesh, not at all. It simply didn't fit with his cavalier attitude at the restaurant or with anything else she knew of him.

"What kind of explanations?" she asked finally, steering the conversation onto what she hoped would be more understandable ground.

"About myself. About Meryl. That was my whole incentive for coming here. I was going to be angry. I was going to tell you to get off my back about my supposed lack of interest in my daughter once and for all. I was going to make you understand so that you'd shut up and leave me alone."

Courtney flinched at his biting tone. She didn't understand it. He sounded angry, angry at her, and she couldn't understand why. One minute she was worrying about pulling her skirt down, and the next he was pacing around, waving his hands at the creek and growling at her.

"Look," he finally continued gruffly, "you may have come up against a lot of negligent parents in your work here"—he waved another hand back in the direction of the house—"but I can assure you that I'm not one of them. I love Meryl, damn it! She's all I've got left. But there's nothing left of *her!* She's not the little girl she was ten years ago when that car went down the embankment and sent glass flying in her face. She was never the same after that. I don't even know her anymore, and I've run out of ways to try to find out who she is.

"It's not just her eyes, although I'd have enough trouble just trying to cope with that. No, it's more than that. She hates everything now. She hates *me.*

"When Andie came up with the idea of sending her to you, I was at my wit's end. If you want to start throwing accusations around, for God's sake choose the right ones. It had nothing to do with wanting her out of my hair. I just couldn't deal with the whole situation anymore. There was nothing else I could do for her, no way to get through to her. I checked you out with Dr. Farber, and I made my decision. I left Meryl here with you."

Courtney sat hunched and shocked on the boulder, still hugging her knees to her tightly and trying to ward off the shivering that had settled into her bones. She felt something inside her cringe at his frustration, because it was deep and desperate. She wanted to go to him, to comfort him much as she would have comforted one of her girls, but she sat frozen and immobilized, terrified of what might happen if she did. She knew that it wouldn't be a mere hug of consolation. For him, perhaps, but not for her. She couldn't find the courage to do it.

"I'm sorry," she murmured inanely.

He paced back to the rock and slid into place beside her again, his emotions seemingly spent. Something primitive uncoiled and eased inside Courtney, and she was selfishly grateful that she was no longer faced with the frustration that he had just displayed.

"Well, that's what I wanted to tell you," he finished, his voice hard. "There you have it. Believe me, Courtney, when I tell you that I do not hate my daughter. I love her dearly. But I can't stand to be around her, to see what this accident has done to her, both physically and emotionally. If that makes me some kind of an ogre, then I admit to it. I can only warn you that I'm not going to change. Don't go knocking yourself out trying to bring me around, because it won't happen. Keep her here. Help her. As I said before, I don't care how you do it, just do it. Bring in the psychologist, if that's what it takes. Just don't bring me into it. I won't allow you to."

Somewhere out on the horizon the sun had slipped

low. The dusk that Courtney had been waiting for had finally arrived completely and was now drifting away again. In the thick purple twilight she could just barely see the hard set of his jaw and the cold, closed look in his eyes. She closed her own against it for a moment before they flew open again in determination.

"You have to," she said softly, urgently. "Don't you see? You're the only person who *can* help her! A psychologist might help, but he couldn't do the whole job. Meryl needs you! You're her father! She needs you to show her that you love her, and not any less simply because she can't see. You can't pull away from her now!" She paused, her own emotions boiling, bubbling close to the surface. Without thinking, she reached out to him and grasped his hand tightly. "Please. I'll help; I'll be there with both of you every step of the way. But you've got to open yourself up to her. If *I* got the impression that you don't care, then what must Meryl think?"

He spun around so suddenly that she gasped, yanking her hand away from his and shrinking back. In the darkening twilight that was stealing her sight just as the sun had, his eyes burned with amber fire. His anger was so intense that she started to struggle off the rock, wanting to flee from him, but he reached out for her, pinning her still against the boulder. His touch sent still another intense kind of fire burning through her.

"For God's sake, woman, didn't you hear what I just said?" He spat the words at her furiously.

"I—" she started, aching to tell him that she only wanted to help, but the words vanished beneath a flood of conflicting emotions. Chaos filled her, and she was acutely aware of his hands holding her close to him, just as he had before. Power and tenderness ran rampant through his touch, and she found that memories of other moments with him were all tangled up with this reality, and that they were smothering her. Something deep inside her began trembling again, and she found herself shivering uncontrollably. She tried to tell herself that it was fear that was causing it, fear of the spitting fire in his eyes, but she knew that it was more than that, that it had to do with his proximity and the totally treacherous way she wanted his lips to come down on hers again, hot and demanding and playful as they had been on that night that seemed like yesterday now. She had one flashing moment of lucid thought before her control abandoned her completely. It was more than simply his virile good looks and his magnetism that was doing this to her—much more. There was simply too much of herself in his eyes.

"Don't look at me like that," he warned her roughly. "I'm not what you think I am. I'm not . . ." All logical thought tumbled away from her as he groaned something else low and indiscernible beneath his breath. The raging strength in his arms as he savagely pulled her toward him didn't come as a shock to her; she had known that it would be like this, just as she had, in some dark, distant part of her soul, anticipated his embrace. Some primitive part of her had been waiting for it ever since they had arrived at the boulder, just as her decision not to fight him anymore had been made when his voice had first intruded on her solitude in the thicket.

As she leaned into him, pressing herself against the hardness of his chest, she abandoned herself to the darkness, accepting it as part of her. He was one with her world now, part of an existence that thrived on touch, on feeling. In the dark, glimmering light of the sunset her other senses came alive in a way they never had before. Huddled in his protective embrace, she could feel everything about him. His thigh pressed hard against her own now, heavy and roughly oblivious of her weaker flesh. The muscles of his chest crushed her breasts with almost brutal force, but within the pain there was a tingling pleasure unlike any she had ever known. Secure and self-assured now in a dark world that had been her constant companion for years, she met his mouth hungrily when it came down on her own, intuitively nibbling at his full lower lip, greeting his tongue willingly and eagerly this time as it darted in and out of her mouth.

It was only when his hands left their place on her arms, the place where they had always rested each time he had touched her, holding her still in the face of his fury and passions, that a dam broke inside her, and an innate sense of fear and pride and self-preservation rushed forth to drown out everything else. Even as his hands strayed beneath her sweater, even as they ruthlessly and impatiently pulled her blouse free of the waistband of her skirt, even as their rough contours found the tender, untouched skin stretched taut over her ribs and thrust their way beneath the lacy confines of her bra, panic galvanized her. She scrambled back across the boulder, her feet finding the grassy turf beside it, then stood, swaying slightly, her heart lurching wildly within her.

"No, don't . . . please, you can't." Her words came out on a long breath, floating free of her without her command.

He slid off the rock, coming to his feet more easily than she had, and when his hands found their old place on her arms once more, he held her still, his eyes burning down on her. "So that's the way it is, teacher, mmm? You want me to take all the chances. What about you? Don't you ever gamble? Don't you?"

He gave her no chance to answer with words, only the opportunity to prove herself. His mouth came down on hers again, and there was a challenge in his kiss this time. Even as his lips pressed hard against hers, she felt it and recognized it for what it was. Something deep inside her, some old, forgotten instinct for risk and daring, was awakened.

"I can," she murmured against his mouth. "I can gamble." The words were as much a reassurance for her as they were a protest to him, and she needed them desperately as his hands left her arms once more to caress the taut flesh of her nipples beneath her bra, the soft skin of her breasts. Still she pressed herself against him, feeling the hard contours of him with each inch of her being, and her fingers, so long accustomed to blazing a trail for her eyes, ran over his face, over the angles of his cheekbones, against the softness of his lips when they left hers. Only a vague, distant part of her traced the path of his other hand, because all of her concentration was centered on the feel of him against her, on the revelations her fingers were finding. When the cool night air brushed against the backs of her thighs as his free hand found the fabric of her skirt and pulled it up and out of the way, when she once more felt the rough callouses of his touch against skin that had never been touched, her concentration was shattered. The magic of the darkness was broken by her sharp intake of breath.

Almost immediately he pushed her suddenly, roughly away from him. The coolness of the early spring air assaulted her everywhere, feeling crystal cold against her still-warm and tingling skin where he had touched her. Courtney stumbled back and hugged her arms to her, huddling in against herself. It wasn't only a defense against the cold, but against his sudden, stony withdrawal as well. She glanced up at him quickly, surreptitiously; she could barely make out that he was running a harried hand over his eyes, and she was wondering desperately where she should go from here when his voice, low and breaking, banished all her indecision.

"For God's sake, what am I doing? Don't do this to me!"

Her gasp echoed over the lonely sound of the water rushing by beneath the boulder. Hurting with a new kind of pain that stabbed at her like nothing else ever had, Courtney spun around in the darkness and ran toward the trees.

She heard his voice faintly over the rushing of her own blood and the pounding of her heart. She could hear him calling her name, but she didn't stop. She ran up the embankment, the darkness fighting against her all the way now, but she couldn't fear it, because all her instincts had her running scared from something else—from Joshua Knight and her thunderous reaction to him.

She careened hard off a tree and moaned softly at the sharp pain that shot up her right arm, but the pain brought her back to her senses. Still panicked, but in control again, she squinted to get her bearings, then bounded off up the path she knew so well. She slowed to a rapid walk as she came out of the trees, breathed deeply and stumbled in the direction of the dim lights glowing from within the house.

Elizabeth gaped at her in amazement as she rushed in off the loggia a few minutes later. Belatedly she realized what a sight she must be. Her hat had long since fallen off, her blouse was pulled completely free of her skirt, and her hair fell wildly over her shoulders and into her eyes. She was vaguely aware of the warm stickiness of her blood on her arm where she had come up against the tree.

"Courtney, what—"

"I'm all right," she gasped. "I'm fine."

"Did he find you? Were you out there with him?" There was no need for names. Their eyes met, and Courtney nodded.

Without any more discussion, she grabbed the handrail and hurried off down the hallway. Taking the steps quickly, she slipped into the welcome, familiar safety of her room.

She shut the door, her breathing ragged but her heart slowing. How could such a thing have happened? She thought back to all of Peter's chaste, boring groping, and a trembling smile slipped onto her traitorous lips.

Shakily, she went into the bathroom and washed the blood from her arm. It was a superficial cut, not bad, all things considered, but her arm ached horribly. Still, it hurt no more than her heart.

What had he meant by "Don't do this to me"? Surely nothing they had done could have gone against the grain of his morals, she thought scathingly. Between Andrea and his brunette, he had had enough of an education. Or perhaps, she thought, feeling as though her heart would explode in its frenzied efforts to break, he simply had an aversion to kissing someone who couldn't see him.

The thought was too much. Her legs collapsing beneath her, she dropped weakly onto the bed, gripping the bedpost to steady herself. One soft, muffled sob escaped her, but she defiantly fought off those that tried to follow.

She was so caught up in her misery that she didn't hear the door open on the other side of the bathroom. She looked up to see Meryl standing in the doorway.

Something of the teacher in her managed to come to the fore. She ran a smoothing hand over her hair, pushing back the wild wisps which had fallen over her forehead, and forced a smile. "What are you doing up here?" Her voice was mildly curious, perfection itself. "I thought you'd be downstairs."

Something in her stomach clenched, denying her casual words. Oh, God, what she didn't need right now was a relapse on Meryl's part. The little girl had taken to going downstairs for meals, although she invariably sat there in miserable, stoic silence. Still, it had been an improvement that Courtney had cherished. Now here she was, when everyone else was undoubtedly downstairs having dinner.

Meryl took another step into the room, running a defiant hand over the eighteenth-century secretary. "Kind of hard to watch TV when you can't see anything on it," she said sarcastically. "I don't know why they even try. Guess they have no more brains than eyes."

"What about dinner? That's what I meant." Courtney was surprised and relieved that only the smallest tremor of anger had crept into her voice.

"Dinner's over," Meryl snapped, then added suddenly, "I knew you were wrong. I knew you were a liar."

"What?" Courtney asked incredulously. Somehow she hadn't been prepared for another attack; she certainly didn't need one now.

"You lied! You said it got better! Well, if it does, why are you crying?" She turned on her heel and disappeared back into the bathroom. The door on the other side slammed with a crack that caused Courtney to flinch.

At that moment she opened her arms wide to all the intense anger she had ever felt for Joshua Knight as it swept back in on her, eager to reclaim its home.

Chapter 5

WHEN COURTNEY AWOKE THE NEXT MORNING SHE was greeted by a heavy, aching feeling that seemed to have settled into each and every one of her bones. She reached out for the alarm clock with a lifeless hand and swatted at it with less than her usual sight, for her head was buried beneath her pillows. Morning. How had it managed to come so soon? Surely it had only been minutes since she had finally fallen asleep!

She poked her head out from beneath the pillows tentatively, feeling like a mole suddenly pulled from underground on the brightest, sunniest day of the year. She had forgotten to draw her curtains the night before, and the room was flooded with early

morning light. She blocked her eyes with one limp
hand and struggled out of bed. Groggily, she made
her way to the windows and drew the curtains.

She had paced the bedroom floor until nearly
dawn as thoughts of Joshua's revulsion toward her
vied for top priority with her thoughts of Meryl's
disturbing accusation. She had zigzagged back and
forth between memories of the two, tormented by
both. Several times she had forced herself into bed,
only to lie there yearning for sleep while her
thoughts forbade it. By four o'clock she had been so
exhausted that she had finally succumbed to sleep,
but each time until then she had ended up throwing
back the covers to resume her frantic search for
answers, trying to come up with a plan of action.

She knew, beyond any shadow of a doubt, that she
had to do something to bring father and daughter
together. For both their sakes, of course, but pre-
dominantly for Meryl's. The child was fighting a
losing battle unless her father would join sides with
her. Of that Courtney was sure. What she wasn't
sure of was how to achieve the apparently impossible
and get Joshua to open himself up to Meryl, despite
the torment and frustration her handicap caused
him.

She slipped into the bathroom, one hand stretched
out in front of her to find the other door, then
pressed her ear up against it. Silence. She knew that
she would have to talk to Meryl, would have to iron
things out, but it would have to wait. She wasn't
about to wake the girl up to do it.

As she washed up, her thoughts pounded at her,
picking up where they had left off the night before,
challenging her less-than-tranquil frame of mind.
The trust between Meryl and herself had been
tenuous at best, but Courtney was the only person at

Winston House who Meryl would condescend to speak to, all the same. Had last night ruined everything? Had that one small sob demolished two weeks' worth of slow, painful effort?

Courtney hoped against hope that the accusation had only been a device on Meryl's part designed to hurt her. Surely she couldn't believe that Courtney had deliberately lied to her. Surely she was wise enough to know that it was only human nature to cry sometimes, and that life, with or without any handicaps it might deem to dish out, was never so easy that a person could dispense with tears altogether. Courtney knew that Meryl's understanding of that truth was her only chance to regain her lost ground.

But what about Joshua? Courtney's racing thoughts came to a stubborn standstill at just the mental mention of his name. The hurt that had seared through her all night was weaker now, but it was nowhere close to departing from her heart. As she pushed clothing back and forth in her closet, a tiny, jabbing pain prodded at feelings which were already tender from abuse. Joshua's final words to her the night before echoed back and forth in her brain. "Don't do this to me," he had said. Those words had haunted her all night long until the intellectual side of her had finally wrenched them away from her heart. Every part of her cried out against it, but she had to accept the truth: Joshua Knight was repulsed by her lack of sight. Hadn't he said himself that he couldn't cope with Meryl's blindness? And she was his daughter, his own flesh and blood! In the face of that, it was preposterous to assume that he could cope with the same handicap in a virtual stranger. And a stranger was precisely what she was to him, Courtney told herself sternly. Anything that had happened out by the creek had only been a temporary aberration on Joshua's part, she was sure, a moment of forgetfulness in the midst of high emotion, when he had undoubtedly forgotten just who she was. And once he had remembered, he had been totally disenchanted, even revolted.

If only it had been such a simple matter for her! Although she had tried all night to deny it to herself, Courtney knew that she had fallen into Joshua's arms with a need that had been shockingly intense and had, ultimately, enjoyed each and every second of her stay there. She had wanted Joshua Knight from the moment he had first started to pace the grassy turf behind the rock, his face so vulnerable and yet so hard. And although she had been shaken by her desires, Courtney knew that she would have confronted them head on if he had only given her the chance. Instead, he had humiliated her with his abrupt withdrawal. The pain of that memory burned her still, despite her attempts to ignore and forget it.

Now, as she pulled a blue skirt over her head and tucked in her silky, tailored blouse, she knew that she would never again dread anything as much as she was dreading another confrontation with Joshua. Still, she would go through with what she had decided. She had to. She intended to call him at her earliest free moment and arrange a meeting with him, no matter how he felt about her. The fact still remained that she had a responsibility to him and to his daughter.

Elizabeth's expression was one of naked relief when she saw Courtney step into the dining room. Courtney stopped dead in her tracks by the table, guilt washing over her. She hadn't come back downstairs at all the night before. Wallowing in her own private misery, she had left Elizabeth to send the girls to bed and close up for the night. Some kind of an explanation was definitely in order, if only out of respect for their friendship.

She put a hand on Elizabeth's shoulder and forced a smile. "It was a lot less exciting than it looked," she whispered. Nonetheless, thirteen pairs of ears almost visibly perked up; thirteen heads swiveled in the direction of the head of the table, where Elizabeth sat.

The woman's eyebrows arched high on her forehead. "I should certainly hope so! For a minute I thought you two had actually been involved in a physical brawl. What happened?"

"Nothing physical," Courtney lied with some difficulty, feeling very protective of the embarrassment she had suffered at the hands of Joshua Knight, even with Elizabeth. It was her own private torture, not to be shared. "But I guess you could say that it *was* something of a brawl," she finished. She stepped up to the sideboard and poured herself a cup of coffee. Balancing that in one hand, she plucked a danish from a plate and started for the door. "I'll be in my office," she called out over her shoulder.

"Before breakfast? Again?" Elizabeth's voice was totally befuddled and more than a little threatening. "You're not going to eat anything this morning, either?"

Courtney waved the danish at her; then, in another effort to appease her, she took a large bite. The smile she volunteered was forced, but she hoped it might suffice.

It didn't. Elizabeth was on her feet in a second, stalking toward Courtney with a look that hunters reserve for prime prey. At the table, Corinne twisted her head back and forth in dismay, knowing that she was missing something. "What's going on? Hey!"

Courtney didn't have a chance to answer the little

girl before Elizabeth pulled her out into the hallway. Her face set in a concerned scowl, she cornered Courtney against the staircase.

"I've kept my mouth shut for weeks, but I simply can't do it a second longer."

"Somehow, I gathered as much." Courtney took another bite of the danish and tried to chew unperturbedly, but Elizabeth was studying her critically. Unable to help herself, Courtney looked away and bit her lip guiltily.

"You look terrible," Elizabeth announced finally. "You didn't get much sleep last night, did you?"

"Enough," Courtney replied, her voice slightly choked. The last bite of her pastry was lying like lead in her stomach. She took a deep swallow of coffee and turned away to hide the embarrassment that flooded her face. Getting dressed earlier, Courtney had decided that she had never looked worse. Her green eyes were banked by dark smudges, and she had lost a bit too much weight to be comfortably slim. Despite her height, she had developed a waifish look that her pale skin and rich, dark hair only accentuated.

" 'Enough,' she says. What, three, maybe four hours?" Elizabeth was asking. "And now you're going to eat that little pastry for breakfast, when you didn't have dinner last night, or the night before that, either! Frankly, I'm worried about you, Courtney. Ever since the Knights arrived on the scene, you haven't been yourself. You've seemed depressed, you're not eating, and now you're not even sleeping. What the devil is going on?"

Courtney sighed heavily and opened her mouth to defend herself, but Elizabeth cut her off. "No, don't answer that." She continued her tirade. "You don't have to. I can sum the whole problem up in a nutshell: Joshua Knight."

Courtney choked on her coffee. "Joshua? Elizabeth, that's ridiculous. I'll be the first to admit that he's troublesome, but he's no concern of mine. I'm only responsible for his daughter. If I haven't been myself, it's just because I'm so worried about her and I hate tangling with him."

Elizabeth sputtered in indignation. "Oh, for heaven's sake! Meryl is coming along slowly but surely. We both know that. She may be fighting progress every step of the way, but it's gaining on her despite herself. She's coming down for meals, isn't she? She's sitting through classes!"

"But she never says a word!" Courtney protested. "Except for last night. We had another run-in, by the way, and—"

"And you were awake all night worrying about it, right?" Elizabeth cut in, her tone heavy with sarcasm, but it turned quickly into concern again. "Oh, honey, I just hate to see you doing this to yourself."

"Believe me," Courtney mused aloud absently, contradicting all her previous protests without even thinking about it, "I'm not the one responsible. At least, not entirely."

A short, awkward silence fell between them while the words sank in, and Courtney was thoroughly prepared to take advantage of it by retreating into the solitude of her office, when Elizabeth made a funny little noise of comprehension deep in her throat. When Courtney turned back to her, she was shocked to see her friend smiling knowingly.

"What? What do you have up your sleeve?" she demanded.

"Courtney, I think the time has come for me to

leave you to your own devices after all. You don't seem to be doing so badly at that. But promise me you'll eat. Please."

"Sure," she answered, but she handed Elizabeth the danish. "Later. I can't stomach this right now. Will you throw it out for me?"

She braced herself for another outburst, but there was none forthcoming. Elizabeth took the half-eaten pastry from her hand complacently. "It happens this way sometimes, I suppose. If I remember correctly —mind you, it's been quite a few years—but I think you should get your appetite back after a few more weeks of this. The early days are always the roughest."

Courtney narrowed her eyes at Elizabeth, squinting at her severely. A glowing halo of light from the windows behind her made her look like an all-knowing angel. The smug smile on her face did nothing to dispel the illusion. Suddenly Courtney understood what the older woman was saying. With her cup in one hand and the railing in the other, she took several irate steps down the hallway before turning back.

"Wrong tree, Elizabeth. You'll have to try barking up another. I harbor many feelings for Joshua Knight, but love is *not* one of them. For heaven's sake! You should know me better than that by now! I would *never* let that happen!"

From where she stood, she could not see that Elizabeth was cocking her head to one side speculatively or that the smile had not yet left her face. "No, you wouldn't think so, would you? But then, you probably didn't have much of a choice in the matter."

"I know so! Elizabeth, there is absolutely nothing going on between Joshua Knight and myself, other than a minor tug-of-war over Meryl. First of all, it would be unprofessional. And most important, Joshua is hardly my biggest fan. He despises me, actually." Horrified, she realized that her throat was closing up with the weight of unshed tears. She spun around quickly, fighting off the subsequent dizziness, trying to hide her reaction from Elizabeth's perfectly capable eyes.

She escaped into the solitude of her office; she had never appreciated it more. Only sheer force of will kept her from slamming the door. Instead, she pushed it closed with the utmost control, then leaned her back against it, everything inside of her aching. It's the sleep, she told herself. That's all it is; that's all that's wrong with me. Elizabeth's right about that, at least. I'm not getting nearly enough of it.

She blinked her eyes to adjust her vision to the dimmer light of the room. Heavy velvet drapes blocked the windows, allowing just the right amount of light in to bolster her failing sight. Still, she thought bitterly, her throat growing tight again, no adjustment in light was ever going to return her lost sight to her, and there was nothing in the world that could guarantee that what she had would stick around. She was trapped in this horrible darkness, its prisoner, and all she had to look forward to was her world growing darker still. It wasn't fair. God, it just wasn't fair! The Andrea Vaughans of the world had everything, and all *she* had were shadows that locked her into a lonely, dark existence!

Scathing indignation and anger ripped through her, and she wanted to throw something, to hear something break. Instead, she went to her desk and sat down heavily, pulling her address book from the top drawer with trembling hands.

She held it in front of her, suddenly not seeing it at

all, not even remembering that she still held it in her hand. With appalled disgust at herself, she dropped it on the desk and got to her feet again.

That business about being trapped in her darkness, and the explosive anger that had come with it! What was happening to her? Courtney closed her eyes and sank weakly into Elizabeth's chair, feeling badly frightened and unsure of herself. She had banished that self-pitying brand of anger long ago, had dispensed with it in the beginning and thought she had seen the last of it. She had been holding herself in check against it for years, resisting the hurt and the indignation at the injustice of it all, that this disease had claimed her rather than someone else. And now it was back. Right on the heels of Joshua's disgust with her, the self-pity was back.

Courtney felt thick tears coursing down her cheeks but made no effort to wipe them away. In the space of one hour spent by the creek, she had lost it all. Her viselike self-control, the bittersweet pride that had kept the self-pity at bay, and the sturdy inner barriers that had kept her pride intact—they were all gone. For a moment, she had peeked out from behind those barriers. She had wanted Joshua Knight; she had wanted him to touch her, to hold her. And what had happened? Exactly what she had guarded against for years, that was what! He had somehow managed to make her handicap more than a small hill that had to be walked around. He had made it into a mountain which was threatening to crumble down and crush her.

Well, she wouldn't let him do it! Her fiery pride came back to her full force, bringing a tiny, trembling smile to her lips, a smile that somehow managed to be just as self-pitying as her tears had been. What choice did she have? It was obvious that he wasn't about to give her one. He had made the choice for her when he had pushed her away from him.

Courtney took a deep breath and squared her shoulders. Gripping the arms of the chair, she pushed herself to her feet. Well, that was that. Time to get back to her old routine. No more self-pity, no more peeking around the barriers. She had work to take care of; there were little girls who depended on her, and they couldn't wait any longer for her to get control of herself.

She decided that she would make her planned call to Joshua, then go back and eat breakfast after all. That should show Elizabeth how wrong her assumptions were! But first she had to make the call to Joshua. The problem with Meryl was not going to go away, and neither would the pained, haunted look in her father's eyes—at least not without a great deal of effort from a third party, namely herself. Joshua Knight's aversion to her was incidental to the matter. There was still a job to be done, and, in founding her school, Courtney had chosen to do it. She moved back behind her desk again and threw open the address book.

It was then, as she contemplated the prospect of calling the Knight house, that another thought flashed into her mind. It was a nagging thought which had been clamoring for her attention all night. Andrea Vaughan. There was a strong chance that the housekeeper would answer the telephone, and the requisite little pang of jealousy stabbed Courtney at the realization, despite all of her stoic resolutions. But it was more than that. It was something Joshua had said about her that had been bothering Courtney.

Andrea had come up with the idea of sending

Meryl to Winston House. Andrea had decided what to do. Joshua had done the final legwork, checking her out with Dr. Farber, but Andrea had come up with the original idea.

Suddenly Courtney's thoughts were spinning out of control, and she got to her feet again. Pacing the small strip of carpet between the davenport and the door, a strip that was almost threadbare from her repeated pacing over the course of two years, Courtney thought hard about what had been bothering her. The letters, all those letters. And the fine, scrawled signature of Joshua R. Knight that had appeared so refined and precise, almost feminine. No wonder she had been so shocked at his initial appearance, for she had been expecting a mousy little man, judging by his signature! Of course, handwriting could be as misleading as voices. Joshua's strange, inappropriate signature could mean nothing—or it could mean everything.

She had nothing but some speculation. If Andrea Vaughan had indeed been the one to sign those letters, if Andrea had gone ahead with Meryl's admission without Joshua's knowledge . . . There was no way to tell, outside of asking him, and Courtney knew that his pride would never allow him to admit it, even if it were true. Unless she saw a sample of writing that was indisputably Joshua's, she would never have anything to back up her suspicions.

No, this jealousy business was just blowing up in her face, making her condemn Andrea at every turn. What basis did she really have for assuming that Andrea had arranged Meryl's admission without consulting Joshua? Just some letters with odd signatures. Joshua had mentioned only that Andrea had suggested the idea, which wasn't really surprising. If she loved Joshua, and she obviously did, then she had every reason in the world to want to combat his troubles with his daughter. So she had mentioned Winston House to Joshua, and he had gone for the idea. So what?

But what if she had done it to get Meryl out of the way? What if Joshua's preoccupation with his daughter was becoming detrimental to his affair with Andrea? What then? Clearly there was no love lost between Joshua's mistress and his daughter, and Andrea had already proved herself to be more than a little callous. But was that any basis for such wild speculations?

Aggravated at her overactive imagination, Courtney swallowed the dregs of her coffee and reached for the telephone again. She had to stop this. She had to remand this ridiculous jealousy to the same place where she had put her thoughts of Joshua Knight: outside the carefully built barriers of her self-preservation. The jealousy was becoming as dangerous as her attraction to Joshua had been. Between the two, she would surely lose the battle for Meryl's welfare if she wasn't careful.

But although she allowed her left hand to rest on the telephone, Courtney found herself reaching for her address book again with her right. She scanned the listings for Meryl, picking out Joshua's business number instead of his home number. She felt at the hands of her watch. It was eight-fifteen. Would he be in his office yet? It wasn't likely, but perhaps she could leave a message with someone who was. It beat the devil out of leaving a message with Andrea.

Courtney tapped the correct numbers, then fell victim to a spasm of doubt. The odds of *anyone* being in the office at this hour were remote.

She was just about to hang up, to battle down her

turmoil over Andrea Vaughan and call Joshua at home, when the ringing stopped and a rough male voice answered, "Knight Enterprises."

Courtney caught her breath in surprise. She had been unprepared for a voice, unprepared for an answer, and she was taken off guard. She thought that her voice sounded uncertain and childlike, not at all like her own. "I'd . . . I'd like to leave a message for Joshua Knight, please."

The only response was a deep silence on the line as Courtney tried once more to steady the erratic rhythm of her pulse. Then the voice returned, with a rugged, low breathlessness that almost prevented her from recognizing it. It was Joshua, and he sounded as though he had spent the morning running a marathon.

"Courtney?"

"Yes, how did you—" How could he have anticipated a phone call from her at eight-fifteen on a Friday morning, especially this Friday morning, after last night? Before she could give voice to the question, he cut her off.

"What do you want? If it's another apology that you're after, I'm afraid I still can't give you one."

There was a razor-sharp edge to his words that threatened to shatter each and every one of her resolutions. Was he speaking of kissing her, or of his words afterward? Did he mean both? Neither?

Her heart launched into its now familiar staccato rhythm as a battle between conflicting emotions raged within her. She wanted no apology. She wanted to know that he had wanted to touch her, that he had meant everything he had done. She needed to know that her lack of sight had made no difference, that he had desired her anyway.

But his words had destroyed the odds in favor of

such a thing, and she knew it, knew that he was almost certainly speaking of his cruel rebuff. He couldn't apologize because he had indeed meant the words. Still, although logic told her that she wouldn't get it, she desperately longed to hear him express remorse for what he had said.

When it became absolutely clear that he was going to offer no such thing, Courtney bit her lip hard, squared her shoulders doggedly and spoke with a calm that she had mastered long ago and only recently forgotten. "Actually, I wanted to arrange to see you. I have to speak with you. Are you free this afternoon?"

"No." The word was short and abrupt, but he sighed, and a further explanation drifted grudgingly over the telephone line. "As a matter of fact, I'm not. I've got quite a full day ahead of me. I couldn't possibly spare any time today."

Only the absolute necessity of doing so kept her rein on her temper tight. He had to know that she wanted to speak to him about Meryl! This was his daughter's welfare they were at odds over! The least he could do was condescend to speak to her about it!

"I'll only take a few minutes of your time, believe me. And it *is* important," she said finally, carefully.

"For heaven's sake, Courtney, it takes more than a few minutes to drive from Philadelphia to Collegeville. It takes forty-five minutes, to be exact. And I just don't have that kind of time today."

"You needn't worry yourself about travel time, Mr. Knight," she answered, her control making her voice icy and formal. "I'll come to you. My last class ends at two-fifteen today. I can be at your office by four o'clock."

"I don't think you understand, teacher. I don't want to see you." His words were sharp and almost

deliberately cruel. Courtney felt her breath ripping
from her raggedly. She gripped the telephone tightly, closing her eyes at the sick feeling that washed
through her, biting her lip even harder until the
immediate pain almost blocked out that in her heart.
So he despised her that much, was that repulsed by
her. Stinging tears burned at her eyes, and she barely
heard his thick, resigned sigh as it drifted through
the telephone line.

It touched Courtney gently, whispering of the
desperation that she had seen in his face only the
night before, and did what the pain of biting her lip
could not do. It melted the pain in her heart, leaving
doubt and confusion to twist in her stomach. She
tried to fight them off, but it was impossible. Finally
she could do nothing but accept their presence and
rationalize it. She would help him. Somehow she
would get through to him and would take away the
hurt. It was, after all, part of her job. She had to
push her own feelings aside.

"You can't come here," he was saying, and she
forced herself to listen. "Look, I'll run over there on
my way home tonight. I'll be late, though. About
seven or so."

"There's no need for you to do that. Really." She
forced a softness into her voice. "You said yourself
that you're busy today. I can be there by four o'clock
and be out of your way again by four-thirty. As I
said, I really just need a few minutes of your time."

"And just how do you propose to get here?" he
asked harshly. "No, don't tell me. You're going to
drive, is that it? Your damnable pride will somehow
keep you safe and sound behind the wheel of a car
when you can't even see where the hell you're going.
Is that what you're trying to tell me?"

Courtney flinched at the hard cruelty that had

once again found its way into his voice. She felt the barriers of her resolve beginning to shatter again with the force of his outburst. It took her a full minute to find her voice, then another to calm it into submission.

"Actually," she said smoothly, marveling at herself, at her control, "I intended to take the train."

The telephone line snapped and crackled into their silence. When he finally spoke again the painful regret she heard in his voice was almost too much for her to cope with. She held the telephone away from her ear for a minute, clutching the receiver with a death grip, fighting off the urge to simply hang up. She couldn't, mustn't, do that. He needed her. Meryl needed her. She had to hold on, had to somehow avoid the pain his revulsion and cruelty brought to her, in order to help both of them. And then, finally, she would be free to walk away from him. She could return to the structured safety of her own little world.

"I'm sorry. I didn't mean that," he was saying.

"I think you probably did," she murmured before she could help herself. "But don't worry yourself about it, please. All I ask is that you see me at four o'clock. Apart from that, I really don't care."

"No, not at four. Listen, we'll compromise. Meet me at my house at seven. That's a halfway point for both of us."

"You don't need to use kid gloves with me!" she snapped at him, her control giving out, her pride bristling. "I may not be able to see very well, but I function just fine. I don't need any special allowances from you. I can get to Philadelphia as easily as anyone else."

"I don't suppose it ever occurred to you that my suggestion wasn't a concession to your sight?" he asked, his own voice cold and angry again. "No, of course it wouldn't. Your pride wouldn't let it. You're more aware of your handicap than anyone else is, I think. Anyway, I don't see as how you have any choice in the matter, teacher." He spat out the nickname with condescending formality. She had forgotten that he could sound like that. In the space of a few kisses, she had forgotten.

"What do you mean?" she asked finally, warily, choosing to ignore his stinging words in an effort to hide from them.

"If you want to see me, you're going to have to do it my way. Be at my house at seven, and don't eat dinner."

"Don't eat—" Astounded, she began to protest, but the line went dead. Immediately she broke the connection and began dialing again. On the seventh unanswered ring she slammed the receiver back into its cradle.

"Damn him!" How dare he! After what he had done to her, how dare he assume that he could condescend to meet with her, feed her dinner and file her neatly into place among Andrea and the brunette from the restaurant. A little high-handed dominance, an invitation to dinner, and she was supposed to melt, to forgive, to forget the cruel words for which he refused to apologize. That tactic might work well with Andrea and whatever other women he had waiting in the wings, but it wouldn't work with her. She would stand him up. She would simply not show. He could just sit there at seven o'clock and stew.

But her seething anger was fighting against an excitement which was making her pulse maintain its pounding. She had gotten what she had set out after: He would see her. And dining with him would be infinitely more interesting than meeting with him in his office. It would be . . . personal, romantic, something other women took for granted, but something she allowed herself so rarely that it was a wonderful gift to be savored. Courtney rose from her desk and went to the window, looking out at the blindingly bright world as something equally shining whispered through her.

Then, just as soon as the feeling touched her heart, she brought a mental guillotine down on it. She would be going to Valley Forge to convince him that he had to begin spending more time with Meryl, and that was the *only* reason. She hadn't forgiven him, and he hadn't asked to be forgiven. No, their meeting would be pure business.

"Business," she murmured aloud, as though to convince her heart of the fact. In all honesty, she had to admit that she would need more than a half hour to convince him of Meryl's need for him, anyway. That, she knew, was going to make for more of a brawl than Elizabeth had ever imagined. She only prayed that Andrea Vaughan would not be a participant in either the dinner or the conversation, but she knew that it was a futile wish. She wanted some time in which to wrestle with her suspicions of the housekeeper, and she knew that she wasn't going to get it. Andrea Vaughan would undoubtedly be sharing dinner with them.

A dull sense of apprehension settled itself in Courtney's stomach at the prospect of such a meal. Facing Joshua after what had gone between them would be difficult enough. Facing Andrea would be positively unbearable. Again, Courtney thought fleetingly of simply not showing up, but she abandoned the idea once more. She told herself that it was because of the image of Meryl which snapped reprimandingly into her mind's eye. God, what a trap! She was damned if she did and damned if she didn't! Courtney fought off yet another overwhelming urge to cry.

Instead, feeling more tired than her lack of sleep could account for, she got to her feet and went to the door. Seven little girls would be waiting for her in the schoolroom, waiting for her to teach them. And she would do it, but first she had one last resolution to attend to.

She stepped into the schoolroom, and the giddy laughter that had been filling the room stopped guiltily. Seven pairs of eyes, some of them operating on instinct only, stared up at her. Courtney gripped the handrail and went to the back of the room.

Meryl was bent over her desk, her head resting on her arms. For a moment Courtney wondered if she could be sleeping, if she, too, had had a long, sleepless night. But as she knelt by the girl's desk, the dark head snapped up and the amber eyes searched hungrily for something she could see.

"Meryl? I need to see you for a moment. Will you come next door with me before class?"

"Do I have to?"

Courtney nodded. "I'd appreciate it—let's put it that way."

"You told me I didn't have to do anything I didn't want to," Meryl reminded her obstinately.

"I'm not *making* you do anything. I just want to talk to you. If you'd rather I do it here with everyone listening, that's fine with me."

Meryl got to her feet abruptly. "You always end up getting your way, no matter what you say."

Courtney stood up as well. "Usually," she agreed. "But I work like the devil at it." She turned away from the other girls, whose ears were absorbing everything in a way that their eyes never could. The room was electric with pitched curiosity, but no one spoke as they left. It wasn't until she and Meryl were out the door that Corinne's voice rang out wisely.

"Something really weird is going on around here!"

Courtney pushed open the door to an empty room and stepped inside. "Come on, let's go in here."

Meryl was silent. She stood rigid and stiff in the center of the room, her back to Courtney, her unseeing eyes trained on the door. Before the quiet could turn antagonistic, Courtney moved around in front of her and leaned back against the door.

"I've been pretty upset about what you said last night," she ventured.

"I didn't think you ever got upset about anything. At least that's what you told me. I thought you were so perfect."

Courtney couldn't restrain her pained laugh. "Oh, Meryl, if you only knew how untrue that is! No, I'm not perfect. I only wish I were. I don't know how you ever decided that; but the truth is, I'm only human, and maybe not even such a great human at that. Let's face it, some of my parts are a bit faulty."

"Okay, so you're not perfect. And maybe you don't even think you are, either. I don't care."

"Maybe you don't. But that's the whole purpose of this conversation, Meryl. Last night you accused me of lying to you because you caught me crying. You threw certain things I had said to you right back in my face—things about life getting easier after a while. And maybe you had a right to, I don't know. But I want to remind you of something that I'm pretty sure you already know."

Meryl sounded curious in spite of herself. "What?"

"Even people who aren't blind cry."

There was a short silence before Meryl asked, "Yeah? So?"

"So how do you know that what I was crying about had anything to do with my eyesight?"

"Did it?"

It was a question that she had been prepared for, and she already knew that she couldn't lie. "It had to do with a lot of things, actually, and that was one of them. But, Meryl, so what if I was crying because I can't see? What then?"

Meryl's voice hedged. "What do you mean?"

"What difference would it make? When I told you things got easier, I meant it. I wasn't lying. They do. Twelve years ago, when I was your age, I spent a lot of useless hours each and every day hating myself because my eyes wouldn't work right, hating my life and hating everyone around me because they could see just fine. But I got older and I guess I got a little wiser, too. Somewhere along the line, I realized that my hatred wasn't doing me an ounce of good. There were still some things left in my life that I could enjoy, but I wasn't doing them because I was too busy crying and feeling sorry for myself. So I wasn't really living at all. I was just cursing fate and sitting around, waiting for something to take me away from it all. So what was the use of being alive?

"All I'm trying to say is that sometimes I do still feel sorry for myself because I can't see, and sometimes I even cry about it. It's not an easy thing to live with. You, of all people, should know that. But the only choice I've got is either to live with it or not to live at all. Given those choices, I'll take the former."

Something proud and strong surged deep inside her with the words and she knew, in that instant, that what she had just said was as much a reminder for her as it was a lesson to Meryl. Perhaps she couldn't have Joshua Knight; perhaps she couldn't offer him what Andrea could. She wasn't going to throw in the towel over it. She could live without him. She *would* live without him.

"So what do you want me to do about it?" Meryl was asking insolently.

"That, Meryl, is up to you. I just wanted a chance to defend myself, that's all. All I want you to do is try to understand that I didn't lie to you. After that, the rest is up to you."

Courtney pulled open the door and stepped into the corridor. "I'm going back to the classroom. It's twelve steps to your left and the door is on your right, when you feel like joining us."

She pulled the door shut quietly, blowing out her tension with her breath. Meryl would understand. She had to.

But would her father be as easy to convince?

Chapter 6

THE FIRE WAS FLICKERING GENTLY IN THE FIRE-
place when Courtney slipped into her bedroom. It
was one of Elizabeth's extra touches which still
surprised Courtney now and again. She pushed her
bedroom door shut softly behind her and stood
staring at the orange and gold flames as they danced
and snapped. Sighing heavily, she moved toward the
flickering light until it grew so bright and consuming
that it seemed to swallow her. Crackling heat caressed her as she sat down carefully on the hearth,
running her fingers over the rough stone to get her
bearings.

With her shoulders hunched inward, her arms
wrapped around her knees and her long hair falling
forward over her face, Courtney twisted around just

enough so that she directly faced the raging fire. It was five-thirty; soon she would have to leave for Valley Forge. As the day had droned on, she had actually begun to look forward to the evening more than she dreaded it, but she felt so spent and drained that she couldn't help wishing that her meeting with Joshua had been planned for some other night. Canceling now, however, was out of the question. She couldn't even conceive of not going. Not now. Not after she had spent all day thinking about it, losing her train of thought in class and absently toying with her lunch while Elizabeth looked on with a mixture of worry and knowing pleasure. No, she had thought only once of standing him up, right after their conversation, and had not seriously considered the alternative since. Although, she thought again as she stared into the flames, it would serve him right for being so high-handed in making the arrangements.

Picturing the annoyance her failure to turn up might bring to the cool, remote Joshua Knight, Courtney almost smiled, but the day had taken its toll on her and she couldn't quite pull it off. It had been a horrendous day, to say the least. Although she had hoped to be able to sneak upstairs for a much needed nap after her last class, that had proved impossible when an early picnic dinner down by the creek had turned into mayhem.

From what Courtney could understand, since she hadn't been at the scene of the crime, Corinne had stumbled and tripped into Meryl sometime during the customary hijinks before the meal. Meryl's temper had exploded, and with a barrage of cruel and cutting words, she had pushed Corinne straight into the creek.

Worse than the lack of sleep which had left her

feeling so lifeless was the heavy mantle of worry that had settled about Courtney after she had returned from the creek. She had been feeling so optimistic about Meryl, daring to believe that she was making some progress with her and that their talk that morning had perhaps been one tiny, creeping step in the direction of change. And now this business with Corinne had erupted to shake her already precarious hope.

Even more nagging was her worry that she was so deeply into the trees that she could no longer see the forest. If it had been Julie or Stephanie who had pushed Corinne into the creek, Courtney was convinced that she would have chalked the incident up to some prank on Corinne's part. But because it had been Meryl, the source of her chief and overriding concern for weeks, and Joshua's daughter, the situation seemed to hint doom.

Exasperated with herself, Courtney smacked one hand irritably against the wall. She was losing her grip on things! First, there were those bizarre conclusions that she had reached concerning Joshua's letters and Andrea Vaughan, and now there was this! Everything seemed to be getting away from her, slipping free of her grasp. She had stepped outside her safely constructed world for just a moment, had taunted fate with a mere kiss or two, and now all hell was breaking loose.

A soft clicking sound from the direction of the bathroom broke Courtney's reverie, and she twisted around toward the door, temporarily blinded from the flames.

Meryl's voice broke into her world, the words tumbling out so rapidly that they reminded Courtney of gunfire. "I'm sorry. That's all I wanted to tell you. I know you won't believe me, but it was an accident, sort of. I—I didn't mean to do it. I just got mad because I didn't see her coming. That's all."

In the next second Courtney heard the scurrying footfalls of Meryl's retreat; then the bathroom door cracked closed again, its echo reverberating in the room. Courtney sat stunned, gaping in the direction of the door.

Gradually a warm, hopeful feeling began to swim through her. Some of the tension and worry slid away, and she smiled, feeling as though her heart would burst for joy. Another step, and not such a small one, either!

She showered and dressed quickly, telling herself that it was in the interests of time that she selected the first outfit she came to in the closet. It was a shimmering silk trouser suit with a long tunic top that fell to her knees and was slit almost to the waist on each side. The pale ivory contrasted wonderfully with her hair; the slender, green metallic belt caught the emerald light in her eyes. The tunic left one shoulder enticingly bare, but the other was plain and demure, a single long sleeve without any elaborate trim to detract from the overall effect. The classical lines gave her a suave grace that was far from what she was feeling. Jade earrings and a matching bracelet added another dimension; with her hair long and free, she looked sultry and almost unintentionally sensual.

Courtney felt herself scowling as she fixed the last of her makeup. Sensual? No, the outfit wasn't sensual, was it? She stepped back from the mirror and stared at a milky, fuzzy reflection that belied the crystal-clear answer she found there. Yes, she did look sexy and sensual and as though she had every intention in the world of seducing Joshua Knight.

What was more, delightful anticipation was beginning to wriggle around in her stomach, and she knew with the utmost conviction that she wanted to look this way; she wanted, if only once in her life, to step out the front door of Winston House dressed to kill and to dare anything that might come of it. For just one evening, she wanted what the Andrea Vaughans of the world would always take for granted. She wanted to play at being Cinderella; she wanted to pretend.

A bright light of warning went off in her heart even as she reached for her hairbrush. Could she dare it? Could she take such a gamble and walk out into a world where she had no business, into a playground where all the other kids were older and wiser and could cope with what they found there? She shuddered almost imperceptibly and was debating the logic of changing into something more severe and businesslike—but after all, this was dinner, wasn't it, and not a meeting at his office?—when Elizabeth threw open the door without knocking and came rushing in, her eyes wide, her mouth hanging open in comical surprise. She started to speak, then clapped her mouth shut again and stepped back into the hallway, looking in the direction of the stairs as if she needed to convince herself of something. When she came back, she pushed the door closed behind her and stood staring at Courtney, her hands planted on her hips.

"What is it? What's wrong? Do you think I'm overdressed?" Courtney asked quickly, troubled and alarmed by the chaos doing battle in her friend's eyes.

"Ah, no . . . no, you look fine . . . perfect, really, considering, ah . . . Where are you going?"

Courtney raised her eyebrows at her. She tried to

continue to brush her hair calmly, but Elizabeth was staring at her hard, with such rapt amazement that Courtney had to struggle to find her voice. Finally she paused in her brushing, knowing defeat when it stared her in the eye.

"Dinner. I'm going out for dinner. I mentioned that, didn't I?"

Elizabeth frowned in severe concentration. "Right, you did. But you didn't say exactly where, at least to my recollection. Anyway, I don't suppose you'd be interested to know that the cab you asked me to call for you won't be necessary."

It was Courtney's turn to look surprised. She went back to her brushing, her strokes deliberate and slow, her eyes focused warily on Elizabeth. "Why not?"

"Because there's a man downstairs in a chauffeur's uniform trying to tell me that Joshua Knight sent him."

Courtney gasped in frank astonishment. Involuntarily, she dropped the hairbrush with a clatter and stared at Elizabeth, her mouth wide, her eyebrows disappearing beneath the heavy fringes of her hair.

Elizabeth's face was calm now, lit up once again with the speculative little half smile that Courtney had seen on her lips earlier. "Why didn't you tell me you had a date with Joshua?"

"Because I *don't* have a date with Joshua!" Courtney answered, her temper flaring into life at Elizabeth's smug expression. "I'm only meeting with him to discuss Meryl! That's all!"

"Dressed like that? You look like Cleopatra must have looked when she set her sights on Antony."

"I'll change!"

"Oh, for heaven's sake, don't do that. You look lovely. Stunning, really. I've never seen that outfit before. You just don't look like you're off for an evening of business."

"Well, I am," Courtney muttered, dragging the brush through her hair again.

"Courtney, Courtney, what am I going to do with you? Come here." In that second Elizabeth's hand was on her arm, pulling her back to the bed and sitting her down. "Will you give me an honest answer to something? Really honest, now?"

Courtney shrugged, her hair slipping back off her shoulders. "Of course."

"Exactly where are you going tonight, and why?"

Well, that was easy enough, Courtney thought with relief. "That's all? I'm going to Joshua's house for dinner because he's given me no choice in the matter. I wanted to meet with him at his office, but he insisted that we compromise on the distance and meet at his place. I've got to talk to him about Meryl."

"Oh? And why's that?"

"Why? I don't understand."

"Why do you have to talk to him about Meryl?"

Courtney scowled and jumped off the bed. "Oh, come on, Elizabeth, you know perfectly well why! Those two need each other. For Meryl's sake, I've got to get them together. I've got to help."

"I see. Feel pretty strongly about that, do you?"

"Of course I do! It's my job!"

Elizabeth reached out and gently fingered the soft skirt of Courtney's tunic. When she stepped away and went back to the door, her eyes were soft and wistful. "No, Courtney, you're wrong. Your job is to teach Meryl, that's all. This is above and beyond the call of duty. This is a matter of the heart. Your heart and your head are doing battle, and your heart is winning, my dear. Now, if you'll excuse me, I'm going to tell Mr. Knight's chauffeur that you'll be down in a minute. By the way, don't change, whatever you do. You look lovely, and don't forget, you've got competition. If you're going to win, you're going to have to fight."

The door swung shut, leaving Courtney to stare at it, stupefied, her heart thumping gently. A matter of the heart? Joshua? She tried to be rational and couldn't; she could only think of her steady, unswerving devotion to Meryl, her heart-wrenching compassion for Joshua, his kisses—*they* surely weren't very professional—her sleepless nights, so many things.

But competition? No, there was no manner of competition involved. The idea was ludicrous. It would be like pitting a race horse against a donkey, and she was most definitely the donkey in this instance. Andrea had eyes. Andrea had Joshua. Andrea had everything, and Courtney was damned if she was going to let it upset her. No, there would be no competition, because she didn't intend to fight. She couldn't.

She grabbed a heavy, fur-lined cloak from her closet and slipped out of her bedroom, still simmering with indignation and anger. Down in the entryway stood a tall, reserved-looking man in a chauffeur's uniform.

The man reached out to take her elbow proprietarily as she approached. "Miss Winston?"

"This is ridiculous," Courtney muttered under her breath, but she allowed him to lead her out onto the porch and down the steps to a classic, pearl gray Cadillac. The chauffeur, who introduced himself as Richard, handled her gingerly and cautiously, and Courtney wondered just what Joshua had told him about her. She fought to restrain a cutting remark which would have defended her remaining, scant sight, for that was obviously the cause of the chauffeur's solicitude. After all, the man was nothing more than an innocent pawn in Joshua's army. She decided that she would save her anger for the general himself.

Oh, for heaven's sake, she groaned inwardly as he helped her into the back seat. The words were more for the car than for Richard's gentle, careful touch. Had Elizabeth seen this? No, surely not, for if she had, she would have warned her about turning into a pumpkin at midnight rather than falling in love. More likely still, she would have been out here, agog with awe and appreciation.

Why was he doing this? Courtney wondered. Why? Agreeing to see her was one thing, but this . . . Her eyes wildly tried to pierce the dark shadows of the car as she fought to understand. The chameleon had changed his colors again; no longer was he the remote, repulsed man down by the creek. Overnight he had gone back to being the cavalier bachelor from the restaurant. Courtney groaned inwardly, her confusion mounting as the lights on the highway sped past, tiny white pinpoints with fuzzy, streaming tails.

All her searching, pondering thoughts stumbled to a standstill as they pulled up in front of a rambling Tudor mansion so much like her own that she felt a small "Oh!" slide from her lips. Without waiting for Richard's help, she jumped from the Cadillac, then went slowly up the walkway, feeling relatively sure of her footing, despite the fact that she had never been there before. Richard rushed to take her elbow again, but she shook him off unceremoniously, watching as double wood-planked doors opened wide. Joshua Knight leaned casually against the doorjamb, one massive shoulder hard against the wood, a glass in his hand.

Courtney stepped closer to him, close enough to look up into his leonine eyes. She knew that she should say something, but the uncertain furor of her emotions prevented it.

"Well, teacher, I'm glad to see you could make it." His words were insolently smug as he swung away from the door and pulled the cape from her shoulders with one deft hand. Courtney was remotely aware of the doors moving shut behind her, but her attention was almost fully captivated by the soft brush of his fingers against her naked shoulder, a brush that left sizzling fire on her skin long after he had moved away from her to put her cape in the hall closet.

Oh, God, is Elizabeth right? she wondered as she stood there watching him, her voice seemingly lost to her, her stomach a haven for thousands of fluttering butterflies. Is it love that's wrong with me? Can it be? How could I have allowed such a thing to happen?

He was reaching into the closet, the corded muscles of his shoulder rippling beneath the stark whiteness of his shirt, and she longed to simply reach out to touch him, to feel those muscles move beneath her fingers, to feel them flex and relax. Instead, she curled her fingers into the palm of her hand and, bemused with her own startling urges and with Joshua's presence as well, watched him as though she had never seen him before. She studied him as much as her eyes would allow, wondering, but not really caring, if it was her eyes or her imagination that told her that his tailored blue slacks were almost straining against the hard width of his thighs, or that, as he turned to face her, wisps of golden brown hair were sneaking out from around the unbuttoned collar of his shirt.

"Courtney?" His voice was low and curious. Embarrassed, she wrenched her eyes away from him and deliberately scanned the walls and ceiling around her.

"Lovely house," she commented, finding gratefully that her voice was still there. "It seems oddly familiar."

He laughed again, and the rippling sound seemed to break the tension between them.

"I almost stopped dead in my tracks the first time I went to your place," he admitted, taking her by the elbow and leading her imperiously toward the back of the house. "It would seem that we have similar taste in architecture, as well as a mutual interest in my daughter. This could have possibilities."

They stopped at the doorway to the den, and his smooth, bantering tone seemed to die. He stepped purposefully up to a long, mahogany wet bar along one wall and poured an ample amount of bourbon into his glass, downing half of it quickly before speaking to her.

"If I remember correctly, you drink brandy."

"How did you know that?" Courtney watched the blur of his body, impressive despite the distance that clouded her eyes and suddenly wondered what else he knew about her.

"You forget that I was at the table behind you the night you told that poor fellow you weren't going to marry him."

"Oh, that." Courtney felt herself flushing and she turned toward the fireplace, feeling drawn to its warmth. The subtle shivering that always seemed to overtake her when she was near him was starting again, deep in her bones. She drew closer to the crackling heat in a vain effort to still it.

She was unaware of the picture she created as she stood there with the riotous firelight catching the metallic jade of her belt and jewelry and the soft, shining emerald of her eyes. Before the orange glow could wreak havoc with her vision, she pulled herself reluctantly away from the fireplace, breaking the spell, and turned back to the bar to catch Joshua staring at her intently, wonder in his eyes.

She took the brandy snifter that he held out to her unceremoniously, wondering if he would notice the trembling in her hands, then sipped greedily at the brandy, seeking solace in its warm depths. Damn Elizabeth, anyway! Why did she have to choose tonight, of all times, to put ludicrous thoughts of love into her head?

"Whoa, custom has it that you're supposed to toast first." Joshua reached out and grasped her wrist lightly as she brought the snifter to her lips again. Something hot immediately shot through her at his touch, leaving an empty, aching feeling in the pit of her stomach and bringing her shivering to an even stronger pitch. She found herself holding her breath against the weakness of her knees as his fingers ran smoothly and carelessly over the soft skin on the inside of her wrist, tickling gently against her hammering pulse. Stop it. You've got to stop this, she thought. The evening was just beginning; she could hardly spend the next several hours quivering at memories of his kiss, his touch.

She pulled away from him carefully, stepping back and holding her glass in front of her with both hands. Even so, the amber liquid moved in small waves with the force of her trembling, and she took a deep

breath, trying to will her control to return. When she
looked up at him again her face was confused and
her voice seemed to come from far away, sounding
tentative and almost shy, as she said, "Oh, is it too
late? Did I ruin it?"

"I somehow doubt that you could ruin anythi ng,"
he answered softly. "No, I think it will still work."
He raised his glass to her and, cursing the liquid
feeling of her bones, Courtney managed to raise hers
as well.

Joshua shrugged; the fabric of his shirt stretched
taut over his shoulders again, then relaxed. "To
Meryl's happiness, I suppose," he said as their
glasses clinked and their eyes locked for a second
over them. "And to peace between her father and
her teacher."

Courtney smiled as she brought the glass back to
her lips, a vague effort to hide the effect his eyes had
on her. "That's apropos, I guess."

She looked away from him then, feeling shy and
uncertain at the sight of him bathed in the flickering
light of the fire, looking like some massive golden
god. He's so perfect, she realized suddenly, the
thought almost painful in its impact. He was the man
she had dreamed about so many years ago when she
had closed tired, seeing eyes against the night,
fantasizing her way to sleep. He was the man she had
wanted before she had learned that she would have
no man at all. She was suddenly grateful that she
couldn't see him better, for she was sure that, if she
could have, all her meager control would have fled,
leaving her even more defenseless than she already
felt.

She wandered back to the fireplace, trying to
avoid looking directly into the flames, but she was
almost captivated by them. When she spoke, it was

with the timid wonder she felt at being there with him at all. "I really didn't have this in mind when I called you this morning."

"I doubt if either of us did. You were the model of professionalism. I certainly never expected you to show up looking like this."

Courtney felt the heat rise to her cheeks, knew she was blushing, and knew also that he was smiling, for she could hear the humor in his voice.

"You look beautiful," he finished, and then, amazingly, the soft humor was gone from his voice and his mockery was back. "If I had teachers like you, I might have been persuaded to stay in school a little longer."

"Stay in school? But—" Shocked at the sudden, icy control in his voice, her own response came out quickly, steeped in confusion, though more at the tone of his voice than at his words.

"I know." His voice was still dry and brittle. "I have a successful business with offices in three states, but I learned it all by the seat of my pants. I never finished school. My father deserted my mother and me when I was fourteen. I had no choice but to leave school and go to work. Luckily, the man I chose to work for knew incentive and determination when he saw them. I finally did get a diploma through night school. That was one of the conditions he set before making me a partner. He died eight years ago, and I took over the business."

"I see," Courtney answered quietly, and she did, although she wasn't sure how. As she stared into the fire, she realized that she wasn't at all surprised at the revelation, for she had somehow known all along that this man had never really been a little boy, and that the hard, cutting edge in his eyes had been born out of necessity. I was right, she thought suddenly.

He's so like me. Something began melting inside her again.

"Do you? Well, maybe you do. I imagine you must have had to claw your way to the top, too. At any rate, there's no sense dwelling on it."

He stood close as he spoke, so close that she could feel his breath against her hair. Instantaneously her heart exploded again, thumping wildly against her chest like a caged bird as she remembered the night before, his kiss, his touch—and his words, so cruel and hurting. Why was he doing this now? Why the brandy? Why the chauffeur? She jumped slightly as his hand came down on her bare shoulder, his fingers warm and electric, stroking the skin there.

She faced him, a world of confusion and uncertainty in her eyes. His own amber gaze stared back at her intently, his eyes startlingly close to her own. Courtney felt herself waiting breathlessly, tremulously, for him to move, to break the spell or send them spiraling even deeper into it, anything that might help her to understand. Still, when his voice came, it brought no understanding with it, just more teasing desire.

"You are beautiful," he said again huskily, and his hand left her shoulder, entwining itself in her hair, pulling gently at its heavy thickness until she had no choice but to tilt her head back, arching into him. "Not a schoolmarm at all," he continued, his voice like velvet fire, hard yet somehow sultry.

Courtney watched him, her legs feeling weak again and strangely empty, as though someone had removed the bones without bothering to tell her. The skin of her shoulder where his hand had rested felt uncomfortably cold without his touch. Without thinking, she reached up and covered his hand with her own, bringing it back against her skin, back where she could feel his fiery electricity once more.

What now? she wondered wildly. Would he kiss her again? No, he was too aware of her, he wouldn't kiss her. Would he? Her yearning was a heavy weight against her heart, suffocating everything else, making it suddenly pause in crystal stillness.

Suddenly unable to bear the torture and the uncertainty of the moment anymore, Courtney broke away. Free of his steady, intense gaze and his silken touch, her heart began its erratic pounding again. Her eyes flew erratically around the fireplace and the mantel, desperately searching for something to latch on to.

Gradually, she became aware that Joshua had moved, that his warmth was no longer there. She turned around again and saw his shadowy form back at the bar, pouring more bourbon into his glass.

Courtney moved toward him carefully, unsure of the terrain of the room. She was halfway around the couch when her shin thudded hard against the corner of the cocktail table. In the second that it took her to cry out in pain and bend to rub at the tender welt, Joshua had barked out a directive to the dining room and had disappeared.

Courtney straightened quickly and, ignoring the throbbing in her shin, searched the room in panic. There was no movement in the diaphanous orange light from the fire. Where was he? He couldn't leave her there! How would she get to the dining room without tripping, without falling? How could she do anything but stand there helplessly? Damn him! How could he do this to her?

"I'm right here." His voice came from behind her, soft and speculative.

"Well, why didn't you tell me?" she asked sharply, relief straining her voice as she spun to face him. "I thought you had just left me here! I thought—"

Her panic was immediately silenced as his mouth came down on hers, hard and searching as it had been the night before. Courtney felt herself stiffening in surprise, afraid to meet his lips with the hot desire that she felt, afraid to reach for him, to touch him. His words of the night before echoed in her brain, even as his mouth broke from hers, even as he buried his face in her hair, his tongue leaving a trail of smoldering fire as his mouth started a downward trek toward her collarbone. And still she stood frozen, her heart exploding within her.

Her control shattered suddenly, falling away from her in a million tiny pieces. The strange but now so familiar weakness began to undulate within her again, threatening to buckle her knees. The splintered remnants of her fear fell into it, leaving her feeling free and daring and exhilarated. Without thought, without deliberation, she reached for him, burying her hands in his hair until he lifted his head again.

The fire sent an orange kind of darkness to shimmer around her and she closed her eyes against it, retreating once more into the familiar corridors of her dark world. Her lips found his easily. She tasted him sweetly and unhurriedly with patient curiosity, until his tongue delved into her mouth, searching for more. The piercing intensity of the night before was gone in the face of something new and exploratory that had taken them over. Courtney felt the slight transition, felt the difference in his touch, and very nearly pulled away from it, the fear rising up in her throat once more. This was different, so different, more gentle . . . more needful, and she wasn't at all sure that she could meet that need. Did she dare? Could she? How reckless had Cinderella been before the stroke of midnight had called her back to her old world of safety?

The choice was taken out of her hands when his hand glided up over her shoulder again, lingering there only momentarily before burying itself in her hair. She let out a sigh that spoke of contentment and peace, forgetting her confusion, her questions, aware only of him and the quivering inside her which finally erupted, filling her with molten lava, hot and searing, devouring her slowly.

He didn't pull back from her in horror this time as she had half expected him to, but eased away from her gently so that she barely knew what was happening. His mouth left hers slowly, only to find her eyelids, kissing each before she had a chance to open them. His hand dropped to her shoulder again and rested there, softly teasing wisps of her hair as he spoke. There was something controlled in his touch, some willpower that seemed to pull him back.

"I was right. There's quite a little wolf lurking around inside the teacher, hmmm?" His voice was like velvet, belying the strength of his restraint. "Too bad you always demand apologies when someone opens the door and lets the wolf out. You know, if you call me tomorrow morning, I won't apologize for tonight."

Courtney reeled away from him in agitation. "I've told you that I didn't call for an apology! I don't even know where you got such an idea! I called on business . . . about Meryl . . . that was all!"

His hand had trailed off her shoulder, and Courtney sucked in her breath harshly and involuntarily as it brushed over her breast, lingering there for the space of a sigh, teasing gently until something hot erupted again and she forgot her agitation. She arched into him involuntarily, grasping at his shoulders with both hands.

"Really, teacher?" he asked idly, as though her reaction had been totally lost on him. Only the shrewd light in his eyes told her that it had definitely been acknowledged, that he was savoring the effect he had on her. His hand moved away, falling down to her waist, then quickly found the slit in her tunic and managed to slide its way to the soft skin that he had discovered once before. Gently he teased, one thigh nudging her legs apart and teasing her toward greater ecstasy with its subtle pressure.

"It . . . was your idea for me to come here." She was breathless, in an agony of controlled desire. "*I* wanted to go to your office. *You* invited me to dinner."

"So I did." His hand kept moving, idly and slowly, as though with a will of its own, until it found her breast again. He cupped it gently, his eyes never leaving her face, not even when his thumb found her taut nipple, teasing it gently until she groaned somewhere deep in her throat and her fingers clawed into the hardness of his shoulders.

"Good idea, too, wasn't it?" he went on smoothly and calmly. "And since you're here, must we argue? Can't we just enjoy something that has the potential of being a wonderful evening? I like you, teacher. I like you a lot. You're an intriguing lady, once you let the barriers down, and I don't really care why you came. I'm only glad that you're here." All the while he teased the sensitive point of her breast until she felt faint with heat and sank down against his thigh, which was still braced between her legs. The deepened contact left her gasping, hoping that the moment would never end.

Suddenly, without warning, his hand was gone. Courtney's breath rushed out, leaving her feeling scorched and explosive. She reached for the mantel as he moved away from her, but he gave her no time to catch her breath, no time to reconnoiter. His hand moved up under her elbow again, and she was concentrating hard on following him through alien territory toward the door, on getting control over her limbs again, when he spoke so quietly that she wasn't entirely sure if she had heard him correctly.

"And I haven't felt intrigued in a good many years."

It wasn't the sort of thing that she could ask him to repeat, she knew that, and yet she wished desperately that she could, for she needed the chance to understand. Her mind was struggling helplessly with words and innuendos, both silent and spoken, that made no sense after his harsh words of the night before. If he hadn't wanted her to touch him then, why had he been tormenting her now? It had all been so clearly a power play, a struggle for control that she had clearly lost, and yet it made no sense. She closed her eyes against the image of him that rose from her memory: his golden brown eyes, burning down into her own with an almost vulnerable yet passionate fire.

Defenseless against her churning thoughts, Courtney's imagination simply staggered away from them. She found herself savoring the feeling of his hand, so strong and purposeful beneath her elbow, and fought to banish the thoughts of the way he had touched her only moments before. Courtney couldn't suppress the smile that played along her lips. When she turned to him, her eyes were bright with pleasure and understanding.

"Some business meeting!"

Before them was a beautifully set table for two, complete with crystal water goblets and the finest china. A vase holding a single long-stemmed rose dominated the table with its simple beauty.

Joshua's mouth seemed to be struggling between a grim line and an almost sheepish smile that tugged mercilessly at the corners of his lips. Ultimately, the smile won. He pulled a chair out for Courtney, seated her, then leaned close over her shoulder. "I wasn't taking any chances that you really did mean business."

Courtney shook her head wistfully, too delighted by the rose and his admission to do anything but smile. The room was lit softly from above, and everything glowed with a soft opalescense, almost like a dream. To Courtney's eyes, everything was fringed with clouds, but for once it was perfect that way. She turned to Joshua and laid her hand over his impetuously. "It's lovely. It really is." It's a dream come true, she thought to herself. My own fairy tale to remember forever.

Joshua's smile remained, but it seemed to grow wavery and uncertain before it froze in place. He pulled his hand slowly and carefully from beneath hers to give gruff orders to the woman who had come in from the kitchen carrying their meal on a large silver tray.

Something sharp stung at her when he pulled his hand away. Courtney slowly brought her own back to her lap, his words from the night before assaulting her again. Although the veal was delicious, the wine better, Courtney found herself sampling both disinterestedly.

"You're not eating." Joshua leaned closer to her, his eyes curious but still somehow distant. "Is something wrong?"

Yes, Courtney wanted to say. Oh, yes. You say you don't want me to touch you, you pull your hand away from mine, but you invite me to dinner and kiss me more sweetly than I've ever been kissed. You've woken me up inside and made me feel things that I've never felt before, but you're not mine, you can never be mine, and you don't want to be mine. Other than those minor issues, everything is fine.

Instead, she shook her head and volunteered a small smile. "I'm sorry. Everything's delicious. It's just that it's been a long, strange day." It was as close to the truth as she could bring herself to get.

Joshua's face clouded even more. "Anything to do with Meryl?"

"In part. But it's not entirely negative. She's showing progress."

He sighed heavily and drained his wineglass with an impatient gesture. "I already know that a good part of the reason you're here concerns my daughter, although I'd begun to believe that my company had something to do with it, too."

"Your company is wonderful," she insisted impetuously, then felt herself blushing. "That is to say, I'm enjoying myself thoroughly. I'm glad I had business to bring me here in the first place."

The smile that creased his face wasn't as mocking as she would have expected, but rather wry and resigned. "But there was business, at least initially."

Courtney nodded. "Of course. That was my reason for calling you, contrary to what you seem to think."

"I don't know what to think anymore, Courtney," he mused. "Look, if you want to talk about Meryl, let's go back to the den where we can at least be comfortable."

She murmured her assent and absently moved

against him as he slipped his hand beneath her elbow again, her thoughts centered on the conversation about to take place. Almost as absently, Joshua moved his hand down to her waist but it was a careless, indifferent touch. This wasn't going to be easy, she thought. Already he was pulling away from her, protecting himself with distance.

She accepted a snifter of brandy from him once they reached the den and was on guard against the disappointment that nudged at her when he leaned back against the far end of the couch.

"Okay, teacher. Hit me with it. What about Meryl?" His voice was hard and impersonal.

"Well, she pushed another little girl into the creek today," she answered him blithely, determined to break through his frigid composure.

It worked. Joshua jackknifed into an upright position, his face a mask of conflicting emotions. "Meryl did that? My God!"

"Joshua!" She reached out a hand across the space between them. "It was progress, actually. She came to me later to explain that it had been something of an accident. She just lost her temper because she hadn't seen Corinne coming at her. Joshua, a week ago she wouldn't have said a word. A week ago she would barely speak to me, much less drop her pride long enough to plead her case with me. In the beginning she wouldn't even come down for meals, but when she pushed Corinne in the creek, it happened during a picnic dinner down there!"

"What are you saying? She's getting better? Is that what you're trying to tell me?" His eyes were hooded slits, suspicious and wary.

"That's exactly what I'm saying," Courtney replied softly. "Oh, the progress is slow, very slow. And I'll admit that I was shattered when I first got down to the creek and found out that it was Meryl who had done the pushing. I was terrified that she'd had some major relapse or something. But when she came to apologize . . . that was the happiest moment I've had in weeks!"

His suspicious eyes softened and he watched her again with the same speculative, wondering look that she had seen in his eyes earlier. Feeling awkward under his scrutiny, Courtney took a deep, fortifying swallow of brandy and plunged on.

"But she still needs you, Joshua. Now more than ever. Sure, she's coming out of her shell a bit, and she seems to accept me, although it's a grudging acceptance. But she's still so lost inside herself, and that's a terrible feeling," she added vehemently. "It's horrible to have to wonder if everyone is feeling sorry for you behind their careful words and to be unable to even see the pity in their eyes. Meryl's living behind some huge, black curtain— she's cut off from everyone. It's like that sometimes. People are hesitant to push the curtain aside; you're too frightened to step around it yourself. That's where Meryl is at now. If someone would just push the curtain aside for her a bit and say hello, it would make a world of difference for her."

"So do it," he growled, springing to his feet and going back to the bar.

Courtney held herself strong against his outburst; having expected the reaction, she was ready to surmount it. She got to her feet and moved tentatively toward him, wary of the furniture around her but determined to get to him, to reach through to him.

"That's not good enough," she said quietly, coming to stand right behind him. "Joshua, if you love her, you've got to help her. I can't do it, because it wouldn't mean as much coming from me. She needs you. She needs your love and your acceptance."

He slammed his glass down on the bar so hard that the bourbon sloshed out in a single wave, splashing upward in liquid amber fireworks. Courtney reeled away in surprise. As her legs carried her backward, she wondered helplessly what was behind her. Would she fall? But then he was on top of her, one strong hand gripping each shoulder, his arms forming a vise around her so that she couldn't have fallen if she had wanted to. There was nothing sensual in his touch now; his strength was built entirely on anger.

"Don't you listen?" He ground out the words through gritted teeth. "Don't you hear what I say to you? This is one mountain you can't climb, teacher. You can't win on this! I can't help Meryl because she doesn't want me to! I can't make myself any clearer than that. She won't let me get close enough to her to open your mythical little curtain." He released her abruptly and she sat down hard on the sofa, but she sprang to her feet again without the slightest hesitation, willing to fight, determined to win.

She drew close to him cautiously, watching as he drew a desperate hand over his eyes, leaning his arm, then his head, on the mantel.

"It's no good," he said, his voice muffled and distant. "There's nothing I can do to help her. Not for you, not for anyone."

"No, there's not," she said quietly, waiting for his head to snap up, for his golden eyes to fasten on her with glittering suspicion before she continued. "Not if you take her at face value. And not if you don't take the risk."

He was beside her in an instant, pulling her around to face him, pinioning her arms again and glaring down at her. "Come on, Courtney. What are you saying to me?"

"I'm saying that what she's saying and what she's feeling are two different things," Courtney responded, fighting to keep her voice calm. "How can she not want you to love her? How can she not want your help? For God's sake, Joshua, she's just too proud to come asking for it, and you're too damned proud to suffer the failure of not being able to help her!"

His reaction was swift and painful to see. The fierceness ebbed and wavered, then finally faded from his eyes; his anger cracked, then crumbled from his face. In their place were an unsteady vulnerability and a tentative hope as he digested what she was saying. His arms drew her close, cradling her against his chest, his chin resting on top of her head.

"I don't know," he said carefully. "You could be right. I guess I have to try."

Courtney felt relieved tears brim in her eyes. She wormed her arms around his waist and held him close, clinging to him and giving him every drop of moral support she had in her. She could feel the heavy drumming of his heart against her cheek as it beat erratically, almost as erratically as her own.

"You drive a hard bargain, teacher. I don't intend to take sides against you often."

Courtney began to smile, a small trembling smile of victory and jubilation, but unexpectedly, the moment again turned from one of comfort to one of sexual intensity. Gone was the tentative searching of his earlier kiss. When his lips came down on hers it was with almost brutal force, as though he were trying to erase some small edge that she had gained over him. One hand slipped behind her shoulder, stroking the soft spot at the nape of her neck, then burying itself in her hair, but this time he held it more tightly, pulling her head back so that her eyes stared up into his own and her lips parted in helpless surrender. Crimson fireworks exploded behind her eyes as she felt his mouth against the hollow of her throat. For a moment time seemed suspended; the room ceased to exist for her, and only the crackling of the flames in the fireplace remained to envelop them, drawing them into the flickering orange shadows.

"Two of you," he murmured, his voice raw with emotion. "Meryl, and you, too. Not just one of you, but two. I don't know if I can do this."

She pulled her head back again, wonder in her eyes, her heart seeming to explode inside of her. All the chained and imprisoned love that she had been denying to herself rained through her, stealing her breath away. The smile that had started on her lips took flight and lit up her eyes. Yes, she did love him. She loved that stiff pride and the vulnerable heart beneath it; she loved the golden sparks in his eyes that could change from anger to serenity with one blink; she loved the feel of his strong hands on her body and the feel of his body against hers.

Not thinking beyond the moment, not caring about tomorrow, she pulled his head down until his lips touched hers, kissed him hungrily, then pulled away again. "Sure you can," she whispered. "You can do anything you want if you want to do it badly enough."

His grin was wickedly enticing. "Anything?"

"Within reason."

"Then tell me when we get past reason," he replied huskily. Then his mouth was on hers again, crushing her lips demandingly with a need she had never known, searching her mouth for a secret she couldn't really understand. She only knew that she felt the same and that she had to have him close to her, touching her. She snaked her arms up around his neck, locking him against her as her instincts took her over. She wiggled her hips into him until, with a small groan, his hands left her hair to slide down her back and crush her even harder against him.

"Don't play games with me, Courtney, not now," he warned her huskily. "No more sheep's clothing."

"No," she murmured, her breath a sigh of surrender. She felt his desire, felt him moving against her, and knew that she was out of her depth, but she didn't care. When he lifted her in his arms to lower her to the sofa she clung to him, afraid that if she let him go for even a fraction of a second the spell would be broken, that something would happen as it had before and she would lose something precious and wonderful that she was only just beginning to learn about.

With his full weight on top of her, his legs entwined with her own, making the evidence of his arousal sure and almost painful, Courtney knew that it was too late to turn back. Somewhere inside she hesitated, then plunged ahead. It didn't matter. Tomorrow didn't matter. She had played with fire, and now she could only welcome its consuming flames. Her heart had been pleading for this for weeks; she had simply declined to acknowledge it.

His hands ran the length of her, touching her everywhere, teasing her, and she welcomed the fire his touch left behind, savoring it even as it astonished her. She molded herself to him and met his savage kisses with equal intensity, catching his full lower lip between her teeth almost playfully, feeling her fingers dig into the muscles of his back and shoulders, muscles that she had wanted to touch for so long. She made no protest when his hand impatiently pushed the single sleeve off her shoulder, arching into him until he had pushed the tunic out of the way, then clinging to him, a soft moan on her lips as his lips found her nipples and he tongued each one gently.

"If you only knew how much I've wanted you," he said, his words muffled against the small hollow between her full breasts. "Last night . . ."

She silenced him with her mouth, finding his and kissing away the words that she didn't want to hear, memories that she didn't want to be reminded of. She didn't want to think about what he had said to her by the creek. She wanted only to revel in the exquisite roughness of his calloused hands on her breasts and in the daring, exalted thrill that rippled through her as he found the button on her trousers, pulling them away from her aggressively so that his fingers could reach to the innermost parts of her, gently teasing, slowly stroking. She caught her breath at the rapturous torture of his easy, deliberate touch and at the growing, gnawing hunger that was enveloping her. Feeling wild and desperate with a newborn passion, she had just slipped her hands inside his shirt, ripping it free of his trousers so that her hands could finally, finally stroke the rippling, corded muscles of his shoulders, when a silken viperous voice shattered the moment with explosive force.

"My, how interesting. Did your business meeting get a bit sidetracked, Josh?"

A small cry of shock escaped Courtney and her eyes fluttered closed; she longed only to hide. Above her Joshua had frozen, his body going rigid and still;

when he pulled away from her, she cringed at the anger she saw glittering in the depths of his eyes.

As he moved away from her, she clutched at the afghan he tossed toward her, clawing frantically at the tunic of her trouser suit behind its protection. She turned her back to the scene in the doorway, but she was unable to shield herself from their voices.

"Andie, I think a little etiquette might be involved here. Have you heard of knocking? How about tact? No? Okay, let's try simple human decency."

"Now, Josh, darling," the smooth voice cooed. "If you had something other than business to transact, I really don't think this is either the place or the proper party. Meryl's teacher, darling? Honestly!"

"Out." His voice was deathly quiet. "Leave. Now. I can't be responsible for my temper if you don't."

Courtney turned around in spite of herself, but she was too far away to see Andrea pouting prettily, one crimson-nailed hand on her hip, the other tossing back her silvery hair.

"Well, will you join me for a nightcap then, after you get rid of her?"

His tone was supercilious in its dismissal. "I sincerely doubt it. Andie, I've warned you—"

"I'm going," she snarled. "I do apologize for disrupting your little sex education class, Miss Winston. Tell me, which of you was the teacher?"

Courtney let out an involuntary gasp as everything began to sink in. Andrea. Joshua's mistress. Oh, dear God, she had almost given herself to a man who had so many women he probably couldn't keep track of them all! A nightcap? Would he leave her and then go join Andrea? He had said no, but had his words been lies meant solely for her benefit? And what did it matter? She had nothing to offer him anyway! This wasn't kind, sweet Peter, who could be controlled and postponed. No, this was a man who would never be controlled, someone who could never be remanded to a back burner while she went blithely on with her life, a life that couldn't possibly include anything that even looked like a romantic entanglement. What had she done?

She had snatched her purse from the bar and tucked it under her arm, her hands clasped together in front of her to still their shaking, when Joshua came back to her. He shook his head wordlessly, reaching out for her again, but Courtney shrank away.

"I'm sorry," he apologized. "She wasn't supposed to be back for quite some time yet, and I never thought she'd interrupt us. I don't know what's the matter with her."

She couldn't believe she was hearing this! She stared down at the carpet, her heart thudding miserably, feeling as though she would give anything to get out of her skin, to be someone else, somewhere else.

"I think I should leave now."

"Courtney, no. It's early. We've only just eaten. We were only starting—"

"I know what we were starting!" she snapped. "And that's why I'm leaving. Go back to Andrea, Joshua. I'm sure she's waiting for you somewhere, ready to bat her great big eyes at you, and you can rest assured that hers can see!"

"What are you saying?" he asked, stark amazement playing across his features.

"Nothing. At least, nothing that shouldn't be said. I'm leaving. Please, let me go."

"I don't understand you," he muttered, more to

himself than to her. Then, spinning around to face her, he continued in a gruff, carefully guarded voice. "Fine. If you insist on leaving, I'll find Richard. I'm not eager to fight you; I mean that. I'd win, but I'm not sure the damage would be worth it. If you want to walk out now, Courtney, do it. But do it for the right reasons. Do it because you're scared or because you don't understand what's happening between us, not because my housekeeper interrupted us and you're embarrassed—although heaven only knows I apologize for that."

"Your *housekeeper?*" she repeated, her temper flaring into even more potent flame. "You're still going to cling to that ridiculous cover-up?" Her anger exploded with such force that she could barely control it. It washed over her, leaving her weak, and she backed instinctively toward the door, knowing that she had to get away before she did something crazy.

"I'll wait outside," she called over her shoulder as she turned, her voice rough with anguish, and relied on her memory to take her to the front door without mishap. She heard an explosion of glass breaking as she slipped through the wood-planked doors and into the chilly night air and flinched at the sound of it. Then she remembered her cape in the hall closet, and immediately recognized the dull clicking of the door for what it was. Knowing it was useless, she twisted around to grab the handle, but it was too late. The door was locked.

Shivering in the cold and feeling shattered, she waited for Richard, praying that he would hurry. The chauffeur didn't arrive soon enough. Within seconds, the tears that had been burning behind her eyes let loose in a deluge of sobs.

Chapter 7

COURTNEY WAS CERTAIN THAT THE LOGGIA HAD never looked lovelier. Someone—undoubtedly Elizabeth—had taken the time to trim the balustrade with bunches of white flowers; in the light that drifted through the windows they shimmered with a ghostly beauty against the blackness of the night. On the lawn below, the fountain gurgled; above, the full moon sprinkled down silvery light to tease her eyes with glimmering splashes of whiteness.

She leaned against the balustrade carefully, trying to avoid crushing any of the flowers, and wished fervently that she could simply stay out there forever. It would be so much easier than going through with what lay ahead of her: searching for a smile somewhere within her, then managing to keep it on all night as she worked her way through the crowds of jovial parents and guests who were arriving even now to celebrate Winston House's second birthday.

Cool air rushed up to her from the lawn, and Courtney turned her face into it, feeling hot and feverish with the same multitude of emotions that had been chasing her ever since she had stumbled through the front door the night before, to shock Elizabeth with yet another frantic run to her room. Of course, that hysteria had long since subsided. The long empty night had afforded her ample time to banish it to its proper place. She had emerged from the night to greet the morning with her determination intact again, and if she still felt shaken and numb, she could only be thankful that she had at least regained some tenuous control over herself.

It had been during the deepest, most desperate hours of the night that she had reached her decision, and she found herself clinging desperately to it, knowing that it was the only alternative that she could even attempt to live with. The hollow, inconsolable feeling that had numbed her when she had left him was still with her. She was a prisoner of her love and her desires; she recognized that fact and knew that there was no help for it.

She could offer Joshua nothing in the way of commitment; fate would never allow such a thing. The protests she had given Peter were real, not just trumped-up excuses to get her out of a difficult situation. Even with Joshua, her personal code demanded obedience from her.

But Joshua had not asked for commitment, nor would he. He had Andrea, he had the unknown brunette, and he undoubtedly had many other women as well. The thought of him giving them all up for her was preposterous. She would be a diversion for him, a temporary one, but if Joshua still wanted her after her outburst of the night before, she would be that diversion for him, with all of her heart.

Part of her cringed at the thought. She wasn't used to being merely one of a crowd. Still, she had no choice. Not really. She couldn't give her life away freely, even had he asked for it, and he hadn't. But she had her love, her heart and her body to give, and give them she would. The alternatives were simple: She could have a short, simple affair with him, treasuring it for as long as it might last, or she could have nothing at all, and the latter was not a situation with which she was prepared to cope. She knew, beyond the slightest shadow of a doubt, that now that she had found Joshua Knight, now that she had experienced his touch, she could not easily let him go.

Of course, there was still the question of Joshua's feelings in the matter. Courtney shivered in the cool night air as she considered the possibilities, her heart still threatening to crack in two, despite her many concessions to it. Had their last encounter disillusioned him about her? She felt certain that the revulsion that had forced him to pull away from her the night by the creek would always be simmering right below the surface. Could her outburst have nudged it into irrevocable eruption?

The only way to find out was to see him, she knew, and that would have to wait, no matter how painful that prospect might be. She wasn't impetuous by nature, but neither had she ever been in love before. The thought of waiting days before she could see him again almost crippled her with desolation. Could she wait that long?

She turned wistful eyes to the bank of windows

glowing softly along the back wall of the loggia, allowing herself a vain wish that he would come to the party. Although he must have received his invitation over a week earlier, he hadn't responded to it one way or the other, despite at least several opportunities to do so. Then there was the fact that the previous night had undoubtedly altered the situation considerably. Courtney knew all about the stiff pride in Joshua's eyes, and she knew that it wouldn't allow him to make the first move after she had walked out on him. No, she would have to go to him. And she would, for she simply could not let him go.

Not even the hesitant voice from behind her could break into her forlorn daydreams as she considered things; it took a tentative, shy tug on the long, flowing sleeve of her dress to nudge Courtney's attention back into place.

Startled, she snapped her head back, her green eyes searching for a moment before they found Meryl's frowning, upturned face.

"You were really out of it," the girl stated flatly.

Surprised at her calm yet purposeful presence, almost unnerved by it and afraid to chance a wrong step, Courtney only nodded. When Meryl placed her own small elbows on the balustrade in an exact imitation of her own stance, Courtney tensed her jaw in a heroic attempt to hide her astonishment.

"You look all right," Meryl said. "I mean, that dress isn't so bad, from what I can see."

Courtney couldn't restrain a surprised look down at herself. Her dress was quaint and very, very Victorian, with a high, ruffled neckline, lacy bodice and long, flowing skirt. A sash around the waist tied in a large bow at the back.

She looked down at Meryl, keeping her voice

carefully nonchalant. "You don't look so bad yourself, but I think the ribbon in your hair is a bit crooked. Either that, or it's my eyes. Either's possible, I guess."

"Probably the ribbon," Meryl announced through tight, frowning lips. "I put it in myself. I asked Corinne to help, but she's still not speaking to me, and even if she was, she wouldn't be such a great help. Blind as a bat."

Courtney grimaced a bit at her words but managed to hold her tongue from any censure. "I'd offer to fix it for you myself, but I don't know if I would be much help, either. I'm not quite as blind as a bat, but I do leave a bit to be desired."

"Hardly anybody's going to be able to see it anyway." Meryl reached up and snatched the ribbon out of her hair. Her long, mahogany curls tumbled down, wild and free. She'll be really beautiful someday, Courtney thought. She's so like Joshua.

As if her thoughts had somehow conjured him into the conversation, Meryl spoke with unexpected temerity. "Will he come? Do you think my dad will come?"

A cold, cruel hand grabbed Courtney's heart and squeezed it with amazing force. Every ounce of control went into battling back the tears that wanted to fall at the child's wistful, trembling words and at the desperate yearning in her own heart. Her wild scramble for a suitable answer almost left her breathless. In the end, the simplest words seemed to be the best. "I hope so," she answered her quietly.

As if horrified at something she considered a weakness, Meryl turned away. One small hand crushed an ivory flower as she kept hold of the stability of the balustrade, but she retained her balance, her back still, her head held high. She marched back into the corridor, a dauntless little soldier.

Courtney found her own chin tilting up and heard herself muttering at the milky sphere of the moon, "If she can do it, so can I."

Moving more slowly than Meryl had, Courtney went back into the hallway. The mercilessly bright lights so soon after the dark shadows of the loggia turned her vision into an unbroken plane of white light. She located the handrailing and followed it until the voices began to sound clearer and closer, then slipped into the dining room. It was set up for a buffet, with the massive table pushed back near the sideboard along one wall. She called her smile wearily and resignedly into place and kept it on her lips with a stoic effort as she recognized the booming, resonant voice of Corinne's father and tried to figure out just where he was.

She huddled back against the wall, waiting for her eyes to clear. Then she heard him.

Courtney's breath froze in her throat as the familiar voice floated through the room. Joshua? Yes, of course it was; she would know his voice anywhere. He had come! She stepped into the room but was immediately shoved by an unknown guest trying to get to the buffet table. Courtney cursed beneath her breath and stepped back against the wall again, frustration torturing her. She was torn between the magical sweetness of a dream come true and the nightmare of the awkward position she was in. Damn her eyes! If only they would clear, if only she could see, if only she could find him!

She listened hard, trying to find him by the direction his voice was coming from, but it meandered and moved, coming first from one corner then the other. Courtney blinked hard, staring studiously down at her toes and waiting. Why didn't he come to her? Was he that angry about the night before? That repulsed? That disgusted with her behavior? She had to go to him, find him, try to explain.

As she moved restlessly against the wall, she heard his voice again, closer than it had been before. Her head snapped up, her eyes straining to see, and finally she could, a little bit. She turned sharply in the direction she thought his voice had come from.

His dark golden eyes were only inches from her own, looking cold and careful and distant. Courtney shuddered as their eyes met, her heart lurching up into her throat, frustration and anguish simmering through her. If he would only give her a chance to talk to him, to explain! She reached out for him, her tentative fingers searching for his arm, for the muscles that she knew would be rigid and tense with anger.

"Hello, Courtney." Even his words were distant and cold. He offered her a tight smile as she reached out for him, then slipped out the door into the corridor.

No! She fought an urge to yell, aware of countless eyes watching her. She glanced around at the blurry faces and offered them her own small smile, then slipped out into the corridor after him, her heart hammering wildly, her stomach sick and weakly fluttering.

She thought she heard him in the living room. Was that his voice? With everyone talking and laughing, with glasses clinking and music blaring, she couldn't be sure. She slipped into the living room, hovering against the wall again. Most of the guests had also edged back against the walls, watching raptly as a few surefooted couples danced. Courtney eased her way through them, moving to the very edge of the

floor, where she squinted out at the dancers intently.
Her eyes searched diligently for Joshua, for the soft
tan of his jacket or the golden brown waves of his
hair, looking for a body that moved with an easy
grace, or shoulders broad enough to be his. Nothing.
She closed her eyes against the clamoring of her
nerves and backed off toward the door again. She
needed another moment of respite, a brandy, a
single breath of silent air in which to reconsider. She
had to think about this, had to figure out how to find
him when her eyes were no help at all, how to tell
him of everything in her heart when he didn't want
to listen.

But people seemed to be everywhere, blocking
her retreat, swarming around her in a confusing blur
of smiles and movement. Where had they all come
from? she wondered almost hysterically as knees
jammed into her own, feet crunched down on top of
hers and elbows jarred rudely into her sides. There
were only thirteen girls, twenty-four parents, not
that many brothers and sisters, grandparents, best
friends. And yet people seemed to be coming out of
the woodwork; disembodied lips moved in greetings
which were indistinguishable in the jovial noise of
the room. A nightmare, she thought; surely this was
some kind of a nightmare. At any moment she
would wake up.

She twisted and plunged head on into the crowd,
determined to get to the corridor, then out to the
loggia, where she could be alone. As she pushed
through the people, one face seemed to blend into
another in a hazy blur. She was only a few feet from
the door when large, beefy hands reached out to
stop her.

"You can't slip out of here now, Courtney, my
girl. You've gotta give me at least one dance."

Corinne's father, his voice just slightly slurred from the effects of alcohol, grabbed her in a bear hug. Courtney tried to pry his arms loose politely, but Albert Klein wasn't having any of it. Doggedly he pulled her toward the dance floor and she was forced to follow him docilely, grateful that at least she could avoid the crush of people by following in his ample wake.

Resigned to her fate, Courtney relaxed in his arms. Unable to stop herself, she scanned the dance floor again, wondering if Joshua would be dancing, not really wanting to know if he was, then almost bumping into him as he slid past her left side. Sylvia Baxter. He was dancing with Sylvia Baxter. Wasn't that her? Of course it was. Who else had that gleaming onyx hair? Who else but Lilith was being raised by a single mother? Who else, of all these crowding people, would Joshua single out to dance with?

Courtney twisted her head around and closed her eyes, but not before Joshua's caught hers again. His face seemed softer now, but then, too, the lights had been dimmed in deference to the music. She was sure that the transformation in his eyes was just the result of soft lighting and her own overactive imagination.

Still, even as Courtney squeezed her eyes shut, the image of him stayed there. She sighed heavily against Albert Klein's thick chest and said a silent prayer that the song would end soon, and that she could sneak away, if only for a moment.

She forced her eyes open again to see that the people still churned about her, their bodies close and clinging as they moved to the strains of the music. Fate had compromised with her, she noticed. The song continued, but Joshua and Sylvia appeared to be gone. Courtney wasn't sure if the new development was a blessing or not. While she no longer had to look at them, she couldn't control her treacherous thoughts and wondered wildly where they had gone.

Missing one awkward step as her imagination took flight, and viciously angry with herself for the understanding smile that her misstep brought from Albert Klein, Courtney closed her eyes again. The dance couldn't last forever. Soon, any minute, it would be over, Corinne's father would release her and she could slide out of the room, leave the band and the people behind, and go out onto the loggia to regain her faltering self-control. She would drink in the moon and the cool spring air, and somehow or other she would figure out how to get through to Joshua. Somehow she would find him and speak to him. If he weren't out there on the loggia, too . . . out there with Sylvia.

Suddenly she caught a glimpse of him again, dancing with Meryl this time. Something wild and joyous sprang into her heart to replace some of the pain that had been simmering there ever since his cool greeting. Thank God for that, she thought. Something is going right. Although Meryl's face appeared closed and careful as they passed by her, the little girl seemed to be following him, allowing herself to be held in his careful arms.

This has got to stop, it simply has to, she thought wildly as once again she was forced to blink back tears from her eyes. But these, at least, were tears of happiness.

With the precision of practiced talent, the band suddenly blended the finale of their song into the yearning melody of a popular love song. Hopelessly

caught up in the new song, incensed that the band
could pull off the transition so smoothly, Courtney
had no choice but to remain in Albert Klein's arms.

Suddenly the burly man released her without
warning. Courtney stepped back in surprise, her
question dying on her lips as Albert spoke.

"Can't say as how I blame you, sir." His words
were jovial and understanding, and yet Courtney
stood still, feeling vulnerable in the swirling crowd,
struggling to figure out what was going on. Then she
recognized the touch, his touch, and she turned to
step into Joshua's arms.

It happened so effortlessly, so easily, that it
seemed as though someone had waved a magic wand
at her, blithely transforming her dancing partner
into the man she had been yearning for. She caught
her breath at Joshua's sudden proximity, at the
musky, sensuous aroma of his cologne and the thrill
of his body moving so easily against her own. One
hand played down her back slowly and thoughtfully,
sending ripples of excitement along her spine; the
other held her close against him, leaving no room
even for the space of a breath. And yet, when she
looked up at him, his eyes still seemed distant and
wary.

"Meryl?" she asked finally, her words steady if
only because she didn't dare to use too many of
them. "You were dancing with her."

"She told me I looked stupid because I was too tall
for her." There was a short silence before he added,
"But at least she's speaking to me."

Their eyes met and held; a small, triumphant smile
was exchanged and Courtney burrowed more deeply
into his arms. "I didn't think you would come
tonight," she murmured.

He laughed, and the sound wasn't entirely cold, only tense. "Neither did I."

He paused, kissing her carefully, his lips perfunctory on her own, sealing some vague, cautious promise that she had yet to learn about. Gently he pushed her away from him, but he didn't release her; his arm remained around her shoulders, impervious to the curious eyes that watched them.

"I came because I have to talk to you. After I got here, I wasn't so sure I wanted to." He shook his head, looking vaguely befuddled. "But I guess I've changed my mind. Come on. Let's go somewhere where we can be alone. I feel like I'm standing in the middle of Veteran's Stadium during a play-off game."

She nodded silently, not trusting her own voice, sure that if she spoke it would ring out with thrilling expectation and sheer joy. He was with her; he wasn't angry. He was hers for the night. One night. One precious night.

They moved down the corridor, close but not touching, and yet it made so little difference. The air was heavy between them, charged with their awareness of each other. The space between them tortured her as she walked beside him, feeling him there and wanting him. When she stepped out onto the loggia she simply stopped and turned into him, desperate for his touch.

He slid an arm around her shoulders and pulled her to the railing. Shivers catapulted through her and she found herself trembling wildly; he ran one hand down her arm in a feathery caress and she trembled even more.

"Cold?" he asked, and yet he made no move to warm her. His eyes alone caressed her, lingering

over the swell of her breasts beneath the ivory lace,
running over the tight satin sash that clung to her
waist, as though he, like her, was remembering his
touch there.

"I'd offer you my coat, but I have a better idea,"
he said finally. With infinite care he pulled her into
his arms. She rested her head against his shoulder
and held on to him tightly, running eager hands over
the hard contours of his back, which she had just
discovered the night before, savoring the feel of him,
gleaning memories.

"Why did you run last night? It's getting to be a
habit with you, and I can't say that I like it much."

Startled at the down-to-earth turn the conversation had taken, she looked up at him, shaking her
head in bewilderment. "Andrea . . ." she began.
Surely he knew. He had to know. Why else would
she have run?

"Courtney, it was embarrassing, but it wasn't any
reason to run out on me."

Something bitter churned in her stomach; she
fought it down. Andrea existed; even now, she was
breaking the magic of the moment. She would
undoubtedly always exist, for she was a necessary
evil. To have Joshua, Courtney would have to share
him with Andrea. Not only would he not be inclined
to give the other woman up, but she herself had
nothing to offer in the way of exclusivity.

"You don't understand," she said at length,
choosing her words with the utmost care. "It *was*
because of her that I ran. Not just because she
interrupted us, but because . . . because . . ."

"Because what?" he prodded gently, tilting her
head up with one finger, his amber eyes burning
urgently into hers.

"I was jealous. She's so . . . so beautiful, poised,

perfect. She can *see!* She can give you so much that I can't," she finished miserably, the words pouring from her in unleashed torment. "She's everything that I'm not."

He drew his head back, jerking away from her, but while it was a sudden movement, there was none of the horror she had experienced from him the first time. His gaze was genuinely incredulous; then laughter burst from him, rich and thick, echoing throughout the loggia.

"Andie?" he asked finally, finding his voice.

Courtney stood staring at him, her heart in her throat, not quite sure if she was astonished, or horrified, or both. Anything she could possibly have said was lost in the turmoil of her heart. She didn't understand his laughter, didn't understand his smile. She felt as though she were swimming blind in black, murky waters that had suddenly turned cold and frigid. Detaching herself carefully from his arms, shivering harder still, she moved along the balustrade.

"Courtney," he called after her, wiping the tears of laughter from his eyes. When he caught up to her, he pulled her back into his arms with a crushing force that surprised her, although she supposed she should have grown used to it. She tried to pull away again, but he had her pinned hard against his chest, his strong arms holding her tightly, as though he were afraid that she would escape again. Knowing that her efforts were useless, she relaxed in his arms, drinking in the musky smell of him and the feel of him against her, not caring if the conversation ever continued, almost hoping that it wouldn't, since it wasn't making sense anyway. All that mattered was that he was here, that he was with her, and that Andrea Vaughan was somewhere else.

"She's Tom's daughter," he said at last, still chuckling. "I shouldn't tell you, not after the way you took off on me last night. I should just let you stew about it, but why not?"

Courtney looked up at him. His eyes were glittering with purpose in the dim light. "So?" she asked finally. "Who's Tom?" Her regret at being dragged back into the conversation when all she wanted in the world was to touch him, to love him, made her words sharp.

"Tom is—was—my business partner. When he died Andie had nowhere to go. This was eight years ago. She was only eighteen at the time and still in school. I took her in, and she's just been there ever since. The situation was supposed to be temporary, but it worked out fairly well, and she stayed. She helped with Meryl when I was at my wits' end, and she really is a housekeeper of sorts, but that's about all there is to it."

"I see," Courtney answered softly, but she didn't, not really. She didn't understand why he was talking about Andrea now. This time was theirs; this hour, these minutes, however much time they could steal away from the party was theirs alone, precious and valuable. He should be kissing her, loving her, and instead he was bringing Andrea Vaughan to stand between them.

"No, I don't think you do," he answered roughly, breaking into her thoughts. He held her slightly away from him, so that her face was only inches from his own. Even in the darkness his eyes caught some of the light drifting in from the windows and they seemed to gleam with a fierce necessity.

"Courtney, whatever there is between Andrea and I, it's superficial. She knows that, and I know it. I don't love her, if that's what you're thinking. I haven't felt the most remote stirring of love in ten years, until . . ."

He stopped abruptly, shaking his head. His dark hair fell down over his forehead, making him look touchingly young and unjaded, but his eyes belied the illusion. He moved away from her, the fingers of one hand tapping out a savage staccato on the marble balustrade. Courtney watched him go, her heart somewhere in her throat again.

Until what? everything inside of her wanted to ask. She wanted to follow him, wanted to find her way back into his arms and wait there until he finished and made some sense of the conversation, but something kept her frozen against the balustrade. She pulled one white flower free, inspecting it as though she could really see it, waiting. Fierce, longing anticipation almost crowded out a vague sense of disquiet in the pit of her stomach but didn't quite do it. Courtney hugged herself, horrified at the way things seemed to be spinning out of control. It's not supposed to be like this, she thought wildly.

"The first time I came here, the night Meryl came here, do you remember the things you said to me?" Joshua asked suddenly, his voice free of the husky emotion that had strained it just a moment before, but still soft and wondering.

Courtney looked up quickly, her eyes playing along the wide splashes of moonlight, looking for a shadow that might be him. The conversation was tumbling away from her like an avalanche, and she tried to fight it with words that were rational and safe.

"I remember. I was way out of line, Joshua. I didn't even know you then—"

"Ah, but if you had known me," he broke in quickly, "you would have had all the more reason to say those things." He began pacing the length of the loggia, a pale ghost when he stepped into the moonlight, a disembodied voice when he was lost in the shadows. Courtney found the flower crushed in her hand. Its cloyingly sweet aroma hung in the air around her and she breathed it in, desperate for something real and tangible to still her whirling confusion.

"I've spent all these weeks wondering about that night, trying to figure it out," he said as he paced, his words coming quickly, as if he thought they might freeze in his throat if he paused. "You just sat there behind your desk, looking so beautiful in your indignation and anger, and even though you'd never met me before, you hit me with words that were so true that I didn't stand a chance. They were like arrows, so incredibly well aimed that I couldn't have dodged them if I had wanted to." Back in the moonlight, he shook his head, looking bewildered.

"You were right," he continued simply. "After my wife died, after the accident, when it became evident that Meryl wouldn't see, and then when Tom died two years after that, everything I had was gone. I started working longer hours, then still longer ones, until at some point I was doing virtually nothing but sitting behind my desk, talking to strangers on the telephone, just some cold, empty financial wizard. No, there was no time for Meryl, none at all. Not that time would have made any difference. By then she was so far away from me that it would have taken . . . well, someone like you to put the pieces back together again.

"But I wasn't just hiding from Meryl, or from the pain of losing everyone close to me. I was hiding from my own vulnerability. It was fear, plain and simple, that kept me in Philadelphia late every night.

It was what had me in there at six o'clock yesterday morning. If I was working, I could keep to myself; I was in a world that I could control. I wasn't risking anything, I wasn't taking chances, and I thought that was the way I wanted it."

He came back to her then, growing larger and more formidable as he emerged from the moon-dappled shadows, and then he held her at a distance, one strong hand on each shoulder. He ravaged her face with searching eyes before he spoke again. Courage, Courtney thought suddenly, and the disquiet inside her blossomed into an ugly flower. He's looking for a way to get around his own barriers. What is he going to say?

"You know, up until this afternoon," he continued, his voice ragged and rough, "I was even going to go to the office tonight. After last night, after you ran out on me, I figured I had to, for my own good. I couldn't come to your party, couldn't see you again, couldn't risk any more of myself on a little mind-reading hellion who was busy hiding from her own ghosts. No way. And then, when I got here, all I wanted to do was turn around and leave again."

She waited wide-eyed for him to continue, but he was silent again, staring out at the moon-shrouded lawn as though he could find an answer there to something that was troubling him. She didn't understand any of this, although a little voice inside of her was nagging a warning in her ear, telling her that something had changed, that something was different, and that the situation was not nearly so out of control as it was going to be. Her shivers were back full force now, racking her slender frame.

When he drew her into his arms again her trembling grew more intense, but this was a trembling that she had come to know well. It wasn't fear and confusion that rocked through her now, but desire, returning to her as strongly as it had the night before, rushing as freely as it had in her memories all day. She tilted her head back, wanting desperately to freeze the moment; she searched for his lips, needing to take matters into her own hands, to spiral them back in time until they could recapture what they had so recently shared.

What she found in his kiss both surprised and frightened her still more. His mouth was tender against her own, and then his lips played over her skin, nibbling at her ear and at the hollow at the base of her throat. His hands found her breasts again, but they were gentle and still there. His tongue didn't part her lips with unharnessed urgency as it had the night before; this time it quietly discovered the corners of her mouth, flickering in and out almost hesitantly. His hand left her breast to smooth her hair back off her forehead, and his other moved to hold her close, pressing against the small of her back just as before, but something was different. There was a distance between them that had nothing to do with physical space.

Lost, not understanding, Courtney pulled away from him, trying to find something in his eyes that would tell her what was wrong. But his eyes were lost in the midnight shadows; she couldn't see them. His features were rigid and closed, telling her nothing.

"Joshua?" she whispered, a plea in her voice. The sound of her words might have been a bullet, for it shattered the deliberate distance that had kept him from her. He groaned deep in his throat, a sound that was animallike in its savagery, the intensity flooding back into him. His mouth found hers again, meeting it with bruising strength, prying her lips apart with unfathomable hunger. His hands came to life again, pulling gently against the collar of her dress until the buttons slipped free. She arched into him desperately as both the cool air and his rough hands teased across her nipples with a feathery touch, and she reached out for him, burying her hands in his hair, needing to feed the fires within him and reveling in his feverish touch.

She was stunned when he groaned again, a despairing, strangled sound, and shoved her rudely away from him. Shocked, she stumbled; then, gripping the balustrade, she stood staring at him, her heart pausing in a fragile stillness. She was afraid to move, feeling that if she did, she would shatter into a thousand pieces.

"Courtney," he said slowly, and his voice was thick and heavy, "why did you run from me last night? I know it sounds ridiculous—" He cleared his throat with ragged force before he continued. "But I have to understand this. I have to know. I could devour you alive right now, but I feel like there's a little more at stake here than that. I need an answer."

"I told you!" she protested weakly, refastening the bodice of her dress with shaking hands. "Andrea—"

"Andrea," he broke in, repeating the name carefully, as though testing it for something. He took a few slow, thoughtful steps toward the corridor door, then paused. The sigh that left him was heavy, carrying back to her eerily and painfully the soft night breeze, and he slid his hands into his pockets again, his jacket jumbled behind him. He didn't look at her when he spoke.

"You were jealous? That's it? It was just an ego thing, with her eyes?" he asked slowly, roughly.

"You know, for the first time in ten years, that's not enough. With you, I want . . . no, I *need* more than that. Much more."

His back was still to her, and although he paused, he didn't turn around. Where was her voice? She had to say something! She couldn't let him go! But her body was betraying her once again; her throat remained closed, tight, all her words of love on the other side of a barrier she simply could not break through.

She had been wrong. He thought she was so clairvoyant, but she wasn't, not at all. He didn't love Andrea, and he wasn't looking for an additional mistress. No, he wanted more than that from her; he was looking for the one single thing that she couldn't give him.

She nearly collapsed at the realization, her knees growing ungovernably weak, and she reached behind her for the balustrade again, holding on to it with a death grip as she watched him, her heart in her eyes, the yearning there plain and clear if only he would just turn around and see what she didn't dare use words to say.

But he didn't turn. He continued to stare at the door, his voice controlled and distant.

"Hell, one of us has to let go of their pride, I guess." Another sigh, harsher still. "I'm falling in love with you, Courtney. God knows I put up the best fight I could, but somehow, every time I've turned around, you've been there, either in the flesh or in my mind. I went to the office early yesterday morning because I couldn't stand it anymore, and you called me. There's been no getting away from you for weeks. You just sat there behind your desk that night with your eyes on fire and you exploded your way right into my life. Last night you did it all over again. And now you stand there and you tell me that you were jealous of Andie's eyes, that your fragile little ego got torn up, so you ran. Fear I could understand, Courtney. I've been grappling with it myself for weeks. If you tell me you were afraid, I can deal with that. But petty jealousy? No, damn it! There has to be more to it than that!"

Suddenly his hand shot out, smacking hard against the roughhewn stone of the loggia wall. When he went on speaking his words were incredibly distant, coming from deep inside himself. "It was a mistake for me to come here. I thought, perhaps, that you've been going through the same things I have. I imagine I misunderstood what I thought I saw in your eyes last night, but that's my own damned fault for looking for it in the first place."

Before the words had left his throat he was moving again, disappearing through the door, his broad shoulders straight and proud, silhouetted by the light inside the corridor. In the second that it took her to gasp his name, he was gone.

Courtney felt the world closing in on her. It started with the hardness of the balustrade pressing into her back, with the thick, wet shadows fogging her eyes, with the distant sounds of the party growing louder, louder, until they enveloped her, forcing her back into the small corner where the balustrade met the wall. She hugged herself, no longer feeling the cold or the shivers, but only an immense wasteland of grief, so vast that she couldn't even begin to try to conquer it.

Gone. He was gone. How could she not have understood? His words out on the boulder, his warning not to do this to him . . . It hadn't been her touch, her kiss, but she herself. He had been falling in love with her, just as she had been falling in love with him. How could she have been so blind not to have seen something with her own heart? Despair rained over her as she watched the blurred light that was the doorway to the house. I'll say it, she thought desperately. Just come back, and I'll do it. Somehow, I'll make the words come out, I'll take the chance. I'll tell you that I love you, and I'll risk ruining your life because I'm selfish and I can't live without you.

No sooner had she thought the words than she knew that they weren't true. She *did* love him, so much so that the knowledge of it filled her. Her love was alive, a tangible thing which was pushing everything else aside, becoming the sole factor of her existence. She wondered inconsolably how she would ever be able to live without him, how she would get through each day with this love so heavy within her, and him so far away.

She'd have to. She had nothing to offer him, nothing. He didn't want her love just for the moment, with no future, no tomorrow. He wanted all of her, but she didn't have it to give him. The darkness had already claimed her for its own, and she couldn't give herself away to another.

As desperately as she wanted to, she couldn't do it, couldn't go to him without her sight, couldn't offer him only half of her. The thought of him taking care of her, pandering to her, sent waves of revulsion washing over her. The thought of ruining his life was unendurable.

It was kinder to let him go. He would never know that she loved him, never. He could walk away, and he would be free. She loved him too desperately to hurt him for the selfish fulfillment of her own love. Tonight, tomorrow, he would begin to forget her.

Nothing had really been ventured, so nothing would be lost.

Not really aware of what she was doing, imprisoned by the torment in her heart, Courtney let her back slide down the balustrade until she sat down hard on the cold marble floor. Huddled there, her arms held tightly around herself, her face buried in the protective canyon between her breasts and her updrawn knees, she let out the tears. Some little voice inside her, so like Joshua's in its mockery, chided her for the tears she had been shedding so often of late. But the tears that had gone before had been different from these. These were the most bitter she had ever known.

Chapter 8

THE FAN PURRED INTO LIFE WITH A REBELLIOUS snapping sound and belched a dark cloud of smoke before it settled down to perform its duty. Elizabeth backed off from it warily, but when the soft humming signaled that it was in working order, she brushed her hands together with a feeling of accomplishment.

"You know, this thing just might last another summer," she muttered.

Courtney looked up from her desk just as the dark plume of smoke drifted out the window into the sultry May air. "If we're lucky."

Outside a car crunched on the gravel and Elizabeth turned toward the door, but not before she gifted Courtney with a small frown and a look that threatened to open up tender subjects. Courtney met the older woman's eyes evenly, but her look did not invite conversation. In the end, Elizabeth settled for a mundane observation.

"Well, the first of the troops seem to be arriving home. I suppose I ought to go downstairs and see about dinner."

"What are we having?" Courtney asked absently, then looked up with an exaggerated grimace. It was one of the few times in months that her face had shown any real expression. "If it starts with the word *barbecue,* I don't think I want to know."

Elizabeth laughed. "No, it starts with the word *cold.* We're having the rest of that turkey you and I started the other day."

"That's encouraging." It was a leftover that she could actually look forward to in the wake of all the parties she had attended over the weekend, trying to keep herself busy. The whirlwind had left her exhausted, but obviously not quite exhausted enough. As she felt the face of her watch to find that it was almost four-thirty, something sparkled into life deep within her, battling off her fatigue as she realized that Joshua would be arriving soon. He invariably returned Meryl at five, when she would career into the dining room just as everyone else was sitting down; Courtney would wait for Joshua near the door and receive one quick greeting from him as he poked his head through. The ritual was always the same. Somehow, she would manage to put a smile on her face before she returned to the dining room, and always Elizabeth would be waiting there for her with sad, questioning eyes.

Courtney had been on very distant, if guardedly friendly, terms with Joshua ever since the party in March. Necessity, in the guise of Meryl, had thrown

them together often. While their own relationship
had deteriorated to a formal, enforced friendship, he
had kept up his efforts with Meryl. The little girl
went home almost every weekend now, and each
time she came back her smiles were just a shade
brighter and a little bit more frequent. She had a
long way to go yet, but she was on the right path,
Courtney was sure. She had even formed a tight
little circle of friends about her, even if it consisted
of little more than Corinne and Courtney herself.

Meryl's progress had been the one bright spot for
Courtney during that dreary and endless spring. She
prayed often, now that June was near, that Joshua
would send the girl back to Winston House next
year, that their own personal entanglements would
not cause him to uproot Meryl once again.

And yet Courtney knew that it would take a
miracle of willpower and uncompromised love for
Meryl for either Joshua or herself to endure more of
the months that had just passed. Their encounters
since the night of the party had been tense; under-
currents flashed back and forth between them constantly, making logical thought difficult and any
amount of sustained composure nearly impossible.
Rather than getting easier with time, as Courtney
had hoped they would, their meetings seemed only
to grow more harrowing and painful as the months
dragged on.

Her halfhearted hopes that her love for him was a
passing thing, and that she had been only a passing
infatuation for him, had been dashed in short order.
Their love for each other blanketed their every
encounter, suffocating them until, when Joshua
would leave, Courtney would long only to collapse
in trembling emotional exhaustion.

She knew deep down that she could spare them

both the frustration and pain of their encounters, that she could often avoid him, and could cut their meetings with each other in half the rest of the time, but she lacked the willpower. She needed to see him, to watch him, if only from a distance.

And so she allowed herself to savor Joshua from a distance, loving the way his shoulders grew rigid and stiff when he got angry, torn apart by the way they hunched sometimes when he thought she couldn't see him. She loved his golden eyes as they skirted the room, refusing to look at her, and when they flashed with burning anger over some dispute they might have had over Meryl. She loved all of him, and if she couldn't have him, she made do with that which she could have: his occasional presence; one shared look over some marvelous achievement with Meryl; an argument; a tentative, strained laugh. It was all she dared to claim for herself, and she cherished it.

Still, despite the torment that accompanied their every meeting, despite the empty feeling of loss that filled her every waking moment, Courtney could not and would not flag in her determination: She would offer him nothing before she would offer herself to him with all of the shackles her failing eyes had placed on her. Her pride would not allow her to do otherwise. Always she flinched at the very thought of tying him down to her when she would be blind, dependent, only half a woman. But her heart was traitorous, and each morning she would open her cloud-filled eyes to hope that he would call, or perhaps stop by. When he didn't, she went to bed empty and aching. When he did, she went to bed full of grudging remorse and guilt because she hadn't avoided him as she knew she should.

In the end, she simply waited for the darkness. She waited for it to come to claim her, her first and final lover. There was nothing else she could do but wait, all the while preparing herself, making sure that her school flourished, that the children learned, and that Winston House's reputation grew. Winston House was all she had.

Elizabeth's voice broke into Courtney's reverie as she appeared in the shadows of the doorway, and Courtney jumped slightly, feeling guilty that she had been caught indulging in such thoughts yet again. She looked up at the older woman, her eyes vacant, just barely discerning Elizabeth's frame. Did she look foggier than yesterday?

"Hey, I said it was a cold supper, not barbecued, remember?"

"Mmmm. So?"

"So we've been waiting for you to join us for dinner for nearly half an hour now. I thought maybe you were boycotting my choice of menu."

"Sorry. I guess I lost track of time," Courtney muttered as she got to her feet. "But I warn you, if I see anything on the table that looks even remotely orange, I'm leaving," she added with a forced grin.

"You will, but it's only candied yams, so you can relax."

They slipped into the shrieks of excitement and tittering giggles that filled the dining room, and as Courtney took her place at the head of the table, she automatically paused to count heads. Twelve. Only twelve? Who was missing?

Quizzically, her eyes rose to meet Elizabeth's before the woman could retreat to the other end of the table.

"Meryl," she informed Courtney.

Courtney thought for a moment, considering. It was five-thirty, but it was also the Monday of

Memorial Day weekend. Which meant that there would be heavy traffic coming back from Atlantic City, where Joshua had mentioned they would be going for the weekend. Courtney's initial worry dissipated a bit. Of course, she could call their house to find out what was keeping them. Surely someone there would know if they had been delayed. She could do it, but she didn't want to. Although it was silly, she simply didn't want to speak to Andrea Vaughan. The long months had done nothing toward easing the envy Courtney felt for the woman's proximity to Joshua, and avoiding her was something that she still did at all costs. Instead of getting up and going back to her office to use the telephone, she bowed her head while Stephanie said grace, then dug into her dinner, thankful for the absence of anything resembling barbecue sauce.

It wasn't until after dinner had been finished, as she took a deep, satisfying mouthful of coffee, that Courtney realized that her sense of disquiet was getting out of hand. What had begun as a niggling little doubt in the pit of her stomach had ballooned into full-fledged concern. She caught up to Elizabeth as they left the dining room.

"I think something's wrong. I'm worried."

Elizabeth looked bewildered. "About what?"

"Meryl—she's not back yet."

"Well, it's only a little past seven. Didn't you say that they were going down to Jersey for the weekend? The entire state of Pennsylvania probably went with them. They're undoubtedly caught up in traffic coming home."

Courtney shrugged, but she still felt a nagging uncertainty. "I guess."

"Look, don't fret about it, for heaven's sake.

You've been doing enough of that lately as it is. Why don't you just call their house and find out if anyone there knows when they're expected back?"

Anyone, Courtney thought. Andrea. But there was no help for it now; she would have to call. Worse than the knowledge that she would almost certainly have to speak to Andrea was the dreadful fear building up inside her, telling her that something was wrong. Calm down, she told herself. It's Memorial Day. They have every reason in the world to be over two hours late. No, they don't, she contradicted herself immediately. Joshua would have called. If they had gotten tied up somewhere, he would have called.

Cold sweat clinging to her now, she moved to the telephone and tapped out Joshua's number, suddenly not caring if Andrea answered, not caring at all, just as long as she could tell her where Joshua and Meryl were and that they were all right.

Joshua answered on the third ring.

"Oh, thank God." The words escaped her in a single breath, grateful and relieved.

"Courtney?" His familiar voice, still as smooth as velvet, still undeniably dear to her, sounded slightly confused. Courtney didn't notice. With her worry behind her she should have relaxed, but she couldn't. Now she was achingly aware of him; she wanted to crawl through the telephone line until she could reach that voice and be loved by it. She knew that she would have to explain why she was calling, but she was unable to do anything but savor the sound of his voice. A week had passed since they had last spoken, and suddenly it seemed like an eternity. Finally she managed to take a deep breath and force out a shaky explanation.

"I—I guess it sounds a little ridiculous now, but

when you didn't bring Meryl back, I was afraid that
something had happened to you. I mean, you're
usually here by five, you know, and it's seven-fifteen
now, so I thought—"

"What are you talking about?" he broke in, his
voice guarded and wary, even a touch annoyed. It
sounded for all the world just as it had when they
had first met.

"Meryl, of course. When you didn't bring her
back, I thought something was wrong."

Suddenly the line was filled with a deep, dangerous silence that seemed to seep out of the telephone
to smother her. Courtney gripped the receiver with
both hands, and the little fingers of fear left her
stomach to traipse up her back and spread over her
shoulders in cold, weighty horror.

"Joshua?" It was the only thing she could manage
to say. Something *was* wrong. Something was dread-
fully wrong, and yet she couldn't ask what, because
her fear had left her breathless.

"Oh, sweet, dear God," he said eventually,
breaking the silence with a voice that was careful and
tight. "What are you saying, Courtney? She's not
there?"

Courtney shook her head, then realized that she
hadn't actually spoken.

"She's not there?" Joshua asked again, yelling.

"No!" Courtney yelled back, terrified by what he
seemed to be saying. "No! When you answered the
phone, I thought she was still there with you. What's
happened?"

"What's happened? Maybe you could try telling
me! I dropped her off there right before five o'clock.
And now you're telling me that she's not there? So
where is she? Where in God's name could she have
gone?"

Courtney only shook her head miserably as a deathly fear spread coldly through her. "I don't know," she moaned softly.

"You don't know? You're supposed to be responsible for her! What do you mean, you don't know?"

Courtney flinched at his words, a new kind of pain tangling with the dull knife thrust of her apprehension. "I don't know," she repeated hollowly, as though she might possibly find some salvation in the words. "I . . . she never came back. She never came in. Where did you leave her? On the driveway?"

"Near the front door. Oh, God, why couldn't I have gone inside with her?" There was a short silence before he demanded, "You looked through the whole house? You're positive she's not there?"

"No . . . no," Courtney stammered. "She wasn't at dinner, so . . . wait, hold on." She dropped the telephone on the desk with a bang and hurried back to the corridor, her heart pounding with sickly intensity. Time could be precious now, she had already wasted so much of it! She should have called before dinner. But hindsight was useless; all she could do was conserve every second she could. Instead of running down the hall to the television room, she yelled Elizabeth's name.

The action was so absurdly unlike her that Elizabeth entered the corridor almost immediately, her arms akimbo, her legs ready to break into a run. When she saw Courtney standing there they did just that; she rushed over, her eyes wide, her breath gasping.

"What is it? What's wrong?"

"Please, you've got to go upstairs and look for Meryl. Get the other girls. If she's not in her room, get anyone else who can see even half an inch in front of them to look, too. Right away, Elizabeth. Hurry!" She started back into her office, but there was no sound of movement from the corridor, and she turned around to plead, "Please, hurry!"

Still, as though in shock, Elizabeth didn't move.

"Joshua says he dropped her off at five," Courtney supplied frantically.

The words seemed to be the catalyst that Elizabeth needed. Her eyes opened even wider and she rushed off toward the kitchen. As Courtney reached out for the telephone again, she heard Elizabeth calling for Lewis, then sounding an alarm for the other girls to come running. She replaced the telephone to her ear with shaking hands.

"They're looking," she announced flatly.

"Courtney, how could this have happened?" In the small space of time that had passed, the panic had left his voice, to be replaced by something desperate, but his words were relatively calm and controlled nonetheless. It was the pain that simmered beneath them that attacked Courtney, becoming her own pain, so thick and heavy that it left no room for breath.

She struggled to find her voice again and tried to keep it as calm as his own, but it wavered a bit, and her words rebelliously defied order. "Joshua, we don't know for sure what the situation is yet. The girls . . . Elizabeth . . . they're looking for her. If they don't find her, I'll go outside and look around myself. Maybe she took a walk or something. Maybe, I don't know, she could have gone down to the creek. Anything's possible. Was everything all right between you two when you dropped her off?"

"Fine," he responded curtly. "She was a little quieter than usual, if that's possible." There was a

short silence, and when his voice came again, it was
deadly and searing with an anger that had finally
proven too much for his tenuous control. "So help
me, Courtney, if anything's happened to her, you'll
pay for it."

Courtney's heart paused in crystalline stillness.
She didn't breath, didn't move, didn't speak. She
simply held the telephone to her ear, her hands
frozen there as they had been when he had spoken;
she thought only of drinking air into her lungs,
knowing that she had to breathe again.

Suddenly Elizabeth appeared at the door, saving
her from further conversation, if only for the moment. Her eyes raked over Courtney's white, drawn
face and acknowledged the situation, then she shook
her head.

"She's nowhere to be found, Courtney. Not in the
house, at any rate. I'm sorry."

"She's not here," Courtney repeated carefully to
Joshua. "I'm going to go outside and have a look
around."

He scoffed loudly and cruelly into the telephone.
His words were heavy with his old mockery. "You're
going to *look* around? Come on, Courtney, give me
a break. Call the police and let them look. As far as I
know, they don't hire blind cops, and they'll be a lot
more effective."

Courtney gasped. "Right, yes . . . yes, I'll do
that," she stammered, numb from the searing pain
in her heart, from the fear in her stomach.

"Where the hell is Andie?" he went on, raging at
no one in particular, as though she were no longer
on the line. "I'm afraid to leave in case Meryl
comes back here. Maybe she ran away; maybe she
just didn't want to go back to you. Where in God's
name did that woman go? Oh, hell, I'm coming

anyway. I'll get Richard to wait. Call the police, Courtney." Suddenly his voice was softer. "Please, don't try to look for her yourself. I don't need you getting lost, too. I'll be there in twenty minutes. Just hang tight."

"Yes," she said again, her lips barely moving, her eyes vacant. She replaced the telephone delicately, then hugged her arms to herself and turned to face an expectant, worried Elizabeth.

"She's gone. I can't imagine . . . Everything was going so well, you know? I don't understand any of this."

Elizabeth merely nodded, her grief very clear on her face. "I know." She came to Courtney and put comforting arms around her, but although Courtney laid her head against Elizabeth's shoulder in quiet despair for a moment, she pulled away again in an instant.

"I've got to go outside and look for her. Maybe she went for a walk and got lost. Will you call the police?"

"Go outside? Courtney, honey, it's getting dark out there! You won't be able to see anything! You'll just get lost too!"

"If I let a little darkness get in my way, I might as well give up on everything," Courtney answered bitterly. "No, I've got to try to find her. Oh, God, Elizabeth . . . it's my fault!"

"Your fault? What are you saying? That's ridiculous!"

"I should have called sooner. I should have waited at the door for her at five o'clock, like I usually do. I should have done so many things that I didn't do."

"No, Courtney! Whatever has happened, you certainly can't take the blame. It's no one's fault."

"No, Joshua's right—"

"Joshua? He said it's your fault? Honey, he's just upset; I'm sure he didn't mean—"

"I can't. . . . I've got to go." She was halfway down the corridor by the time Elizabeth got to the door. Before the woman could open her mouth to call out to her, Courtney had been swallowed up in the deepening dusk.

Chapter 9

ELIZABETH AND JOSHUA HAD BEEN RIGHT IN THEIR estimation of the crippling effect the darkness would have on her, but it was too late for Courtney to admit it, and she was too desperate to try to go back. It wouldn't have made any difference anyway. Dusk had given way to a consuming cloak of blackness that was much more powerful than she was, and moving back was as dangerous as going forward.

Infinitely wary, her hands out in front of her in stiff caution, Courtney struggled to make her way through the trees. She had nothing but her sense of direction and her ears to guide her, and neither seemed to be working right in the face of her panic. Trees and unrecognizable objects—bushes, a boulder—confused and impeded her; finally, despite all her care, her ankle twisted in the tangled root of a tree and she went down hard, her wrist bending back painfully as she tried to break her fall, her head cracking against the trunk.

Gasping at the pain, she sat there and ran her good hand through her hair, only vaguely curious when it came back moist and sticky with blood. She took a deep breath and tried to quiet the pounding of her heart. Her desperation to find Meryl wouldn't allow her much logic, but what she had managed to hold on to was enough to force her to admit that the odds were against her, that Meryl probably wasn't out there at all. The best thing she could do was simply calm down and get her bearings, then check the creek and go back to the house, where she would surely be needed.

Persistently, she got up again to move through the trees, and as she did, she called out Meryl's name, not really expecting an answer. When the gurgling rush of the creek greeted her, she was filled with faint relief. At least she knew for sure where she was. Still shaking a bit, she moved slowly until her knee thumped hard against the boulder. Letting out another small cry of pain, she sat down, her back to the babbling water, and stared into the pitch.

"Meryl?" she asked softly, her voice faint in the darkness. It was useless and she knew it. Meryl wasn't there. But where could she have gone? And why on earth would she have gone anywhere besides right through the front door and into the dining room? Unless . . . unless someone had taken her.

No, the windows had been open, and Courtney's ears were too acute to have missed the sounds of such a scuffle. Clearly, Meryl had left of her own volition, and if that was the case, there was still a small, remote chance that she was hiding somewhere. Out here by the creek was as good a place to look as any. Intent upon exhausting the possibility, she got to her feet again and began moving carefully through the trees.

And then she heard it: a twig snapping, something brittle cracking, something moving. She froze, not daring to move, listening hard.

More movement—a lot of it now. Branches thrashed and footsteps sounded hard against the earth.

"Meryl? Meryl, is that you?" Her plea took flight on the night air, then was swallowed up by the trees.

In that instant rough arms grabbed her from behind, spinning her around so quickly that her arms hurt from the force of their angry strength and a wave of dizziness swept over her. She started to scream, terror boiling up in her at the shock, but Joshua's voice stopped her.

"What do you think you're doing?" he growled, but there was more panic in his words than the biting cruelty that had been there earlier. "Elizabeth said you'd come out here. My God, Courtney, it's pitch dark! Something might have happened to you!"

"I had to try to find her." She had no choice but to touch him, to seek the solace of his arms. She held on to him weakly, willing the dizziness to pass.

"We will, we'll find her, but killing yourself in the process isn't going to help any of us. Courtney, don't ever do this to me again. All I could think of was that you were both lost out here somewhere. I couldn't stand it." His voice was warm and throaty now, and something of his old vulnerability throbbed through it as well. Courtney found herself wanting to wrap herself around him, a buffer against all that could cause him pain, never mind their careful distance and his vicious words.

And yet she drew away from him, wary and suspicious, remembering his hard and cutting words on the telephone, remembering that she couldn't allow herself to get too close to him, for her willpower seemed to be a remote and dreamlike thing out here in this fantasy world of darkness.

"But—" she began.

"I know what I said."

Before he could go on, police floodlights bathed them and she looked up into his golden eyes, so naked in their anguish and pain. When he pulled her to him tightly, touching her for the first time in months, her willpower fled entirely. She wrapped her arms around his waist, for the moment undaunted by their love or its implications, even temporarily forgetting about Meryl. She wanted only to hold him, to huddle against him in the bright floodlights, and to savor the firm hold of his arms, the closeness of his body against hers. Then he spoke again, and although he didn't release her, the moment was shattered as reality crashed in on her.

"I'm sorry about what I said. I was upset, and God knows I didn't mean any of it. I just— No, come on. We've got to go back inside. We'll talk there." He brushed tenderly at the hair that had fallen over her forehead, one arm hesitating around her shoulders, as though he knew that once he let her go, once he retreated to the other side of their careful distance, his pride would force him to stay there. Slowly, regretfully, he took his arm away; only then did he notice the tacky, drying blood on his other hand.

"What the—" he began in incredulous alarm.

Instinctively Courtney's hand flew to her forehead. There was a good-sized lump there, but it wasn't overly painful. Then she reached out to cover his hand with her own, as though to hide the evidence of her fall.

"It's nothing. I fell and hit my head, but I'm fine, really."

He pulled his hand away from hers, staring down at the blood, then up at her eyes, his own eyes thin slits that hinted of anger.

"Courtney, why didn't you tell me that you were hurt? No, never mind. I don't need your protests right now. Come on, we're going back to the house where I can take a look at that cut and maybe get a doctor if we have to—"

"No!" Courtney snapped. "No . . . it's nothing, and it's not important. We've got to find Meryl!"

"Practically the entire police force is out here looking for her with floodlights, dogs, you name it. They'll find her." His voice was jagged with pain, despite his dictatorial assurance. Courtney felt herself crumbling again, but now it was her own impotence that was threatening to destroy her.

"Oh, Joshua, I'm so sorry."

"It's not your fault," he said tightly. "I should have made sure that she went inside. I didn't want to come in because I knew you'd be standing there in the hallway, and I was sure that if I had to play that little game of ours even one more time I'd go crazy. If anyone's to blame, I am. If I hadn't been so concerned with avoiding you, this wouldn't have happened."

Courtney allowed herself to cling to him again, her arms tight around him, not sure if she was comforting him or herself. She only knew that he was wrong, totally wrong, in his assumption of guilt.

It had been her fault all the way down the line, the fault of her stupid game, as he had referred to it; for if she hadn't been trying to maintain their distance, if she had just avoided him completely, if she had just made their distance so vast that it maintained itself, then he might have come inside with Meryl. But no, she had to have those little meetings between them, had to try to savor what little of him she could from a distance. And now, because of that, disaster had struck. Yes, he was right. She had been playing a game, and it had turned out to be a deadly one.

But his hands were on either side of her face, and his eyes ravaged her. Courtney couldn't have pulled away from him if she had been gifted with all the determination in the world.

"The way Elizabeth was carrying on when I got here," he continued, "I thought for sure that something had happened to you, too." He shook his head as if surprised at what he was saying. "And I didn't know what to do, you know? I didn't know if I should go after you or talk to the police about Meryl, and so I just stood there, feeling like if I died right then, it wouldn't matter, because the two of you are my whole world and always will be, no matter how hard you try to stay away from me. If I had lost you . . . if I lose her . . ." He broke off, his voice betraying him, drifting away.

"I'm okay, and we *will* find Meryl," she whispered, loving him, her heart breaking for him. "Come on, let's go back and see if they've found anything."

He nodded his agreement, his eyes still clouded and almost vacant in their misery. Courtney reached out for his hand impulsively, hoping that somehow, if they touched, they could draw on each other's flagging strength. Guided by the searchlights, they made their way back to the house to find Elizabeth waiting for them on the loggia.

Courtney released Joshua's hand to squeeze Elizabeth's reassuringly, and as she did, their closeness seemed to fall away, their love was hidden again. She felt it, knew that she had to let it go willingly, and somehow kept her voice calm as she spoke to Elizabeth.

"I'm still all in one piece. I may not look it, but I am. Sorry to scare you."

The woman's eyes darted back and forth between the two of them, looking for something, then shifted away still confused. "Did you find anything?"

"No, but then, I was the only one who thought I would. You were both right. Without my eyes, I was useless." Her voice cracked over the words, and she turned and made her way quickly into the hallway, leaving the two of them to stare worriedly out at the commotion on the lawn.

The glass of brandy she poured herself once she was back in her office was fuller than usual, and she swallowed much of it immediately before topping it off again. At her desk, she put her head down wearily on her arms, fighting back tears. No, not now. Right now she had to think. She had to forget Joshua's presence, forget her guilt, and figure out what could possibly have happened. Why would Meryl run away, if that was indeed what she had done? Why? Things had been going so well for her! She and Joshua had embarked on a tentative new relationship; Courtney herself had wormed her way into Meryl's life as a friend. And now this! Why, in heaven's name? Why?

She sensed rather than heard someone else in the room and looked up with bleary, worried eyes.

Corinne's slight form was silhouetted in the doorway, a dark, reed-thin spot in a sea of light. She crossed to Courtney's desk timidly, her old exuberance gone.

"It's Meryl, isn't it? What's happened?"

Courtney looked at her blankly for a moment before she spoke, her eyes unfocused, her emotions exhausted. "We don't know, honey. Maybe you can help us. Was she upset about anything lately that you know of?"

Corinne seemed to be thinking about it, her head cocked to one side. "No, not really," she said finally. "She likes you. She thinks you're a little weird for a teacher, but I told her you weren't really like a teacher, you know, just a friend, sort of, who taught us things. Why? Do you think she ran away?"

Courtney felt a small smile tug at her lips, warmed by the somewhat bizarre description of herself, but reality soon dragged her down to earth. "That's just it—we don't know. That's why I wondered if she's been upset about anything."

Again Corinne shook her head. "Nope. She was excited about going to Atlantic City with her dad; she said that they were going to go on the boardwalk. She was glad that lady wasn't going, because she's been bugging her lately."

"What lady?"

"The one who lives with her dad. It's not her stepmother. I don't know who she is, really. Meryl doesn't talk about her too much 'cause she doesn't like her. But anyway, she's been bugging her lately."

"Bugging her how?"

Corinne shrugged. "Beats me. That's all she said."

Courtney reached out and ruffled the little girl's hair, trying to stay calm. "Thanks, honey."

"Did I help?"

"I'm not sure, to tell you the truth. We'll have to see."

Suddenly Corinne's voice became choked and thick tears streamed down her cheeks. Courtney got up quickly to go to her, pulling her into her arms.

"She's got to be all right! She's just got to!" Corinne cried.

"Shhh. She will be. We'll find her. We'll figure this out. Look at all the police her dad's got here. With all of them on our side, how can we go wrong, hmmm?"

A small smile flickered across Corinne's face. "I hope so," she said, her words hurtling over a hiccup.

"I know so," Courtney said with much more assurance than she felt. "Now, will you do me a favor? Could you make sure that everyone got to bed okay? With all of this commotion, I don't want to have to worry about where the rest of you are."

Corinne nodded and Courtney pushed the girl away a bit, shooing her toward the door. "Thanks, honey. I owe you one."

Halfway to the door, Corinne paused, her small face working again. "You'll wake me up if anything happens, won't you?"

"Cross my heart."

Corinne murmured something indistinguishable, then turned to squeeze past Joshua, who was standing in the door. His arms were crossed in front of him, and something soft mingled with the closed look of pain on his face. Without asking, Courtney poured a large glass of bourbon and handed it to him.

"Nothing new?"

He shook his head but didn't speak to her.

"I talked to Corinne. She says—" Suddenly

Courtney paused, wanting to think about Corinne's reference to Andrea just a bit more before she told him about it. It could mean everything, or it could mean nothing. Was it just her jealousy, or were her suspicions actually making more and more sense? Had Andrea taken Meryl away somewhere? But why? And could Courtney dare to entertain such an idea simply because of a vague reference on Corinne's part?

But then, there were still those letters, all those letters. Not once had she ever really forgotten about them, but Meryl had been doing so well lately that they hadn't seemed important anymore. Still . . .

Either way, it wouldn't do any good to have him lashing out at anyone right now, as he surely would. As much as she despised Andrea, she hesitated to bring Joshua's wrath down upon her head needlessly; neither was she sure that Joshua wouldn't turn on her instead for maligning a friend. His words on the telephone still burned somewhere deep within her. She knew that he was still volatile with emotion, and she hesitated to put his control to another test.

Instead of mentioning what Corinne had told her, she leaned back against the bar on one elbow, keeping a careful distance between them. When she spoke, it was with a cool detachment that belied the pounding of her heart.

"Corinne said what we've been saying all night: that Meryl has seemed happy. If anyone would know, I think it would be Corinne. Those two have been as thick as thieves lately."

Joshua only nodded, his eyes distant and far away as he sank into a chair, and if it hadn't been for the slight movement of his dark head, Courtney would have sworn that he hadn't heard her. She retreated to her desk and sat down on the edge of it, watching his blurry outline broodingly. She felt so helpless, so impotent. She could do nothing for him, nothing at all. She couldn't comfort him; she couldn't allow herself to love him. She couldn't even tell him of her suspicions yet. She had to think, but everything was so tense, so nerve-wracking, and she had her hands full just trying to hold each thought still for long enough to consider it.

She buried her face in her hands, fighting off yet another urge to cry. Footsteps sounded in the doorway, seeming distant and remote, and Courtney wearily lifted her head to see Elizabeth standing in the corridor. She entered the room slowly, her shoulders hunched. When she reached the center of the room, however, she planted her hands squarely on her hips and scowled at them with a formidable ferocity that showed no signs of her weariness.

"Now what?" she asked suddenly.

Courtney looked at her blankly and downed another mouthful of her brandy.

"According to the police," Elizabeth went on, "there's not much we can do now except wait. Are you two planning to do that sitting in here all night?"

"Would you rather we went out on the town?" Joshua asked scathingly, his tension brimming again.

"You could try to get some sleep," Elizabeth snapped, not in the least cowed by him.

Courtney snorted loudly and clearly. Not only did she surprise herself, but Joshua and Elizabeth raised their eyebrows at her as well.

"Sleep?" she repeated when she finally found her voice. "You've got to be kidding!"

"I'm not kidding, not in the least. Listen to me, both of you. There is absolutely nothing to be gained by the three of us sitting here all night, hanging by the telephone, listening for the door to open. One of

us can do the job quite well, and I intend for that
someone to be me." There was a strict authority in
her voice, and even Joshua seemed affected by it. He
leaned his dark head back against the chair and
watched her with glittering amusement.

"You're both going to need all your wits about
you tomorrow," Elizabeth continued, then amended, "that is to say, if nothing breaks tonight. And it's
already after midnight. Joshua, you do have someone standing by at your place, don't you?"

"Yes, of course. Richard is there. And Andie
should be back by now."

"Good. Call them." She was at the desk, pushing
the telephone at him. "Tell them that you won't be
home tonight."

"Pardon me?" He blinked at her, looking tired
and drawn, his face bewildered because someone
was actually telling him what to do.

"Elizabeth—" Courtney began, not at all sure
what she was going to say but spared the necessity of
finding out.

"Look at you two!" Elizabeth mimicked Courtney's snort. "You're both so frayed at the edges that
neither one of you knows what you're doing. I'm
going to stay up tonight in case something happens,
but you two are going to sleep. Don't you trust me to
wake you up if anything happens?"

"Wake me? Elizabeth, you're forgetting one
thing." Joshua spoke with amazing patience, the
pulse at his temple throbbing and his hands balled
into fists. He relaxed one hand long enough to finish
the remainder of his bourbon in one long swallow,
and Courtney hurried back to the bar to get him
another, preferring to stay out of the conversation.

She wanted him to stay . . . God, how she wanted
him to stay! Guilt swamped her anew as she realized

how very little that yearning had to do with Meryl. She simply longed to have him under the same roof, ached for the comforting knowledge that he was close by. Selfish, selfish, said the little voice inside of her. Let him go. You've done enough damage already by hanging on to him.

"I honestly don't think sleep is a possibility tonight," he was saying now. "My daughter—"

"Yes, I know," Elizabeth broke in quickly, her voice so thick and soothing that even Joshua seemed to relax a bit. "We're all very upset, Joshua, but you really do need to get some rest. It's imperative. You're going to want to be out there with the search party tomorrow—"

As though it had been his idea all along, Joshua reached for the telephone. When Courtney returned with his glass, she handed it to him, then moved behind her desk, still deliberately careful to preserve their distance, the space between them. She leaned back in her chair as he spoke into the telephone, not even trying not to listen, anxious to hear what he would say.

"Richard? . . . No, no, nothing . . . Andie hasn't returned yet? . . . Of all the damned times for her to take off. I can't remember the last time she did something like this. . . . Do you mind? . . . Just until she gets there. . . . No, I'll be staying here, but I want both fronts covered. . . . Tell her to call me as soon as she gets in. . . . Yes, of course you will, that goes without saying. . . . Thanks; good-bye."

He stood thoughtfully for a moment, his hand dangling the receiver over the telephone before he dropped it with a clatter. When he turned back to Courtney she was sure that the hurt in his eyes would kill her, too.

"Andie's still not there. And there's been nothing

new from that quarter, either. Richard will stay there, of course, until Andie gets back."

Courtney cleared her throat, knowing that she had to tell him, that she had to give voice to her suspicions, and never mind the consequences. She still wasn't sure how he would take any of it, not now, not in the midst of all this turmoil. Still, she pushed the words out.

"Joshua, Corinne did mention something else . . . something that I've been thinking about."

Something in her voice seemed to alert both him and Elizabeth; the woman seemed to freeze as she poured herself a drink, turning her head and peering back over her shoulder at Courtney with shrewd, comprehending eyes. Joshua collapsed in the chair again, his legs spread wide, clutching his own glass, his eyes riveted on her. She could feel them on her as she got up and crossed the room, wondering how to tell him of her suspicions.

She cleared her throat and started again. "I'm not sure if it makes any difference, actually, but Corinne told me that Meryl has been complaining about Andrea 'bugging' her—her word, not my own. Actually, she didn't say Andrea, she only referred to that woman who was living with you." At the description of Andrea, Courtney felt her throat close up and her voice crack. Her heart thudding heavily, she turned back to the window, hiding the torment on her face.

"Bugging her? What exactly does that mean?" Joshua asked with a careful calm.

"I don't know that. Corinne couldn't say. It was just something that Meryl mentioned."

"Are you suggesting that Andrea has something to do with this?" Joshua asked harshly, the understanding just coming to him. Courtney fought an impulse to cringe away from his voice, for it was snapping with anger, and she had no idea just who the anger was meant for, herself or Andrea.

Then, suddenly, it didn't matter anymore. Angry fire burned in her eyes as she realized that she was so tired of hiding things from him. He could do what he pleased with the information; she refused to care what he believed. She spun back to face them, standing still for a moment as sudden nausea and dizziness swept over her.

"Yes, that's exactly what I'm saying! We've exhausted every single angle and we've come up with nothing. The only alternative left to consider is Andrea. I think we ought to find out just what she was doing to bug Meryl—when and if she ever decides to turn up, that is. Personally, I think it's highly suspicious that she's chosen tonight to disappear into the sunset. Some coincidence, isn't it? Meryl's gone, and so is Andrea!"

"But what in the hell would she have to gain by it?" Joshua thundered.

"I was wondering the same thing," Elizabeth contributed softly, her quiet tone restoring some sanity to the scene. "I'm sorry if I offend you by saying this, Joshua, but I have no real affection for your friend. I simply don't care for her, and I don't trust her. But, Courtney, I don't see how she could have any reason to be behind Meryl's disappearance."

"Joshua," Courtney said suddenly, her voice hard, for she was determined to make her point now. "All those letters you wrote to me when Meryl was admitted. Why? Why not a single telephone call in all that time?"

Joshua dropped his face into his hands and massaged his temples, looking so defeated that it tore her heart out. Part of her wanted to stop, to drop the whole issue. He doesn't need this, she thought, not now. But another part of her knew that it was imperative to continue if they were going to find Meryl and salvage everyone's sanity. Look at us now, she thought wildly. Joshua's like a wounded animal, and I sound like a shrew!

Suddenly he sprang to his feet again, breaking her thoughts. He started pacing toward her, then pulled up as though afraid to get too close.

Clenching his hands into fists, he spat out, "Because I knew nothing about it! Does that jibe with your suspicions? I had no idea what was going on, Courtney, no idea at all! Andie wrote the letters and signed my name. Andie arranged Meryl's admission. I knew nothing about it until I came home from work that Saturday, and by then Meryl was gone. Andie told me then, showed me your letters and told me that you could help her. She said she hadn't told me before because she was afraid I would refuse to go along with it, and she was probably right. But I checked you out with Dr. Farber, and he had nothing but good things to say about you. Then I came here, and no matter what you said to me that night, I knew that you would be good for Meryl. I decided that the best thing to do was to leave her here.

"Now, if you can find something in that to base your suspicions on, then please tell me what it is, because I sure as hell don't see it! The way it looks to me is that Andie had nothing but good intentions!"

"I don't think she did it because of any concern for Meryl!" Courtney cried vehemently, determined to finish. "I think she did it because she wanted Meryl out of the way!"

"What?" His eyes were incredulous now, but no less infuriated.

"She's . . . in love . . . with you!" she gasped, her words fighting past the sobs that tore through her suddenly. "I . . . ought to recognize . . . the . . . the symptoms . . . because . . . because . . . I am too!"

Oh, God, what had she said? What had she done? She was horrified at herself, standing outside of herself and staring back at some stranger who had suddenly taken over her voice, her body. But she knew, too, that she had hit a breaking point. It had all become too much: Andrea, Meryl's disappearance, Joshua so close that she could almost touch him. If she simply reached out her hand, it would meet with his warm skin, would brush the soft, downy hairs on his arm, and yet she had to stand back from him and pretend to be indifferent. She simply couldn't do it anymore.

Everything had collapsed in on her at once, and all she could do was move shakily toward the door, unable to look at him, determined that she would not fall apart, not totally. She had done enough damage already! Three months of careful behavior had been dashed! Somehow, she held back the rest of her sobs. She had said her piece—much more than she had ever intended to say—and now she would just leave him to Elizabeth. If there was any sense at all to her suspicions, once the jealousy and the love had been removed from the issue, unclouding it, Elizabeth would see it and would act accordingly. Courtney sent a desperate, beseeching look at her friend, then turned toward the door.

"I'm going to follow your advice, Elizabeth, and try to get some sleep." She spoke quietly, with amazing surface calm, never once turning back to face them. "I doubt it's possible, but I'm going to try. Joshua, if you do care to stay after . . . well, after all, I suppose you might as well use Meryl's room. Either that, or the davenport is free, if you decide you want to stay down here."

She was astounded at the cool steadiness of her words, in awe of the way her shoulders squared of their own volition, without any prodding from her pride. Resolutely she made her way down the corridor. Her emotions and her love for him were racing through her freely now, pounding against her heart, making her feel that, by all rights, she should explode long before she reached her bedroom.

She didn't. Miraculously, she made it, and only the smallest whimper escaped her as she passed Meryl's empty bedroom. She let herself into her own room carefully, unsure how long her control could last, and shut the door quietly behind her.

The bed looked vast and inviting; she wished that she could simply lie down there and forget everything. For the first time she regretted the day Meryl had first screamed her way into the entryway, regretted ever meeting Joshua, this man whom she would always love no matter how hard she tried to stay away from him. Always there would be the torment of not having him. Always she would suffer with the pain of his loss. And now the time had finally come when she didn't think she could stand it anymore.

She moved around the room with trancelike slowness, turning back the covers on the bed, dropping her jeans and tee shirt on the pink velvet chair. She reached into her closet and took out a nightgown, pulling it over her head, only vaguely aware of the comfort of its silky folds caressing her skin. She moved carefully into the bathroom, and despite the perfect lighting there, she found herself groping along the edge of the counter until she came to the sink.

Somehow she managed it all. She brushed her teeth, washed her face, cleaned the small cut on her forehead where she had hit the tree. She paused only once to look out the black window at a world she couldn't see, wondering where Meryl was, what she was doing, and almost praying that she *was* with Andrea, because if she was, she would be safe. Finally, pulling herself away from the window, she went back to the dresser and began loosening her hair.

Perhaps it was the lack of anything else to do that was finally her downfall. Suddenly, with her hair free and nothing else to turn to, the barriers collapsed inside her. Courtney dropped the hairbrush she had been holding and moved her hands until they were flat against the smooth surface of the dresser. She could feel her shoulders sagging, the release of giving in to it all, and she told herself she would just cave in for a second, just a second, that was all. She dropped her head until she could see nothing past the dark waves of hair that shrouded her face and let the tears come.

So devoured was she by her own torment that she didn't hear his footsteps in the bathroom, and she couldn't know that he paused there, frozen, when he understood that she was crying. She hadn't thought to close the bathroom door, and he stepped over the threshold as something soft and lingering spread over his face.

Nothing alerted her to his presence; she simply knew that he was there. She turned, her hands limp at her sides, her face tear-stained and faintly pink, looking fragile and delicate.

He was only a blur in the doorway, filling it with shadow; he was far away on the other side of the room, and yet even so he was too close. Something exploded in Courtney, and still more of her barriers collapsed. Just for tonight, she thought. I need him. He needs me. Oh, God, I could love him now, just for a little while.

"Courtney." Her name was a throaty murmur coming from deep within him. She stepped toward him without thinking, just wanting to see him more clearly, and what she saw nearly tore her heart in two. He half turned away from her, running one hand over his face slowly and carefully, his golden eyes dark with torment. ·

"Why didn't you tell me? All these months . . ." he asked, more to himself than to her.

"I couldn't. I just couldn't."

"It doesn't matter, I guess. I know now. But God, all that wasted time . . ." Before the words had slipped from his throat he had turned around again and came toward her slowly, each step measured, each one pausing just enough to allow him to turn again at any moment. But he didn't turn, he kept coming; seconds ticked by, and then he was right in front of her.

Another brittle, weak barrier inside her cracked. With a resigned sigh at its fate, it trembled and fell away. Courtney felt it go, but it didn't seem important; she was too immersed in his eyes to care. Soft gold radiated from them, and she thought that she could drown in them easily. Perhaps she would never come back to reality, and then tomorrow wouldn't matter.

With a yearning that made her shudder delicately and hold her arms out to him, she knew that she had been waiting for this all along, that it had been the driving force behind her game. It was inevitable, and no amount of inner strength or willpower could have kept her from it. In the second when he started toward her, it had long been too late to turn back.

Greedily, hungrily, she took him in her arms, sliding her hands beneath his shirt and up along his spine. Her touch, so soft and yet so desperate, seemed to ignite him; when his arms came around her it was with the unleashed necessity of months of torment. The muscles beneath her hands tightened convulsively as he drew her to him.

"I do love you," she whispered against the soft mat of hair on his chest as she freed the buttons of his shirt. The words came easily, free at last of the barriers. "I always have. I've always wondered how you couldn't know . . . how you couldn't see it."

"I'm just glad you finally decided to let me in on it." His words were careful and guarded well by the old mockery, but then something inside him seemed to collapse as well. Before his lips came down on hers with fierce possession, he murmured, "I've already told you that I was falling in love with you. I was wrong. I wasn't falling. . . . I fell. I was just too proud to admit it then. Too proud, and too frightened, too, I suppose. But it's hopeless, Courtney. I can't live without you. You've got to know that."

She barely heard his words. There seemed to be no reality but that of his hard arms around her, crushing her against him even as he lowered her onto the bed. In the darkness of her swirling vision, everything seemed right and perfect. Tomorrow was far and distant from her heart, a matter of little consequence which she would deal with later.

He had to free himself from her desperate grasp to rise up on his elbow, sliding out of his shirt, and even then her fingers feathered over him, needing him with a cavernous desire that was simply too strong for restraint. She pulled him back to her immediately, molding herself to him, moving with him as he tried to pull away again, releasing him only one last time to allow him to pull her nightgown over her head. As he came down on top of her again she knew only that she wanted him, and that for now, for this moment, she would give him all of herself.

His hands traced along the silken curves of her breasts, blazing a reverent trail for his lips before his mouth found her taut nipples, pulling and teasing at them much as he had on that single night in his den that had been shining in her memory for months. Courtney moved against him, moaning softly as she locked her hands behind his neck, holding him to her as though her strength could freeze him to her forever, sealing their love tightly against the evil and treacherous march of time that she knew, even in that moment, would ultimately steal him from her.

She arched into him even more, holding him more tightly as his fingers brushed gently and seductively against her thighs, touching her intimately. Her love for him exploded within her, finally, blessedly, crowding out all logical thought until nothing else existed but the two of them. His hands belonged to her and they owned her, igniting a fiery response within her that made her finally release her hold on him ever so slightly, just enough so that her fingers could find the buckle of his belt and work at it feverishly. Even as his clothing joined hers on the floor, even as his fingers drove her yearning to a pitch of ecstasy, she needed more. She turned into him, clinging to him.

"Please." It was the only word she could say, for she had almost forgotten how to speak. He leaned away from her slightly, looking down at her with a small, teasing smile, and she relinquished the effort of words and returned to the sanctity of touch, back into her own darkness and her own world, guiding him into her.

As he took possession of her, her eyes flew open in exquisite rapture, and she fell into the golden depths of his eyes. She cried out softly with a pain that disappeared almost before it was realized, feeling it drowned out as something hot and scorching flashed through her, making her tremble more than she had known was possible. Her heart lurched wildly, then seemed to break free as he moved slowly within her, seeming to tease her with infinite care and endless time. Finally, when her hunger seemed to consume her, when it ached and throbbed within her so that she cried out his name and clutched at him wildly, he, too, lost his hold on control. His movements came harder and faster until she felt rended by him, torn and devoured by his love for her. Still, she met him as he moved into her, desperately trying to drink in all of him, needing him as she had never needed anything else in her life, until her darkness grew golden bright and shattered within her. In that instant their eyes locked, and they spoke together the only words they would ever need to explain a springtime full of agony and longing.

"I love you," they whispered in unison.

Chapter 10

SOMEHOW, THEY SLEPT. FOR COURTNEY, IT WAS A fragile sleep, filled with both nightmares and dreamy bliss. Meryl was gone; the horrendous fact haunted her every waking and sleeping moment. It was a dark, cloudy specter on the fringes of her consciousness, taunting and tireless. But Joshua was beside her, and the miracle of that suffocated the horror of Meryl's absence, blanketing the worry and pain with something sweet and precious.

She awoke once, in the very darkest hours of the night, aware of him there beside her even as she struggled out of her dreams. As her eyes opened to the blackness she remembered their lovemaking and a tinge of fear thrilled within her. Her barriers had gone; she had let him in. She was alone now, vulnerable and unprotected against the loss of him. Even now, she couldn't conceive of staying with him forever, couldn't allow one rapturous night of love, no matter how beautiful and right, to destroy his life. Nothing had changed. She felt more compelled than ever to spare him her blindness and to spare herself the indignities of depending on him. Her only weak consolation in the smothering pitch of the night was that she now had the ultimate memory, one that would last with her until the end of time.

But the night wasn't over yet, and he was here. She still had some precious time left, time that she clutched to her heart savagely. He was beside her, faintly asleep and very restless. One dark lock of hair fell over his eyes; one arm was outstretched and hanging over the edge of the bed, as though he were reaching for something. His other hand lay against her thigh, warm and heavy, making her think of his touch as it had been when he was awake. Small shivers coursed through her and she found herself smiling into the darkness, then reaching down to take his hand in hers. She held it against her heart with infinite longing, wishing fervently that she could think of a way to freeze the night for eternity.

Even as Joshua slept he frowned, and even as he frowned he awoke. He moved against her; despite the misty darkness, she knew that his eyes were on hers. She could feel them burning into her and she shivered again, almost imperceptibly. As if to reassure both of them that they weren't dreaming, he reached over and pulled her close to him, one hand deep in her hair, pressing her head into the hollow of his neck, the other running smoothly down her back, caressing her, loving her.

Courtney escaped into the night again. She reveled in the exquisite touch of his long, lean body against hers and savored the heat of his hands as they caressed her with their silken touch. Her nipples tightened with pleasure at his touch, her breasts swelling in his hands. She moved restlessly against him, only half-awake herself, but knowing that nothing she had ever done in her life had felt so right as this. When one hand slipped lower to part her thighs she trembled with expectation. Then she, too, moved one hand lower, tracing the line of hair down his abdomen to touch him with a boldness she would never have expected from herself, a boldness she had been too shy to exercise the night before.

He groaned against her skin, and she felt the sweat-slickness of his cheek against hers, tasted the musky maleness of him as she nipped gently at his own flat nipples while her hand continued to play its own tune below. Joshua shuddered convulsively as she invited him into her secret recesses, moving with restless urgency within her until they both cried in unison, clutching each other with the explosive ecstasy of the moment. As they settled back to earth she nestled quietly in his arms, feeling the rightness of it.

Still, she was frightened. She wanted this moment to last forever, she never wanted the night to end, yet she knew that it was impossible, that morning would come eventually, and that the dream she had nourished for months would be stolen from her. The knowledge filled her with something bitter and heavy that leaned against her heart with weighty inevitability. Gradually she fell asleep again, clinging to him, afraid to let him go.

When she awoke again, he was gone. Frantic, wondering if it had only been an exquisite dream, her arm flailed across the bed, coming to rest against the cold emptiness where he had lain. Panicked, she rolled over and sat up; the sheet fell to her waist and the cool morning air from the open windows caressed her breasts, reminding her that she was naked, reassuring her that the night had happened after all. Delicious joy raced through her, but right on its heels was the nagging heartache that wouldn't let her go. She sent frantic eyes to search around a room that she couldn't see.

Joshua was silhouetted against the window, a dark shadow against the earliest morning light. As he stood there, his broad shoulders blocking the pale sun, he seemed to hunch a bit in defeat.

He must have heard her move, for he turned back to her. Wonder, so lovely, fresh and exquisite, filled her at the knowledge that he was there. After all these months, they had come to this, and they had shared more than she had ever hoped to share with him. Yes, it was a crowning memory, one more precious than any she had ever known, and in the darkness of his shadow Courtney prayed fervently that it would be enough.

His voice whispered through the lingering darkness and broke the miraculous existence of the night. "She's out there somewhere," he said softly. "And I haven't the faintest idea where. Do you know what that's doing to me? Just a second ago, I found myself hoping that you're right, that she's with Andie. At least that way she won't be afraid. At the very least, I know that Andie would never hurt her."

He turned away from the window, leaving the light behind and stepping into the obscurity of the darkness. Her eyes searched helplessly for some movement that would locate him for her, and then he was sitting next to her on the bed. She couldn't help it. The moment was a serious, sorrowful one, and she knew that she should be comforting him,

trying to make the pain go away. She wanted to
more than anything in the world, and yet her hands
moved to his chest of their own volition, entwining
themselves there in the soft mat of hair, lying softly
against the faint throbbing of his heart. Shocked,
even angry at herself, for there were things to think
about other than the virile, enticing leanness of his
body only inches from hers, she tried to pull her
hand away, but he caught it in his own and pressed
her palm against his lips with a subdued outpouring
of emotion.

"It's like a flower growing out of the snow," he
said finally.

In the silvery morning darkness Courtney cocked
her head at him, waiting for more.

"This. . . . Us," he explained. "So much pain,
another loss, and yet somewhere in the middle of
it all, this blossoms up. When I woke up a little while
ago, I thought, somehow, that I had dreamed it all.
It wouldn't be the first time. But no, you were there,
and your hair was all over like a dark cloud, and you
looked so beautiful." He moved closer, pulling her
to him, cradling her against his chest.

"I won't lie to you, Courtney. I thought about
leaving, about slipping out of here before you woke
up. I just feel that this love I have for you could
devour me, and it scares the hell out of me. Especially now, when I'm dying inside over Meryl. I wanted
to hide from you, because I can't for the life of me
imagine losing you, too, and I know how easily that
could happen. One minute you could be here, the
next you could be over an embankment, gone,
vanished. Part of me—a big part of me, if the truth
be known—just doesn't want to take that kind of a
chance. But another part of me knows that I've hit a

point of no return. I'm in love with you, and there's no way I can change that. Not for all the safety and security in the world."

Courtney listened to him, enraptured by his soft voice, enthralled with his warm skin beneath her hands, melted by his words; and yet the panic fluttered deep within her. The little voice inside her was active, harping. It's too late, too late, it said. The game's over. Meryl's gone, and your love for him has run rampant. Too late, Courtney. You can't turn and run any more than he can. Darkness or no darkness, you just can't do it.

And yet she knew that she had to deny the voice, had to fight against it, had to triumph over it. There was no place for him in her life.

"No, I can't run," he was saying. "It would make a mockery of all you've meant to me. I fell in love with you because you're so brave, because you try so hard. I can't let you go because of a lack of those same things in myself."

His words echoed through her, hurtful and sharp in their ironic truth. Oh, God, she thought, he'll never understand. If it was just me, if I only had to be responsible for myself, then maybe I *would* be brave, maybe I'd chance it. But it's more than that. I love him too much to drag him down with me. When the darkness comes, it has to be mine alone. I can't share it, and I can't give it away.

Brighter light was spilling through the window, and she pulled away from him, her sorrow painful and throbbing. Still she managed to slide her legs over the side of the bed, and when she spoke, it was with relative complacency, although her voice was husky with her love for him—love that seemed, as he had said, to have devoured her.

"It's almost seven," she said stiffly. "The police should be back soon to organize that search party."

The pain of Meryl's loss seemed to settle back over him like a cloud. His shoulders rigid, he rose from the bed and moved quickly into the bathroom without answering her. As he left, Courtney felt an overwhelming sense of loss boil up in her, crushing her heart, tearing her breath away. Thick tears coursed down her cheeks as the sounds of the running shower drifted out of the bathroom. He was gone from her. The memory was over, complete, ready to be stored away.

It would be harder now than ever to break away from him. Hopeless agony filled her at the realization, but she had no regrets for the night behind her. It had been the most beautiful night of her life, and she would make it last a lifetime. Never would she forget a single moment of it. Always she would carry it with her in her heart.

By the time he came back from the bathroom her tears had dried and she had succumbed to the grim determination that had settled over her. When he gathered her to him in arms that were as demanding as they were reverent and kissed first her forehead, then each eye, and finally her mouth with sweet, tantalizing slowness, she remained impassive, wrestling with the passion that filled her at his touch and somehow forcing it down. Reality was on the other side of the door, waiting for her, mocking her in a way that Joshua's eyes never could.

"I wish we could stay here forever," he said huskily as he released her. If any part of him had noticed her lack of response, it was buried deep beneath his fear for his daughter. "But we can't. I have to find Meryl. You'll meet me downstairs?" His eyes raked over her nakedness, and something started to smolder before he wrenched away from her and moved toward the door.

Courtney nodded bleakly, agony spearing through her as she watched him slip away. Already his eyes were far away and clouded with worry. He was more father now than lover, and it was just as well. Feeling empty and dead, Courtney went through the mechanics of taking a shower.

When she got downstairs her pain was no less vast or encompassing, but she had harnessed it. She found Joshua and Elizabeth at the butcher block table, their conversation tense, their faces drawn. Yet when Courtney entered the kitchen, Elizabeth looked up with a smug, complacent smile. She knows, Courtney thought with a start.

It only made the whole thing worse. She found herself battling a lump in her throat as she poured herself a cup of coffee with trembling hands, only half listening to their conversation, more caught up in her own private misery. When she turned back Joshua was leaning across the table, speaking to Elizabeth with earnest intent. Beneath the thin fabric of his shirt Courtney could see that the muscles she had so recently touched were hard with tension. A fine pulse throbbed in his temple, and there was a shiny urgency in his eyes. And yet, as she sat down, one of his hands disappeared below the table to rest warmly against her knee, as though to comfort her. Despite the obvious lack of sensuality in his touch, Courtney still felt her limbs growing weak; quickly she put her cup down and tried to catch her breath. She realized he noticed the faint blush working its way up her cheeks. He smiled at her faintly, his lips twisted in wry amusement, one eyebrow raised almost imperceptibly in suggestive humor.

"Well, then, I'll stay here," Elizabeth was saying, oblivious to the electricity that was flashing back and forth across the table. "Courtney and I can run home base. By the way, I took the liberty of canceling classes today," she said, turning to Courtney. "Lewis has been saddled with the unenviable chore of taking the girls to breakfast at the diner and then to the shopping mall. If he never comes back, we'll probably be able to find him at the nearest funny farm. I did call Barbara Rolphy, however, and she's agreed to take the morning off from her own classes and meet him at the mall. She'll be some help, if Lewis can manage to survive breakfast first."

Courtney only nodded and sipped at her coffee, her thoughts chaotic.

"What time did the police say they'd be back to organize the search party?" Joshua asked. "I can't seem to remember. Everything's been so crazy."

"Any minute now, I would imagine," Elizabeth answered him. "They said first thing in the morning."

On cue, the door upstairs banged open and shut, and the sound drifted down the kitchen stairs to fill them with fresh urgency. Elizabeth got up abruptly, placing her cup in the sink and grabbing the plate of pastries off the table. Joshua jumped to his feet as well, downing the rest of his coffee in one swallow.

"You'd think those badges of theirs give them immunity from courtesy," Elizabeth muttered, in something of a temper from her lack of sleep. "The least they could do is knock instead of just walking in."

Courtney murmured a vague agreement and got to her feet slowly, her heart still weighing her down. She looked up at the door expectantly, half expecting to see the large blue blur of a police officer standing there, but there was no movement from the head of the stairs. She splattered the rest of her coffee down the sink and retreated toward the steps.

"I'll go upstairs. I heard them come in, but who knows where they've gone."

Joshua was close behind her, his breath warm against her neck, making his presence so potentially volatile for her that it took everything she had to remain cool and unflustered. They moved up the stairs as quickly as her limited sight would allow. When she missed a step in her haste to get to the top his strong arms came up to catch her around the waist.

"What did you do without me all these years?" he asked lightly as she regained her balance, but his casual words only sent more pain shimmering through her. *I survived, she wanted to say. I fell sometimes, and I stumbled, but I always landed on my feet, and I always will. I'll live without you. I have to.*

Instead, she only offered him a small smile and pulled away from him, keeping her distance as they made their way into the corridor. The ground floor of the house was steeped in quiet. Expectantly, Courtney cocked her head, listening for voices or something that would tell her where the police had gone, but there was only silence.

"What the—" she began in confusion.

From somewhere upstairs a door banged loudly. Courtney jumped slightly, her nerves raw, then turned to Joshua with her eyebrows raised high. "I don't get it. I gathered from Elizabeth that the girls had left already."

Joshua shrugged, but the gesture froze before it

was completed. Before she could say anything more, he was on the stairs, his long stride carrying him upward two steps at a time.

"So did I," he called back over his shoulder. Courtney barely heard him, for his words were almost lost in the rush of his breath as he rounded the hall toward her room.

Courtney stood stunned for a moment, staring at the bleary emptiness on the stairs where he had been only a second before, then gradually understanding dawned on her. Only three people were in the house. The police weren't on the ground floor, and even if they were as brazen in their authority as Elizabeth presumed, they wouldn't have gone upstairs. Elizabeth was downstairs in the kitchen, she was here, and Joshua had only now run upstairs.

Courtney broke into a run with the same instantaneous force that had carried Joshua, and if her steps were slower, it was because her panic had robbed her of her usual sense of direction. It took a second longer than usual for her to find the handrail, and although she was normally capable of taking the stairs two at a time, her feet stumbled over each one this time, as if she had never climbed them before. As she headed toward her room she heard their voices, loud and strident.

Joshua's pulsed with frightening anger. "What the hell did you mean by this? Did you think I wouldn't worry? Wouldn't care? Dear God, Meryl, I've been beside myself! We didn't know what to think! Meryl, talk to me. Tell me—"

Courtney paused outside the door, a flood of emotions drowning her. Relief was predominant, overwhelming her so that she sagged weakly against the wall. And then a small smile came to her lips.

Meryl's voice rang out with equal intensity, just as angry, just as vehement. What a match they are for each other, Courtney thought.

"Well, do you think it was my idea? If you do, you're really stupid. It wasn't something *I* decided to do! Andie talked me into it!"

"Explain then. Go ahead. I want to hear every last little detail. Everything. You got that? Sit down. Talk. Where the hell is Andie now? Why in the world would you go with her, anyway? Why didn't you tell anybody where you were going?"

"If you'd just shut up, I'd tell you!"

"All right. Talk."

Meryl's voice came back more softly. "Well, Andie came up with this plan, see. Do you remember that time I told you how Corinne fell and broke her wrist?"

There was no answer from Joshua; either he didn't remember or he had nodded within the walls of a room that Courtney couldn't see.

"Well, Corinne told me that Courtney thought it was her fault or something. I told you that, too. And Andie heard me tell you, and she got this idea that if something happened to me, it would be Courtney's fault and you wouldn't like her anymore. She said it would be a good way to get Courtney out of the picture."

More silence. Courtney could visualize Joshua gaping at his daughter. His eyebrows would be lost under the dark fringes of his hair; his mouth, so tender and provocative the night before, would be open in surprise. Only the smallest flicker of shock passed over Courtney's features. She had never stopped considering the possibility of Andrea's involvement.

"So that's it." Joshua's voice came back filled with awe and a faint touch of amusement. "But I thought you liked Courtney."

"I do. A lot. But there's more. Andie told me that if I went with her I wouldn't ever have to come back here. And I didn't want to come here in the first place, but nobody would listen to me! So yesterday, when you left me here, I just waited on the steps and then went back down to the street and went with Andie."

"Why? Why would you be a part of something like that? Do you hate it here that much? Why didn't you just tell me, if that was the case? Damn it, Meryl, we've been spending weekends together for months. Why didn't you ever tell me that you still hated it here? You never said a word!"

"If you'll just listen to me for a minute, I'll tell you the rest!"

"I'm listening, damn it. Go on."

"No, you're not! You're yelling at me!"

"Meryl, I'm warning you! Tell me the rest. Where did you go?"

"She has this friend. Some artist guy in town."

"Some artist guy? In this town? In Collegeville?"

More silence. Courtney could only imagine that Meryl was nodding her assent. When Joshua's voice came again, it was incredulous. "How did you get back here?"

"I sneaked out."

"But how did you get *here*?"

"I walked."

"You *walked*? Where exactly did you walk from?"

"Kellehy Street."

"You could have gotten yourself killed!"

Courtney nodded into the murky shadows of the

hall but was no less astounded than Joshua seemed to be. That was a distance of at least a mile.

"I can still do some things, you know!" Meryl retorted. "I'm not some cripple. Everybody wants to make me into some kind of a cripple, and I'm not! The only ones who don't treat me like that are Courtney and Corinne."

When Joshua's voice came again, it sounded softer and less tense. "Is that why you came back?"

"Mostly. It's not so bad here." It was a sullen, guarded answer, but her next words sounded alarmed. "What are you doing?"

"I'm going to find Courtney and tell her that you're back."

"Will you—" Meryl began, and then her voice broke off. Courtney found herself waiting, holding her breath. "Will you tell her I'm sorry?"

"I think you should tell her yourself. Later. Right now I have to tell her that Andie's plan backfired on her. Courtney and I have something to straighten out."

It seemed to be only Courtney who caught a warning in his words, something that boded ill for her resolve to break off with him completely. Meryl's voice was eager and inquisitive, but Courtney only gaped at the door, her heart pounding wildly, something inside trying to make her run before she had the chance to hear more.

"Straighten what out?" Meryl was asking.

"I'm going to marry her, Meryl."

"Marry her?" Meryl repeated, her voice unreadable.

"Marry me?" Courtney croaked from outside the door. Oh, Lord, how had it come to this? Everything was snowballing on her. She felt the blood drain from her face, felt her knees going weak. She leaned back hard against the wall, groping for the handrail and the support it would offer her.

Suddenly the door flew open, banging hard against the wall, and Joshua nearly ran over Courtney in his haste. He stopped just short of knocking her down, but his arms reached out for her anyway. Even in the turbulence and excitement of the moment, Courtney felt a small shiver go through her at his touch, although her own problems ached right below her skin, tantalizing her heart.

She managed to triumph over them enough to open her mouth and murmur, "I heard."

"You little witch," he answered. "You were right. Andie took her."

And then the smile left his face and he was watching her shrewdly, his eyes thin slits of suspicion. "You heard everything?"

Courtney only looked up at him, her eyes wide, her heart thudding heavily with sick dread. She clasped her hands in front of her, giving the greatest attention to each finger, staring down at them. Suddenly everything was very unreal. Surely this situation hadn't arisen so soon, without giving her a chance for preparation, futile though it might have been.

He hooked his finger under her chin, and if it wasn't a completely gentle touch, neither was it demanding. He tilted her face up until it was close to his, and there was more curiosity in his expression than anything else. His lips were just inches from hers, and Courtney fought against the urge to touch them with her own, to come against them with all of the desperation she felt, to lose herself in his arms again and never let him go. His eyes stared back into hers with golden intensity, yet when he spoke, his words were careful.

"I'm sorry you had to hear it like that."

"What?" she asked senselessly, buying time, trying to get her feet on the ground again. Somehow she had to harden herself, but how? She had to move away from him. She couldn't do this while she was so close to him, feeling him even through the inches that separated them.

"My proposal." They were two short words, clipped and very wary. He feels it, she thought.

"Yes, well . . ."

"I have no excuse except that I didn't know I was going to say it until I said it. Oh, I was thinking along those lines, of course, but not in so many words. I've known all along that I had to have you, but you were keeping yourself so far away. I was confused, so I went along with it. But now, after last night, I'm never going to let you retreat again. I once swore that I would never marry again, but I don't see as how I have any choice now. You've got to be mine. I want you legally, physically, emotionally, every way there is."

"No." The word was torn from her throat, choked and painful.

"What?" There was no time for anger in his golden eyes. Despite the warning her distress had flashed, they were stunned and perplexed. His eyebrows were lost beneath his hair, and his lips twisted into a threatening grimace.

A dreadful agony erupted inside her at that grimace, and Courtney made a run for the stairs, stumbling down them blindly. Distantly she heard his footsteps behind her, but she ran in pursuit of their old distance, craving it, for without it she was lost. She crashed through the door to her office, holding her hands up and flinging the door open as she moved. Yet even as she pushed it closed behind her, it slammed open again as Joshua pushed his way through, sending her reeling backward as she understood that there was to be no escape from this.

She hugged her arms to her and tried to talk, tried desperately to explain as he stood watching her, his eyes burning with that old golden fire, but there was only agony inside her. She wanted him so badly; she wanted to share every second of her life with him until eternity caught up with them. Without him, there was nothing. An empty wasteland loomed ahead of her, dry and barren. She forced herself to take her first step into it.

"I can't," she whispered painfully.

"Can't? Or won't?"

"Can't."

"Would you mind telling me why?" His voice was hard, frightening in its barely concealed anger.

Her own anger was nothing more than a shield against her anguish, contrived and desperate. "You eavesdropped well enough that night at the restaurant! Surely you found out more than just my preferences in food and alcohol! What I said to Peter then goes for you, too. I'm sorry. I can't. The answer is no."

"You didn't love Peter."

"No."

"You love me. You said so. Last night—"

"I lied!" she shouted, hating herself, hating him for pushing her to this. Dear God, would she live through this? Did it matter?

He crossed to her with one long stride, pinning her against her desk. His hands gripped her arms painfully, and she knew that she was on dangerous ground. His control was gone. Throughout the night it had been tenuous at best, and now it had vanished.

He shook her so hard that her hair flew around her face in a dark cloud. And though she tried to pull away from him, his strength, unleashed, was amazing. He held her there, close to him, his golden eyes on hers with glittering scrutiny, and then his lips bore down on hers, bruising her with their punishing insistence. His hand tangled itself in her hair, pulling her head back painfully; the other crushed her against him with such force that exquisite pain tingled through her limbs and her breath was driven out of her. Despite herself, despising her weakness for him, Courtney responded to his overwhelming strength and desire, going weak and pliant in his arms, meeting his kisses with equal ardor.

Then, suddenly, with a movement so swift and angry that it stunned her, he tore at the hem of her thin sweater, yanking it quickly and roughly up to her neck. Courtney froze in fear for a moment, knowing that she had pushed him too far, that she was swimming in waters far too deep, but then his rough hands were on her breasts again, not as gentle as they had been the night before, but harsh and demanding. His touch was different, so different from any she had known from him before, and yet it still had the power to destroy her. She sank weakly against him as he broke the front hook of her bra simply by pulling on the cloth; the little plastic hook dropped silently to the carpet, and her fear dropped just as quietly away from her heart. She reached for him in a way that was at once new and old to her, remembering his lovemaking as it had been, needing him again, feeling the old hunger creep up inside her.

But this wasn't the Joshua who had made love to

her in the darkest hours of the night. His anger and
frustration were real and tangible between them.
They had consumed the touch that had once been so
gentle and treasured by her; now he spent no time
on tentative searching and learning. He ripped open
the snap on her jeans, then released her from his
grasp.

Courtney staggered away from him, the fear back,
running thickly through her lungs so that she
couldn't breathe. Carefully, slowly, she moved toward the door, but then he had her again, holding
her, his eyes dark gold in their anger.

"You lied?" he hissed at her. "Well, then, my
love, you're one hell of an actress. That was no lie
upstairs last night."

She only shook her head, confused and frightened. He released her suddenly, and she sat down
hard on the davenport. Then, just as suddenly, he
leaned over her, pulling at her jeans with one strong
hand, then dispensing with them, tearing at the small
pink scrap of her bikini panties. Courtney gasped
and tried to scramble away from him, but in the
breath of time that it took her to realize the unfathomable degree of his frustration it was already too
late. He came down on her, crushing her back
against the davenport, removing his own jeans
quickly and effortlessly. Then, finally, there was
something familiar in his touch; beneath the anger,
there was his need for her, desperate and searching
and determined not to be denied. When his hand
found the secret place between her thighs again
there was the old gentleness there, igniting her in the
same way it had the night before. Still he kept her
apart from him, holding her down with one strong
hand as she struggled to reach for him. Even as he
plunged into the depths of her, he stayed far enough

away to see her eyes, to see her need for him flaming there.

Courtney struggled against the hand that held her down, finally twisting herself around as he moved within her, and in a final frenzy of the hunger that was working through her again she pushed his arm away until he sank down on top of her. Then, only then, was she able to feed her desire for him. With him close, with his arms wrapped around her, she could feel all of him, and she moved up to greet his every touch greedily. The cause of his anger was forgotten; she knew only that this man was her life and her world. The agony of living without him was momentarily smothered by the exquisite fire of her passion.

Even so, as she clutched him to her and held on to him desperately, she couldn't find the magic to push time away, couldn't freeze the moment, couldn't stop it from thundering on to its inevitable conclusion. With a small cry she could feel her hunger stealing through her, finding the escape it needed to crash over her in one final crescendo. Above her Joshua moaned deep in his throat, and then her respite was over, another chance was lost to her. When she opened her eyes to look up at him, his features were only a foggy blur, and she knew, in that one agonizing second, that she would never truly see him, that nothing would ever change, and that he was lost to her.

"That was no lie just now, either," he said, his voice dangerously quiet. "No way. More of your little game, perhaps, but no lie. Are you trying to drive me crazy? Is that your aim? Can you actually lie there and deny that any of this has meant anything to you?

"You enjoyed every last minute of it," he went on,

his control more frightening than his anger as he pulled away from her and began to dress. "Do you take me for some kind of a fool? Do you think I was born yesterday? That was the first time for you last night! Are you telling me that you would throw that away on the wind, when you don't love me?"

"Yes, that's exactly what I'm saying!" she spat back at him, grabbing for her anger again as she grabbed for the tattered remains of her clothing, for it was the only armor that she had, and still it wasn't strong enough. The pain of losing him was back, gnawing at her heart and tearing her breath away.

"Go ahead, Courtney," he said suddenly, cunningly. "Let's hear your little speech again."

"What speech?" Confusion ebbed back in on her.

"The one you gave Peter. You're right, I heard every word of it that night, but since I'm going to be the lucky recipient this time, I think I deserve to hear it firsthand."

"I . . ." she began, but froze again. He was leaning across the davenport, his eyes on fire with a golden fury and pain the likes of which she had never seen before. She flinched, and despite her most heroic efforts, tears began to collect in her eyes.

"Okay!" she shouted, wild now, springing from the davenport and pushing past him with startling strength. "Right this second, I can see you. I see a great big brown blur. It's not much, but it's all I've got, and I can live with it. But it won't always be there! Damn you! I'm going blind! Don't you understand that? It's going to happen! Someday . . . I . . . won't be able to see anymore!" Sobs choked her voice and she fought desperately to beat them down. When she continued, her voice was wet and thick, but steadier.

"It's going to happen, Joshua. I've never deluded

myself for a minute. It's going to happen, and when it does, I don't intend to fight it, because I can't! It's bigger than I am! I've got to live with that, but I'm the *only* one who's going to live with it. I'm not going to drag someone else down with me! I refuse to make your life as miserable as my own will be, no matter how much I love you and want to have you with me! It would be selfish and horrible and cruel!

"You say you want to marry me." She laughed harshly, and the sound was ugly. "Well, think about it. Think how wonderful it would be to have a wife who can't even cook your dinner because she can't see what in the hell she's doing, someone you would have to take care of, someone you would have to worry about all the time. Not just Meryl, Joshua, but a wife, too. Two of us. Your life would be a joke! You'd be tied down to two people who would be lost without you! You're not even thinking about that! You want me as I am now, but this is only a mirage. It's just temporary. For the majority of my life, I won't be like this!

"I can't give you anything," she continued, determined now and unable to stop the words. "Children? Do you think I would ever take the chance of bringing some little girl or boy into the world to live in the dark? No way! I can't even give you that!

"I can't marry you, Joshua. I can't. You've got to go away. Send Meryl to school somewhere else next year. Just go. Please."

The words had barely escaped her before the sobs started again, heavy and wracking her slender frame with grieving force. She gripped the edge of her desk hard, her knuckles white. She prayed that he would turn and walk out the door, but agony blazed through her at the very thought that he might.

He stood rigidly still, a coiled spring ready to snap

again, and when he spoke it was with a voice so soft that it was all the more treacherous. "Sounds good, but I don't buy it. That other sap may have swallowed it hook, line and sinker, but I think I've already mentioned that I'm no fool. No, what *I* said to *you* that night stands. I thought I was wrong, but I wasn't. You're afraid. You're talking about fear, pure and simple. That's all it is.

"You know how to be so strong and uncompromising when it comes to someone else, but when it comes down to yourself, you're nothing! Nothing! Maybe what I've been loving simply isn't there. You made me open up to Meryl again. You forced me into it. And you made her open up to me. Risk it, isn't that essentially what you said? You need each other, you told me. Go ahead and risk the hurt. And I did.

"But it's all for the other person, is that it, Courtney? Are you too damned scared to take your own medicine?

"You don't want to marry me because it's easier to hide in the dark. You've got some experience with that. It won't ever leave you, won't betray you. It's coming, and you can count on it, and that's that. You're a coward, Courtney. The biggest chance of your life is looking you right in the eye, and you're running away from it! You're a coward!"

His words cut through her like knives, sure and deadly. She gasped, and it was enough to make the sobs stop. She stared at him, her heart breaking, as he moved to the door.

"Go ahead, Courtney. Hide, if that's what you want to do. Get out of my life. You're a fraud, and I was just stupid enough to fall for your act. Don't worry, I'll take Meryl away. I'll leave you to your precious darkness."

He moved away from her down the hall, his footfalls more distant with each passing second.

"No," she moaned aloud into the empty room, speaking of everything and nothing. She collapsed back down onto the davenport, clutching her clothing to her as the pain of losing him rocked through her and fresh tears clogged her vision. She heard his footsteps hard and heavy on the marble in the entryway. She waited, tense, for the sound of the door opening.

There was a slight hesitation, then it did, slamming shut again as it crushed all of the remaining light out of her life.

Chapter 11

ONE MORE CAR SLID PAST THE WINDOWS OF THE
entryway; one more small, shining face pressed
against the glass of the back window; one more little
hand waved gleefully at the house. Courtney sighed
heavily and leaned against the front door. Eleven
down, two to go. Only Lilith and Meryl remained
upstairs, the lone stragglers on this last day of the
school year. Their voices rang out from somewhere
above Courtney, but she closed her ears to them,
trying not to hear them, not to think about those last
two walking out of her life and leaving her alone for
the summer.

Not for the summer, came the small voice that
never let her rest. Forever. One of those girls was
Meryl. She would leave, and she would not come

back. She and her father would disappear from Courtney's life forever. Forever.

Gone. Joshua was gone. There had been no more shared smiles across her desk, no more arguments. His golden eyes had slipped from her world, and they would never mock her again. He would never touch her again. Everything she loved about him— his strength, his vulnerability, his caution, his passion—all of it was gone. He had left her to her darkness, as she had known he would have to. She had wanted this, hadn't she? This was right. She was being selfless and strong. Someday he would see it, if he hadn't already. And then he would thank her for it.

From the floor above her Lilith squealed and Meryl laughed, and Courtney felt the frozen hollow that sat in place of her heart growing more cold, more empty. She bit her lip and pushed herself away from the door, moving down the corridor toward her office. She couldn't be there waiting when Joshua arrived for Meryl. She didn't dare see him, not even one more time. It would, quite simply, be more than she could bear.

The grief that filled her at that realization left her no chance for breath. She sat down hard on the chair behind her desk, everything inside her trembling, breaking, collapsing. She felt it in her bones, a physical ache, and in the pit of her stomach as it clenched, trying to force her morning coffee out. Even sitting, her legs felt weak and empty.

I'm right, she tried to tell herself. He's better off. Let him go. He was wrong. I'm not hiding from my own ruin, but from his.

The words sounded hollow and empty in her heart. They banged against the very perimeters of her being, and she hugged her arms to her. Once, days ago, even hours ago, she had been able to embrace those words and derive some small comfort from them. Now they teased her, sounding like blatant lies. Now that he would be arriving at any minute, any second, to take his daughter away, there was no hiding from the torture they wrought within her. She tried to cringe away from them, burrowing more deeply into her chair, but it was impossible. They haunted her and mocked her.

Out in the entryway the door banged open, and every muscle in Courtney's body stiffened, waiting. Her breath froze in her lungs yet again, sticking painfully there. A voice should come soon, some greeting, some words. Would it be his? Oh, God, would it finally be his?

No. She heard Sylvia Baxter's piping voice exchange greetings with Elizabeth, heard Lilith come squealing down the stairs, her suitcases thumping against the bannister. Courtney's breath flew out in a spasm of relief and she collapsed back against her chair.

But there was to be no surcease from the horror that grew within her with each passing minute. Even before she could take another breath, even before she could try one last time to calm herself, the door banged again. Sylvia and Lilith leaving? No, no, there was his voice. Flat. Hard. Careful.

Elizabeth said something indistinguishable.

Meryl called down from upstairs.

The door banged still one more time; Sylvia and Lilith called out their farewells.

Courtney held on tightly to the arms of her chair, grasping them until tiny pinpoints of pain raced through her knuckles. The pain seemed to shoot through her heart, shattering it and destroying it, making it weak. Shakily, she got to her feet.

She had no choice, really. She was only human, only a woman with a backbone that could hold up through almost everything, but not this. Live without him? Let him walk back out that door again and be gone from her until the stars burned clear of the sky? The very thought made her weak again, and she knew that the days she had spent without him hadn't made her any stronger. No, they had only opened the floodgates of her heart, and she couldn't step back and escape the torrents of emotion that ran free. Just as he had once said that he couldn't turn and run, neither could she. She couldn't do anything but love him. Yes, it was selfish, but it was inevitable, as well.

The first step was the most difficult, for her conscience still fought her, trying to make her stop. You'll ruin his life, it said to her. You'll bring him down, tie him down; he'll be miserable.

He loves you, said another, kinder voice. Don't be afraid. Go on, go to him. Take that risk you made him take with Meryl. Go on.

Her feet started moving of their own volition, and then her heart was with them all the way. She ran into the corridor, then stood blinking, struggling to make something of the shadows at the end of the hall. There was no one there. Had they gone? Oh, God, was she too late?

No, there was Meryl's voice again, and Elizabeth's, both upstairs now. Where was Joshua? Where had he gone?

And then she knew, simply and without thought. She understood. He was waiting for Meryl. He wouldn't wait in the corridor and risk seeing her. He would go off somewhere alone. Outside. The creek? The loggia?

She ran down the corridor, missing the handrail on the first grab, then finding it and hurrying on. As she reached the door to the loggia she put one hand straight out in front of her. The other grabbed the knob. She burst through the door like a whirlwind, then suddenly froze, uncertainty immobilizing her.

He was there, as she had known he would be, sitting on the steps that led down to the lawn. His hands were clasped in front of him carefully, and his shoulders were rigid yet stooped, trapping something inside of him which he didn't dare let free.

As if in a trance, she moved closer to him, wanting to turn back, afraid to, yet afraid to keep going. When she was close enough to touch him, she stopped and spoke his name, her voice soft and trembling.

"Joshua?"

His head spun around, his dark gold eyes snapping as they raked over her, and then he got to his feet, moving down the steps, stopping only when he reached the lawn.

"Damn it, Courtney," he growled suddenly. "Damn you! Is your heart only for your precious little girls? Try to spare some for me, hmmm? Get the hell out of here. Leave me alone. I came out here for a reason."

She closed her eyes, her heart hammering wildly within her, but she didn't move, for she knew that he would back away from her with every step she took toward him. Instead, she rested her hands against the balustrade and finally, finally, released the chains that had been holding in her love for him.

"So did I," she said finally.

"What?"

"I came out here for a reason, too. I . . . have to talk to you."

"No." He spat the word out quickly before turning on his heel to move away from her across the lawn.

"Yes!" she yelled at him. Her restraint and caution gone, she ran down the steps, rushing across the lawn toward him, oblivious to any cloudy obstacles that might trip her.

"Wait! You have to listen to me! I—I'm not a coward. I just love you too much to hurt you, to tie you down to me. But maybe you were right about what you said last week, in a way. I was trying so hard to be brave, to accept my lot in life, that that was all I could accept. Maybe I've lived with it for so long that I was afraid to try for anything else."

"What are you saying?" He was wary and guarded, but at least he had stopped moving. He stood still, listening to her, trying hard to look casual with his hands in his pockets and one foot tapping against the lawn. The wind fluttered his hair and his shirt rippled against his chest, and her heart lurched into her throat at the sight of him. Everything about him was so dear to her, so special. She took a deep breath and spoke.

"I love you. I'll marry you. I'll take the chance."

Something soft and almost shadowlike fell across his face. He didn't rush to her, but moved slowly, his hands still deep in his pockets, his face creased with thought. Even when he reached her he stood like that, separate and apart from her, watching her.

"It's not a chance, Courtney. It's a giving in, like I did with Meryl. You said that she needed me and I believed you, and you were right. Well, *I* need *you*. Do you believe that?"

Slowly she nodded, overwhelmed by the love she

saw in his eyes, at the dawning peace and happiness there.

"Then be my wife."

Again she nodded, but the gesture was stopped midway as he reached out to her. She fell into his arms, allowed them to swallow and crush her, and clung to him, tilting her face up to his.

His kiss was almost chaste in its sweetness, and his eyes still ravaged her, looking for something, searching for an answer in her eyes.

"I'm still afraid to do this to you," she said at length, pulling away from him hesitantly. "Can you live with it? Without my being able to see?"

"Courtney, something tells me that between you and Meryl, I'm going to be the outsider. I love you. I always will. I love those witchy green eyes of yours, even if they can't see a damned thing."

It was all she needed to hear. Tentatively, like a baby bird testing its wings, she reached out for him again. Her arms went around him in an embrace that was full of trust and passion, and somewhere deep inside, the last, lonely barrier came crashing down.

The smile she gave him was one of humor, trust and love. She shrugged slightly into the wind and rested her head against his chest.

"What the devil," she said lightly, but her voice was sweet and thrilling with joy. "As long as I've got you, who needs to see? I'll be too busy using my other senses. . . . Like touch," she finished, but the words were muffled as his lips came down on hers.

Silhouette Intimate Moments

Available Now

Serpent In Paradise by Stephanie James

At first Jase Lassiter had promised Amy paradise, offering her nights of love and days of sheer delight. But then she thought he'd betrayed her and she wondered if paradise would ever be found.

A Season Of Rainbows by Jennifer West

Christopher Reynolds was a genius on the brink of realization—realization that beneath Lauren's cool exterior beat the heart of a woman waiting to be awakened by passion!

Until The End Of Time by June Trevor

The private wilderness of Rafiki was Reed Kincaid's haven, until Elise brought the outside world to his door. He hadn't wanted to love again, but she was woman enough to change his mind.

Tonight And Always by Nora Roberts

Kasey was an anthropologist, but her knowledge of men in general hadn't prepared her for one man in particular: Jordan. Together they did research for his novel, and found something even more precious than knowledge.

Silhouette
Intimate 🖤 _Moments_
more romance, more excitement

Special Introductory Offer $1.75 each

#1 ☐ DREAMS OF EVENING
Kristin James

#2 ☐ ONCE MORE WITH
FEELING Nora Roberts

#3 ☐ EMERALDS IN THE DARK
Beverly Bird

#4 ☐ SWEETHEART CONTRACT
Pat Wallace

$2.25 each

#5 ☐ WIND SONG
Parris Afton Bonds

#6 ☐ ISLAND HERITAGE
Monica Barrie

#7 ☐ A DISTANT CASTLE
Sue Ellen Cole

#8 ☐ LOVE EVERLASTING
Moëth Allison

9 ☐ SERPENT IN PARADISE
Stephanie James

#10 ☐ A SEASON OF RAINBOWS
Jennifer West

#11 ☐ UNTIL THE END OF TIME
June Trevor

#12 ☐ TONIGHT AND ALWAYS
Nora Roberts

LOOK FOR _THE PROMISE OF SUMMER_
BY BARBARA FAITH AVAILABLE IN AUGUST
AND _THE AMBER SKY_
BY KRISTIN JAMES IN SEPTEMBER.

SILHOUETTE INTIMATE MOMENTS, Department IM/5
1230 Avenue of the Americas
New York, NY 10020

Please send me the books I have checked above. I am enclosing
$_____ (please add 50¢ to cover postage and handling. NYS
and NYC residents please add appropriate sales tax.) Send check or
money order—no cash or C.O.D.'s please. Allow six weeks for delivery.

NAME _____

ADDRESS _____

CITY _____ STATE/ZIP _____

Get 6 new Silhouette Special Editions every month for a 15-day FREE trial!

Free Home Delivery, Free Previews, Free Bonus Books. Silhouette Special Editions are a new kind of romance novel. These are big, powerful stories that will capture your imagination. They're longer, with fully developed characters and intricate plots that will hold you spellbound from the first page to the very last.

Each month we will send you six exciting *new* Silhouette Special Editions, just as soon as they are published. If you enjoy them as much as we think you will, pay the invoice enclosed with your shipment. **They're delivered right to your door with never a charge for postage or handling, and there's no obligation to buy anything at any time.** To start receiving Silhouette Special Editions regularly, mail the coupon below today.

Silhouette Special Edition